JAN   2022

LIFE WITHOUT PAROLE

Also by Elaine Viets

Angela Richman, Death Investigator

BRAIN STORM
FIRE AND ASHES
A STAR IS DEAD *
DEATH GRIP *

Dead-End Job

FINAL SAIL
BOARD STIFF
CATNAPPED!
CHECKED OUT
THE ART OF MURDER

Josie Marcus, Mystery Shopper

DYING IN STYLE
HIGH HEELS ARE MURDER
ACCESSORY TO MURDER
MURDER WITH ALL THE TRIMMINGS
THE FASHION HOUND MURDERS
AN UPLIFTING MURDER
DEATH ON A PLATTER
MURDER IS A PIECE OF CAKE
FIXING TO DIE
A DOG GONE MURDER

* *available from Severn House*

LIFE WITHOUT PAROLE

Elaine Viets

**SEVERN
HOUSE**

First world edition published in Great Britain and the USA in 2021
by Severn House, an imprint of Canongate Books Ltd,
14 High Street, Edinburgh EH1 1TE.

Trade paperback edition first published in Great Britain and the USA in 2022
by Severn House, an imprint of Canongate Books Ltd.

severnhouse.com

British Library Cataloguing-in-Publication Data
A CIP catalogue record for this title is available from the British Library.

ISBN-13: 978-0-7278-5028-7 (cased)
ISBN-13: 978-1-78029-827-6 (trade paper)
ISBN-13: 978-1-4483-0565-0 (e-book)

This is a work of fiction. Names, characters, places and incidents
are either the product of the author's imagination or are used fictitiously.
Except where actual historical events and characters are being described
for the storyline of this novel, all situations in this publication are
fictitious and any resemblance to actual persons, living or dead,
business establishments, events or locales is purely coincidental.

All Severn House titles are printed on acid-free paper.

MIX
Paper from
responsible sources
FSC® C013056

Typeset by Palimpsest Book Production Ltd.,
Falkirk, Stirlingshire, Scotland.
Printed and bound in Great Britain by
TJ Books, Padstow, Cornwall.

For Alison McMahan. With thanks.

ACKNOWLEDGMENTS

Even though I spent hours in front of my computer to finish this book, novel writing is a team effort. Many people helped me write Angela's latest adventure, *Life Without Parole.*

Most important is my husband, Don Crinklaw, my first reader and best critiquer.

Thanks also to my agent, Joshua Bilmes, president of JABberwocky Literary Agency, and the entire JABberwocky team. Joshua reads my novels and gives me detailed suggestions to improve them.

Investigating a murder is difficult and intricate work, and I tried to give a taste of that in *Life Without Parole.* Special thanks to Detective R.C. White, Fort Lauderdale Police Department (retired) and licensed private eye, for his many hours of advice and help on police procedure. Thank you, Dr Sharon L. Plotkin, certified crime scene investigator and professor at the Miami Dade College School of Justice, who read my crime scenes for accuracy. Thanks to death investigator Krysten Addison and Harold R. Messler, retired manager-criminalistics, St. Louis Police Laboratory. Nurse Gregg E. Brickman, author of *Imperfect Friendship*, helped me kill off my characters. Award-winning author Greg Herren was another big help. Sarah E.C. Byrne made a generous donation to charity to have her name in this novel. She's a lawyer from Canberra, Australia, and a crime fiction aficionada.

I'm grateful to my friends Alan Portman, and Jinny Gender, as well as two award-winning writers, Joanna Campbell Slan, author of *Love, Die, Neighbor*, and Marcia Talley, author of *Done Gone.* And thank you, Carol, my behind-the-scenes proofreader.

Thanks to the Severn House staff, especially Editor Sara Porter and Commissioning Editor Carl Smith. Their suggestions greatly improved this novel. Copyeditor Loma Halden made some excellent catches. I'm also grateful to Publishing Assistant Natasha Bell. Cover artist Piers Tilbury perfectly captured my book.

Special thanks to the many librarians, including those at the Broward County library and St. Louis and St. Louis County libraries. I could not survive without their help and encouragement.

All these generous people and more helped me write *Life Without Parole*. Any mistakes are mine.

Please enjoy Angela Richman's latest adventure. Email me at eviets@aol.com

ONE

Four in the morning. I was wrapped in the arms of my lover, sleeping the sleep of the satisfied, when my work cell phone rang.

Damn. Someone was dead, probably murdered. Why couldn't people die at a decent hour?

I gently pried myself from Chris Ferretti's arms, and forced myself awake. I'm Angela Richman, a death investigator in Chouteau County, Missouri, a pocket of white privilege some thirty miles west of St. Louis. I work for the medical examiner's office.

Officially, I'd been on call since midnight, but I'd hoped everyone would stay alive. I scooted across the warm bed to check the phone's display – Detective Jace Budewitz, one of the good guys. I padded across the room, flipped on the bathroom light, and answered the phone. 'Jace, what's happening?' I asked, closing the door and keeping my voice low.

'We've got a bad one, Angela.' I heard the worry in his voice. 'Tom Lockridge is dead. Three shots to the head.' I couldn't help wincing when he said that.

'The Ghost Burglars have turned deadly,' he said.

'They were bound to start shooting soon,' I said. 'Did they kill Tom's wife, too?'

'No. Cynthia is OK. Claims she was on the other side of the house.'

Claims. Hm. Sounded like Jace didn't believe her.

'I'll be there in twenty minutes,' I said.

I hung up, yawned, stretched, and turned on the shower. Cold water first, to shock me awake, followed by soothing warm water.

Tom's death would have a big impact on Chouteau County's social life. Tom was sixty-six, and his sexy wife was thirty-four years younger. Tom and Cynthia were the closest stodgy Chouteau County had to jet-setters, and gossip swirled around them. I'd heard that in summer, Tom's plane – loaded with his friends – flew to his house at the Lake of the Ozarks, about 175 miles away in the Ozark Mountains. From there, the party piled into Tom's boat and headed for the lake's 'Party Cove,' a floating sin spot notorious for public sex, drugs and nude sailing. A local paper condemned Party Cove as a 'giant petri dish of debauchery.'

Wild child Cynthia and her freethinking friends fostered the colorful gossip: rumor said they drank, they drugged, and they hosted onboard bacchanals.

Until he met Cynthia, Tom – Thomas J. Lockridge – had been a hardworking contractor. He still worked hard, but now he partied harder. In the winter, Tom and Cynthia flew their party pals to Telluride, Colorado, for skiing and lots of powder – and I don't just mean snow.

Tom was generous, and not only to his friends. He was a major donor to every local charity and was frequently photographed in a penguin suit, presenting a hefty check to a smiling, sequined socialite.

Now he was dead.

I rinsed the shampoo out of my long dark hair, and didn't bother blow-drying it. Instead, I pulled it into a practical ponytail, then dried myself with one of Chris's fluffy towels. I'd spent the night with my new lover. Chris was a Chouteau County patrol officer. He understood why I'd also brought my black DI pantsuit and shoes – sensible black lace-ups – 'just in case,' and plugged in my work cell on his night stand.

When I emerged from the bathroom dressed for work, Chris's love-rumpled bed was empty. I could hear him banging around in the kitchen.

I hurried downstairs and saw him in his black bathrobe, scrambling eggs in his cast-iron skillet. He had strong tanned features and brown hair cut short, but not too short.

I kissed him good morning. 'Is that coffee I smell?'

'Duty calls, right?' he said. 'Who is it?'

'Tom Lockridge. Jace Budewitz told me Tom was shot dead in his bedroom. Jace thinks it was the Ghost Burglars – just what we were talking about last night.'

Chris shook his head. 'I knew that situation was headed for tragedy. Twelve burglaries in two weeks, and now the Forest's trigger-happy home owners are armed with everything from shotguns to AK-47s.

'The man who was killed – Lockridge. Is he the guy who lives in the marble palace on Windsor Court?' Chris asked.

'That's him,' I said. 'The Lockridge mansion is a copy of an Italian palace. Tom bought it for his bride, Cynthia.'

'Do you know him?' Chris asked.

'I've seen Tom and Cynthia enough to recognize them, but I don't really know them. I've never been in their house.'

Two slices of wheat toast popped up in the toaster. Chris deftly removed them to a blue plate and forked the scrambled eggs on top.

'Breakfast,' he said.

'Looks delicious, but can I get it to-go?'

He wrapped the egg sandwich in a paper napkin, handed me the Thermos of hot black coffee and kissed me again. 'I wish you could stay with me.' His kiss was long and lingering and I wanted desperately to go back to bed with him.

'I really have to go,' I said, forcing myself to leave.

'Will I see you tonight?'

'I don't know yet.' I broke free of his embrace and headed for the door. 'I'll call you. Thank you for a lovely time. And breakfast.'

And I was outside in his condo parking lot, in the cool early morning air. Moonlight gave the prosaic blacktop lot a shimmering shine. Soon it would be another warm May day. I chirped open my black Dodge Charger, leaned my head against the steering wheel and sighed with happiness. I'd been widowed for more than two years when I'd met Chris by accident – for real. Someone had tried to run me down in a parking lot.

Chris was the officer on call, and it took at least another month before we started dating. When my husband, Donegan, died suddenly of a heart attack, I knew I'd never love again. I was too broken. But Chris courted me slowly and patiently, and I began to come back to life.

I poured myself a cup of coffee from the Thermos, and took a long drink. I felt the caffeine flowing through my veins. I was finally awake.

I'd finished my sandwich and the first cup of coffee by the time I turned on to Windsor Court. Tom Lockridge's bone-white marble mansion glittered in the moonlight. The four-story faux Renaissance palace was designed to impress, overwhelming the other mansions on the court. Perfectly sculpted shrubbery lined the wrought-iron fence. The mansion looked slightly less forbidding with lights blazing in the tall windows.

Mike, a sleepy-looking uniform cop, stopped me at the gate. 'Morning, Angela,' he said. 'Follow the driveway around to the side by the garage. You can park there. You'll need to suit up and wear booties. The whole freaking place is a crime scene, and there's blood everywhere in the bedroom.'

I signed the crime scene log and got the case number, then drove through a moon-silvered forest that opened on to a vast velvet green lawn. Finally, I reached the parking area. The garage was big enough for eight cars. The parking area held a dozen official vehicles, and there was still room for my car. I parked next to Jace's gray unmarked sedan that screamed 'cop car!'

About an acre of the backyard was marked off with yellow crime scene tape and lit by the glare of portable lights. Uniformed officers were doing a grid search.

I pulled my death investigator case out of my trunk. It went with me everywhere. The kit was a black rolling suitcase packed with the paraphernalia I needed for a death investigation: Tupperware containers for evidence, plastic and paper evidence bags, evidence tape, my point-and-shoot camera, and more. I donned a white disposable Tyvek suit and rolled my suitcase toward the sunroom off the kitchen. The glassed-in room was a riot of green plants, from palms to giant split-leaf philodendrons. I sat on a teak bench to put on my booties, and saw – and smelled – the basil growing in clay pots.

I heard Jace talking to a woman in the kitchen. Her voice was thick with tears. Cynthia, the victim's wife? Too bad the kitchen door didn't have a window.

'Tell me what happened again, Mrs Lockridge.' I could hear the skepticism in the detective's voice.

'But I've already told you a hundred times.' More crying.

'I need to hear it again.' Jace's voice was polite but firm.

'I was upstairs, on the other side of the house, in my office, working on the plans for the Chouteau Forest Christmas Ball. I'm the co-chair.'

The charity ball was the premiere social event in Chouteau Forest. Cynthia was definitely in high cotton if she was co-chair.

'I was planning the menu.' Cynthia's voice was wobbly with tears. 'The Forest Inn wanted to charge too much for filet mignon, and we have to have some kind of red meat. The men demand it. I was figuring the cost of petit filet appetizers, and chicken for the main course, when I heard a popping sound – three pops – and then footsteps running down the back service stairs. My dog started barking and growling. I ran over to the back stairs and saw two men running toward the door—'

'Did you have a gun or any protection when you went running after two adult males?' Jace interrupted.

'I told you. I had Prince, my Malinois.' Now the tears had changed to impatience.

I had one bootie on, but I hesitated putting on the other. I wanted to hear what Cynthia had to say.

'Why didn't you turn on the alarm system last night, Mrs Lockridge?'

'I wasn't thinking. Besides, I had Prince with me.'

'You weren't thinking about the Ghost Burglars, even though they've been hitting every big home in the Forest?' I heard the disbelief in Jace's voice. 'You weren't thinking your husband might need protection?'

'No!' Cynthia gave a tear-drenched shout. 'My husband had his gun. And this isn't the ghetto, Detective. I'm not used to living under siege.' Now she began wailing. 'My husband is dead! My poor Tom is gone! And you wouldn't let me give him one last kiss.'

Jace was right to prevent the widow from contaminating the crime scene.

'We're done here!' A male voice, commanding and self-assured.

'Mrs Lockridge is my client, Detective. She's suffered a terrible shock and the loss of her husband. She's been through enough. I'm taking her to my home. My housekeeper, Mrs Mason, will care for her.'

'Fine,' Jace said. 'But don't leave town, Mrs Lockridge. I'm going to be talking to you again in the morning.'

'And I'm going to be there with her,' the man said.

'You do that, Counselor,' Jace said.

I'd just put on the other bootie when the side door was flung open and out stormed the owner of the male voice. Wesley Desloge, an ambitious Forest lawyer trying to make a name for himself. He had his arm protectively around the new widow. Cynthia's eyes were red and swollen, and her mascara left black streaks on her face, but she was still glamorous. Her black hair tumbled down her back, and she wore black silk lounging pajamas with a black lace peignoir.

Wes guarded her like she was made of gold.

TWO

I rolled my DI case into the kitchen and found Jace pacing the floor. The big detective with the boyish face and short buzzed blond hair looked angry.

'Something's not right,' he said. 'The victim was shot at 1:08 this morning and his wife didn't call nine-one-one until 1:53. A forty-five-minute gap. What was she doing during that time?'

'How do you know the exact time of death?' I asked. TOD – time of death – was almost unknowable. Unless someone saw a murder and had a clock nearby, it was difficult to determine the exact time.

'I'll show you. Let's go upstairs,' he said. 'The service stairs are part of the crime scene, so we'll use the main staircase. Have you ever been in this place?'

'No. I've just seen it from the road.'

I rolled my DI case down a short hallway. Jace opened a carved oak door and we were in a vast marble foyer with a four-story domed rotunda and a forest of marble columns.

'Wow!' I said. 'It looks like a museum.'

The crystal chandelier was the size of a piano. On the vaulted ceiling, cherubs frolicked on cottony clouds. The curved double staircase led to the second floor.

'The crime scene is upstairs,' Jace said. 'Can I help you with your suitcase?'

'No, thanks,' I said, a bit too sharply. I'd had six strokes and brain surgery two years ago, and they'd nearly killed me. But I was lucky. I was ninety-nine percent cured – and touchy about accepting help.

Pride had its price. I was panting slightly by the time I'd dragged my heavy suitcase up the stairs. I hung on to the handrail all the way up.

'The master bedroom is the first door on the right,' Jace said.

Inside the bedroom, I opened my DI case and gloved up, putting on four pairs. I would strip them off as I examined different parts of the body, to keep from contaminating it.

'Nitpicker's here,' he said. 'She's working the back staircase right now.' Sarah 'Nitpicker' Byrne was our best tech.

'The bed has been printed, photographed and videoed,' Jace said. 'We're waiting for you to finish before we take it apart.'

The bedroom looked more like a royal reception chamber. The carved marble fireplace was big enough for me to stand in, and I'm six feet tall. The walls were pale yellow silk and the tall windows were draped in yards of shimmering gold fabric. One window was open, bringing in welcome cool air. A vast four-poster bed was the centerpiece.

On the bed was a squalid scene: A fat, bald, hairy-chested man wearing striped pajama bottoms appeared to be swimming in a pool of blood. He was lying on his left side in the fetal position, his head facing north.

Jake pointed to the gunshot wounds in the victim's head with his gloved hand. 'Three in the skull – two in the parietal and one in the occipital.' The parietal is the bulging bone in the back of the skull. The occipital is right under it, and completes the curve.

'No sign of an exit wound,' I said. 'Must have used a small caliber weapon.'

'Probably a twenty-two,' Jace said. 'That would scramble the poor guy's brains. Mrs Lockridge said her husband kept a twenty-two in the drawer next to the bed and it's missing.'

'Did you find it?'

'No. Mrs Lockridge claimed her husband slept with the windows open and the burglar must have thrown it out the window into the backyard. We're looking for it now.'

'Did you find anything when you did the GSR test on her?' That's gunshot residue. Jace was the kind of careful detective who would check. He wasn't intimidated by money or power.

'Nothing. I allowed her to change out of her bloody clothes, under the supervision of a female uniform, and bagged her clothes.'

'So what's her story?' I asked.

Just what I'd heard at the kitchen door: Cynthia Lockridge had been working in her office on the other side of the building, with her Malinois for protection. 'The dog, Prince, started barking,' Jace said. 'She heard three pops, came running into the bedroom and found her husband. She says he was dead and she saw two men running down the service stairs.'

'Let me guess, the infamous unknown black intruders.'

'No, but her description is just as useless. She said one of them turned around, and she thought he was a white guy, wearing a black stocking mask. Average height, average build. The men didn't say anything.

'Here's how I know when her husband died.' Jace pointed to a round inlaid table with one drawer open beside the bed. The ornate gold clock had been knocked over and was lying face-up. It had stopped at 1:08. The clock face, as well as the table, was spattered with blood.

'Who uses a wind-up clock any more?' I said.

'Looks like some kinda fancy antique,' Jace said.

'Did the burglars get anything?' I asked.

'No. When the burglaries started, Mrs Lockridge was smart enough to store her good jewelry, including her diamond engagement ring, in a safe deposit box. Most of the victims used the safes in their homes. Mrs Lockridge kept some costume stuff in that jewelry box on the floor. Looks like the burglars stomped on it when they found out it didn't contain anything of value.'

The demolished box appeared to have been an antique with fine marquetry. It was splintered now. Crushed rhinestone earrings lay in the remains, along with gold-colored discs. A pearl necklace had been torn apart, and the pearls ground into the carpet.

'She was pretty broken up about those pearls,' Jace said. 'They were a graduation gift. But they gave us a boot print.'

'The burglars must have been furious when they didn't get her diamonds,' I said.

Jace nodded. 'When Mrs Lockridge saw her husband was dead, she called their friend, Wesley Desloge, for help. A friend who happens to be a lawyer.' In Jace's eyes, that alone made her guilty.

'Wouldn't most people call nine-one-one?' I asked.

'That's what I'd do. Mrs Lockridge says she was upset and Wes is a good family friend.'

'Any idea just how good a friend Wes Desloge is? Were he and Cynthia having an affair?'

'Don't know,' Jace said. 'But I'm sure going to find out.'

I could make out small bloody footprints, about a woman's size four or five, on the carpet and the bedding. Cynthia Lockridge must have been barefoot when she discovered her husband. Each print was marked with a numbered yellow plastic tent.

'How did she get blood on her feet, Jace?'

'She's a small woman, Angela, no more than five feet tall, and you can land aircraft on this bed. She went up those steps there' – he pointed to three carved oak steps leading to the tall bed – 'and she says she held her husband. According to her, he was lying face-down and the blood spatter on the headboard seems to bear that out. You can see where she moved him.' The blood pool showed the marks of her husband's body being dragged so he was resting on his side.

'She got on her knees there' – Jace pointed to the marks in the blood – 'and pushed her husband on to his side, the way he is now. You can see her bloody handprints on his back and arm, where she touched him. She said, "I held him as if I could will him back to life."'

'Very dramatic,' I said.

'She says she was afraid someone might still be hiding in the room.'

'So she tried to hug her husband back to life, and then feared for her own?'

'So she says,' Jace told me. Again, I heard the skepticism in his voice.

'She walked through her husband's blood, and grabbed that right bedpost to have a look-see. By then, Wes the friendly lawyer came running to the rescue. He entered by the open back door, ran up the service stairs and into this room.'

'Thereby trampling any evidence on the stairs,' I said.

Jace nodded. 'That's her story, anyway.'

'Do you believe it?'

He shrugged, but before Jace could say more, one of the techs working on the stairs called out, 'Detective, you need to see this,' and Jace left to check what they'd found.

I opened the Body Inspection Form on my iPad, and started my examination. The victim was lying in the fetal position in a four-poster bed in the northwest bedroom. His head was on two pillows, and the yellow silk coverlet with a fleur-de-lis design had been pulled off the bed, along with the beige top-sheet, exposing the body. The victim appeared to have been asleep at the time of death. He was pronounced dead by Detective Jace Budewitz at 2:12 a.m. There were no attempts to resuscitate the victim.

I photographed the scene first, then the victim himself, documenting the scene with long shots, medium shots and close-ups. I took the room's ambient temperature – a comfortable seventy-two degrees, and photographed the thermostat near the door, which had the same reading. Tom Lockridge was a white male, aged sixty-six, a once-muscular man gone to fat. His height was five feet eight and I estimated his weight at about two hundred eighty pounds.

I saw his wedding picture on the bedside table. Jace told me the date was seven years ago. Tom looked distinguished in black tie. He was bald and fit. I guessed his weight at that time at about one hundred sixty pounds. Cynthia, his tiny bride, was clearly at least thirty years younger than her groom. She wore a glittering wide-skirted white gown and looked like a fairy princess. They were smiling dreamily at each other. Now the dream was dead.

I started the body 'actualization,' beginning with the victim's head.

Some hairstyles hide gunshot wounds. Since Tom was bald, his wounds could be seen clearly. There was 'tattooing' – black powder marks – around the wounds from the gun barrel, which meant he'd been shot at close range, probably less than three inches away. I measured the gunshot wounds and the blood on the back of his head. I hoped he didn't feel anything, and had died when he was asleep.

Tom did not appear to have been beaten: there was no bruising or blunt-force trauma on his face, neck or shoulders.

He did have 'raccoon eyes' – his upper eyelids had hemorrhaged, creating a dark mask around his eyes. Raccoon eyes are often found with gunshot wounds or skull fractures. Both eyes were closed. I lifted an eyelid. Tom had brown eyes.

On his right trapezius, Tom had four healing claw marks. The longest was four inches, and the others were three inches. Did Cynthia – or someone else – claw his shoulder in a moment of passion? I hoped so.

I measured the patches of blood on his back, and photographed the small bloody handprints up close. Jace and Nitpicker had confirmed the prints belonged to Cynthia.

Tom wore a yellow metal ring on the third finger of his left hand – a plain gold wedding band. On the fifth digit of his right hand he wore a yellow metal ring with a large square-cut clear stone.

That's the official way I reported his rings. I don't appraise jewelry, but even I knew Tom sported major bling on his pinkie. That square-cut rock was worth a fortune. Why didn't the Ghost Burglars take it?

The decedent's hands were clean and had no injuries. His nails were freshly manicured. Like many men who work in the supervisory side of construction, his nails were buffed to a shine, but he didn't wear clear polish. He tried to bridge the business and the construction worlds. His workers would not have respected him if he'd worn 'unmanly' clear nail polish, but bankers and other business people expected well-tended nails.

Tom's chest was nude and covered with a thick black-and-gray pelt.

He wore super-soft gray-striped Hanro drawstring pants that sold for a hundred and seventy bucks – I'd seen them online. There was one bloody handprint – also his wife's – on the right knee of his pajamas. His feet were bare and clean, with no visible injuries.

I'd wrapped up my body inspection and was checking the decedent's medications in the bathroom when Jace came running into the room and said, 'Hey, Angela, look at this!'

THREE

'd been cataloguing the decedent's medications on my iPad in Tom Lockridge's luxurious gold and marble bathroom, when Jace rushed in. The medicine cabinet was behind a gold mirror fit for a Medici prince, but the prescription medications inside were all too modern. Tom had been taking Zocor for high cholesterol, a hypertension drug called Procardia XL, and Plavix, which helps prevent blood clots. Judging by his medications, Tom had had serious heart trouble – and at least one heart attack or stroke. With his weight, the man was a medical disaster waiting to happen.

Jace was outraged. The usually good-natured detective had gone from angry to irate. His face glowed red with fury. Even the tips of his ears were red.

'We found the weapon,' Jace said. 'No fingerprints. Just smudges.'

'What? Were the burglars wearing gloves?'

'Probably. I'm guessing the smudges belonged to Tom Lockridge.'

'Why would the Ghost Burglars kill him?'

'Rage?' Jace said. 'They came here for Mrs Lockridge's diamonds, and got rhinestones instead. You could tell they were furious by the way they destroyed that jewelry box.'

'So why didn't the burglars take that big honkin' diamond off Tom Lockridge's finger?' I said.

'Maybe Mrs Lockridge didn't want them to. Maybe she hired them to kill her husband. That's one question I'm going to ask her.'

Jace had just started his tirade. Now he paced up and down the vast chamber – past the double sinks adorned with cupids, the Swedish shower and the marble whirlpool bath.

'I've got a lot more questions for Mrs Lockridge,' he said. 'Why didn't her dog Prince bark when the intruders entered the house?'

'Because Prince didn't hear them?' I said. 'It's a big house.'

'Not that big. And a dog's hearing is way better than ours. Dogs can hear sounds a quarter of a mile away. So either Prince alerted Cynthia about the burglars and she ignored the dog, or she and the dog knew these so-called burglars.

'I also want to know why the alarm system was off, especially when all the local bigwigs are so afraid of burglars. I don't buy her story that she forgot because she doesn't live in a bad neighborhood. Even a rich nitwit must have some sense of self-preservation. She might as well put out a neon sign that said "Housebreakers Welcome."'

'How did the burglars get in the house?' I asked.

'Supposedly, they broke a basement window. They tried to make it look like they came in that way, and did a piss-poor job. I checked. The window was broken all right, and from the outside. But that window's right over a dusty work table – and there are no footprints on that table, just broken glass. Besides, the basement door to the upstairs was locked. So how did the killers get into the house?'

'What about Cynthia's knight in shining armor?' I asked. 'Did the lawyer lock the basement door when he came charging inside?'

'Oh, so the burglars just floated to the basement stairs, without touching that table? Maybe they really are Ghost Burglars.'

Hm. Sarcasm. I kept quiet. Jace was wound up. He finally quit pacing up and down and sat on the edge of a marble cherub sink with gold fixtures. Six cherubs supported his rear.

'No, the lawyer had no trouble getting inside. He had a key to the house,' Jace said.

'A key? Who gives their lawyer a key? That's weird.'

'That's not all that's strange, Angela. That lawyer – Wes Desloge – stopped me from talking to Mrs Lockridge because she was "upset" and hauled her off to his house. How do they get by with that?'

Jace was a Chicago transplant who'd patrolled that city's scariest neighborhoods. Now that he worked in the Forest, he was learning the rich were gangs in classier clothes.

'This morning, I'm going over to Wesley's house at ten

o'clock to see Sleeping Beauty, and I don't care if she has a battalion of lawyers with her!'

Jace's cell phone chirped and he answered it with a terse, 'Budewitz.'

Then I heard, 'The housekeeper is here? Have a uniform escort her inside. I'll meet her in the small room off the kitchen. It's been cleared. And don't let anyone tell her what's going on.'

'That was Mike at the gate,' he said. 'The Lockridges' housekeeper, Harriet Timmons, is here. Do you know her?'

'Vaguely. My mom knew her better,' I said.

'Come sit in while I talk with her,' he said. 'She may feel more comfortable talking when someone she knows is there.'

I checked my iPad. It was 6:31 in the morning. I'd been here two hours. I made sure that Tom's medications were safely packed in my DI case, then followed Jace down the marble steps to the breakfast room, rolling the case with me. I didn't want any chain of custody problems with the medical evidence.

The 'small' room off the kitchen was a good thirty feet long, and furnished with an antique oak round table with lion-paw feet and a matching sideboard. Cheerful yellow chintz curtains revealed the side lawn and a garden with a gazebo. I could barely make them out.

Harriet Timmons looked older than I remembered. She was a sturdy sixty-something, with tightly permed gray hair. She was dressed for work in a white nylon uniform and thick-soled white nurse's shoes. The right shoe was slit across the bulge on her foot, possibly to ease a bunion. Harriet carried a fat black leather purse and a canvas bag jammed with cleaning supplies, which she set on the floor. She kept her purse on her lap. Her light blue eyes were clouded with fear and worry.

Jace introduced us, and Harriet said, 'I knew your mama, Angela. She passed way too young. She was a fine woman.' She managed a smile.

'Yes, she was,' I said. 'I miss her every day.'

The social niceties over, Harriet got down to business. 'What's wrong, Detective? Was it them Ghost Burglars? Did they hurt Mr Tom?'

'Now, why would you think it was burglars?' Jace asked.

'Because that's all anybody can talk about. People are shaking in their shoes, wondering who's going to be hit next. I was talking to Mr Tom just the other morning at breakfast and I said, "It's just a matter of time before they hit this house."'

'And what did Mr Lockridge say?' Jace asked.

'He laughed and said, "You worry too much, Harry" – that was his nickname for me, Harry. "We've got old Prince here" – and he tossed the dog a piece of his breakfast bacon – "and I keep a gun in my bedside table. We're perfectly safe."

'Call me superstitious if you want, Detective, but I crossed myself then. I knew he was tempting fate with those words. Now tell me, please, is Mr Tom OK? Why are all these police here?'

I noticed she didn't ask about Mrs Lockridge. So did Jace.

'Aren't you worried about Mrs Lockridge, too?' he asked.

'That one.' She rolled her eyes. 'She can take care of herself. Cindy Lockridge is like a cat. She always lands on her feet.' Harriet's eyes narrowed, and I thought there was no love lost between her and Cynthia Lockridge.

'What time do you usually report for work, Mrs Timmons?' Jace asked.

'Six thirty. I bring Mr Tom his coffee at seven a.m. in his room. He's an early riser. His married daughter, Victoria, brings his breakfast at seven thirty. They always eat together. Victoria is a sweet girl, devoted to her daddy. They finish up about eight thirty and she leaves for her job – she's an insurance adjuster. Then I fix Mr Tom what he calls his real breakfast – fried eggs, bacon, hash browns and a loaf of toast with butter and my homemade jam.'

'Why the two breakfasts?' Jace asked.

'Victoria is a health nut – eats all that organic stuff. In the last few years, Mr Tom put on some weight and had a heart attack. Victoria's worried about his diet. She wants him to eat healthy, so she bakes him what she calls heart-healthy food – oatmeal raisin cookies, zucchini bread, and bran muffins. She cuts up fresh fruit for him, too. They have breakfast together in the gazebo, if the weather's nice. Mr Tom says those healthy muffins taste like ceiling insulation.'

'Why does Mr Lockridge eat his daughter's food if he doesn't like it?' Jace asked.

'Because Mr Tom loves her, and this is their time together. I've known Victoria most of her life – she's always been a daddy's girl, and after her mother died of cancer, they were closer than ever.'

'How did Victoria get along with her stepmother?' Jace asked.

'She never complained, but I know her stepmother didn't treat her well. Not well at all. Victoria wanted to get along with her father's new wife, for his sake. When Mr Tom announced he was marrying Cindy, I thought it would be a happy time for all of them. Victoria was newly engaged to a nice young man, a banker, Ashton Du Pres. Do you know him?'

'I know the name,' Jace said. 'Victoria married into a powerful Forest family.'

'Yes, she married well. Mr Tom was thrilled by the match. He promised the couple a destination wedding in Paris. He'd fly in all their friends and they'd have a big party. But that didn't happen.

'Instead, Cindy talked Mr Tom into giving Victoria and Ashton a wedding at the Ritz-Carlton in St. Louis – which was nice, but not the same – and a two-week honeymoon in Paris.

'I asked Victoria if she was unhappy with the change of plans, and she said, "It's still Paris, and Ashton and I will have more time to be together." That's the kind of person she was.'

'What happened to the money Mr Lockridge saved from the Paris wedding?' Jace asked.

'Cindy used that money to renovate Mr Tom's vacation home at the Lake of the Ozarks. Turned it into a party place for her and her low-rent friends.' I could see the anger in the housekeeper's eyes.

'I felt like Cindy was in competition with Victoria,' Mrs Timmons said. 'Cindy's engagement ring had to be bigger than Victoria's. For Victoria's first anniversary, Ashton bought her a new Beemer. Cindy insisted that she get a new car, too. Mr

Tom gave her a red convertible Jaguar. When Victoria got a cocktail ring from a local jeweler, Cindy had to have one from Harry Winston in New York! Everything Cindy got had to be better than Victoria's.'

'Did the women fight?' Jace asked.

'No, but they weren't all huggy and kissy, either. I guess you could say they were civil to each other.'

'One more question,' I said. 'Why would a rich woman like Victoria work as an insurance adjuster?'

'Because she wasn't raised to be rich and useless.' Something flared in the housekeeper's eyes: anger? Determination? I wasn't sure. 'Victoria started working as an insurance adjustor right after college, and liked the job. She was good with numbers. And sometimes, if she could get by with it, she'd use her power to help people. When the trailer park where Cindy grew up was hit by a tornado, Victoria made sure the residents got a good deal when their homes were damaged. She couldn't do that all the time, but she helped when she could. She wasn't one of the idle rich, like you see too often here in the Forest.'

Harriet Timmons said, 'I've answered your questions, Detective, and you still haven't answered mine. What happened? Is Mr Tom OK?'

I could see by Harriet's stricken eyes and her white knuckles gripping her black purse that she was expecting bad news. Jace's answer was swift.

'I'm sorry, Mrs Timmons. Mr Lockridge is dead.'

FOUR

Harriet Timmons froze at Jace's words: 'Mr Lockridge is dead.'

'What?' she said. It wasn't a question. It was a denial.

Jace repeated himself: 'I'm sorry, Mrs Timmons. Mr Lockridge is dead.'

The housekeeper clutched her chest and went as white as her uniform. She was breathing in short, sharp gasps. She slumped in her chair and began rocking back and forth.

'No!' she cried. 'No! Not Mr Tom! That slut killed him. She and her lawyer boyfriend. They've been plotting this for months.'

Jace kneeled down next to her. 'Mrs Timmons, are you feeling OK? Can I call a doctor for you? An ambulance?'

'No.' Her voice was a weak gasp. Jace looked at me, sending a silent message. I nodded yes. I understood his signal – a woman like Mrs Timmons would not want to 'make a fuss,' but her breathing problems could not be ignored. I slipped out of the room and called 911.

'I have asthma. I just need my inhaler. In my purse.' She fumbled with the clasp, but couldn't open it. Jace gently took the purse, the size of a small suitcase, rummaged around inside for the inhaler, then handed it to her. By the desperate way Mrs Timmons handled the puffer, I was glad I'd called 911 for her.

'Would you like some water?' he asked.

Mrs Timmons nodded. Jace said, 'Angela, would you mind? The techs have cleared the kitchen.'

In the kitchen, I filled a glass with cool water from the fridge and hurried back. Mrs Timmons gulped down the water. Her reddened, work-worn hands trembled when she held the glass. I didn't like her color or her raspy breathing.

When she was calmer, Jace said, 'You've had a terrible shock, Mrs Timmons.'

'Better now,' she said with a wheeze. She could only talk in short phrases. I wondered if Jace should be questioning her before the ambulance got here. 'I'll help. Any way I can. Mr Tom was a good man. A kind man. Apologies for my language, Detective. I should not have used. The S-word. Not even for. That woman.'

'I understand.' Jace's voice was soft and he leaned toward her. 'What did you mean, when you said uh . . . Mrs Lockridge . . . and her lawyer boyfriend were plotting against the victim? Who is the lawyer?'

'That Wes person.' Mrs Timmons spat out his name. 'He has a key. To this house. Comes and goes at all hours. He's supposed to be helping That Woman' – Mrs Timmons said it like she couldn't bear to use Cynthia's name – 'with the financial part. For her committee. Those big-deal charity events. Have money. Lots of money. The top tickets. This Christmas ball. Fifty thousand dollars for a table. More than I make in a year.'

She gave a kind of wheezy laugh and started coughing. I wanted her to stop talking, but didn't dare say anything.

'Wes and That Woman. Constantly together in her office. Alone. I may be old. But I'm no fool, Detective. He and she were . . . uh . . .'

Mrs Timmons stopped, and said, 'They were . . . they did . . . she was . . .' Red with embarrassment, she burst out: 'They were doing it. On the couch. In her office.' Mrs Timmons shifted uncomfortably after that revelation, and studied her white shoes.

'They were having sex?' Jace asked.

'Yes! I heard them! I couldn't help it.' Another wheeze that was painful to hear.

'Is that why you think Mrs Lockridge was plotting to kill her husband? She was having an affair with the lawyer?'

'Yes. She has expensive tastes. Look around here – all this fancy stuff is her work. That lawyer liked to throw money around, too. They were two of a kind.'

Mrs Timmons sat with her hands crossed, quietly pleased after this revelation.

'Was Mr Lockridge unfaithful?' Jace asked.

'Never looked at another woman,' she said. 'Poor Mr Tom, as he got older and heavier, he was having problems in the bedroom department. Popping Viagra like M&Ms. But it wasn't helping.'

'How do you know that?' Jace asked.

'I found all those empty Viagra bottles in his dressing room trash.' Now her color was high. 'And if you want more proof, I wash their sheets. Nothing on them, if you know what I mean.'

Mrs Timmons was talking faster now, as if she wanted to unburden herself. 'That lawyer, Wes, was only thirty-five. Much closer in age to That Woman. One day, when I was dusting the hall table outside her office, I heard him talking to her. He said, "Why don't you ditch the old man and marry me? He can't satisfy you the way I can." That Woman said something I couldn't hear, and then Mr Tom came down the hall with Prince and I starting dusting again.'

'Did Mr Lockridge know his wife was unfaithful?' Jace asked.

'I don't know. Mr Tom never mentioned her having another man, not even when they had disagreements. He was friends with Wes, something about they were in the same college fraternity and Mr Tom was trying to help Wes's career. Mr Tom said working on the financial part of those parties for That Woman would introduce Wes to the "right people." He wanted Wes to meet the local movers and shakers. It hurt my heart to see Mr Tom laughing and joking with the man who put the horns on his head. I can't tell you how many times I wanted to tell him, but I never did. If I'd had any gumption and spoken up, that nice man might be alive today.'

Mrs Timmons started weeping. Jace handed her his pocket handkerchief, and she mopped her eyes. Then her tears turned into wracking coughs, and she grabbed for her inhaler again. The poor woman was wheezing and couldn't talk. The inhaler clattered to the floor.

'Mrs Timmons!' I jumped up and handed her the inhaler, but it wasn't much help. She was panicky and gasping for breath.

Jace's cell phone rang and I heard him say, 'Yes, Mike,

send the ambulance up here ASAP – lights and sirens. It's an emergency. The housekeeper is having an asthma attack. And call Ken will you? Send him to me quick.'

Now Mrs Timmons was clawing at her chest, trying to breathe. I tried to soothe her and hold her hands to keep her from hurting herself, but it didn't work.

Within two minutes – though it seemed like forever – the ambulance arrived. Two paramedics the size of minivans put Mrs Timmons on a gurney, and clapped an oxygen mask over her face. Now the sturdy housekeeper seemed very small and frightened.

'Should I go with Mrs Timmons?' I asked.

Jace looked at me like I had two heads. 'Angela, no. Chain of custody, remember? You have to stay here to finish the DI paperwork, and arrange for the pickup service to remove the body after we clear the scene. That's why I sent for Ken.'

Ken, an older uniform with thick gray hair, was at Jace's side.

'You woke me up at four a.m.,' I said. 'I'm not too sharp when I get up at that hour. I wasn't thinking, Jace.'

'Does Mrs Timmons have any family we can contact?' Jace regarded me as his local Forest expert.

'Her sister, Patti Russell, works at City Hall.' I could see the woman in my mind's eye, behind a desk covered with pictures of her grandchildren. She was a good-natured brunette in her mid-fifties who wore bright pink lipstick.

'Hey, Ken, do you know Patti Russell at City Hall?' he asked.

'Sure. Patti and I go way back.'

'Mrs Timmons here is Patti's sister,' Jace said. 'She's Tom Lockridge's housekeeper and she's pretty upset. Why don't you see if there's room in the ambulance for you to ride along and head over to the ER with her? I'll call Mrs Russell, then pick you up when I leave here.'

'No problem,' he said with a smile. Ken was divorced, and I knew he'd escaped a boring grid search. At the hospital he could drink bad coffee and flirt with his nurse girlfriend.

By now, the paramedics seemed to have Mrs Timmons stabilized and were pushing the clanking gurney out the door. Ken ran after them.

Jace turned to me. 'I'll call the sister and send her over to the ER. Stand by, will you, Angela?'

Jace hit the speaker button on his cell phone so I could hear the conversation. Patti answered the phone cheerfully, but when Jace told her about Harriet, I could almost imagine the blood draining from her round face. 'Did something set her off, Detective?' Patti asked.

'Yes, Mr Lockridge was shot to death.'

Patti lowered her voice and said, 'By that lying, cheating missus of his, no doubt. I heard about her and her lawyer boyfriend.'

I wondered if Patti had gotten that information from her sister.

'Thank you, Mrs Russell.' Jace cut her off. 'When you see your sister, tell her we're pulling for her.'

Jace hung up. A young crewcut uniform waited hesitantly in the doorway. 'Detective,' he said. 'Breakfast is here.'

'Good. Put the food in here. And tell everybody this room's been cleared.'

Breakfast? What time was it? I checked my iPad: almost seven o'clock. I'd been here nearly three hours. I needed another infusion of coffee.

'We might as well get some food, Angela,' Jace said. 'This is going to be a long day.'

On the carved oak table were two huge containers of hot coffee, paper cups, napkins, and an array of bagels, plus whipped cream-cheese spreads: plain, honey-almond, strawberry and jalapeno pepper.

I didn't realize how hungry I was until I spread a cinnamon-raisin bagel with honey-almond cream cheese. By the time I poured myself a large cup of black coffee, my stomach was growling.

Jace and I pulled our chairs over to the long buffet. I kept my voice low. 'Do you think Cynthia killed her husband?'

'That's how it's looking now. Either that, or she hired a hitman. Maybe those Ghost Burglars. What I'd like to do next is—'

Jace's cell phone buzzed and he took the call. 'Yeah, Mike, what is it? The daughter's here? OK, have her sign the log and call a uniform to escort her here. I want to talk to her. I'm in the breakfast room. And don't tell her what's happened.'

'Lockridge's daughter Victoria is on the way.' Jace poured himself more coffee.

'Maybe she can tell us who killed her father.'

FIVE

Victoria Lockridge Du Pres was a beauty, even with her face pale and pinched with worry. She was tall and willowy, and everything about her said money, power and style: her long blonde hair was expensively cut. She had a slim black pantsuit and a sleek black briefcase tucked under her arm. Despite her high heels, she quickly outdistanced her cop escort and loped inside to speak to us. I should have hated her on sight, but there was something likeable about her. As she got closer, I saw she was carrying a platter covered with a blue cloth napkin.

'Detective,' she said, a bit breathless. 'Is my father OK? Why are all the police here? Was he robbed by the Ghost Burglars?'

'Please, sit, Mrs Du Pres,' Jace said, and introduced us.

'Victoria,' she said, as she sat in a chair and tried on a wobbly smile. 'Please call me Victoria. The police cars are all over the place. On the way here, I saw an ambulance speeding toward SOS. Was Daddy in there? Was he hurt?' Now she was holding the platter in her lap. The briefcase was propped next to her chair.

'No, Victoria,' Jace said. 'Your father wasn't in the ambulance.'

Victoria paused. 'Was it Timmy? I mean, Mrs Timmons. Where is she? Timmy's been like a mother to me.'

'It was Mrs Timmons,' Jace said. He saw the alarm in Victoria's face and quickly added, 'I don't think it's serious. She had an asthma attack and she's on her way to the hospital for a breathing treatment. Her sister will be joining her.'

'What about Daddy? Why wasn't he with her?'

'That's twice you've mentioned your father,' Jace said. 'You've also asked after your housekeeper. What about your stepmother?'

Victoria looked blank. 'What about her? Is she hurt?'

'She's fine. But your father is dead.'

'No,' Victoria shrieked. 'Not my daddy!' The platter slid off her lap and crashed to the floor, smashing into pieces. Brown muffins rolled across the polished wood floor and a bowl of cut strawberries landed with a splat.

Now her long hair hung like a curtain over her face, hiding her tears. Rocking back and forth, Victoria said, 'She killed him. I knew she didn't love Daddy. All she wanted was his money. Damn her! Damn her to hell!'

Victoria reached into her briefcase, and pulled out a packet of tissues. Jace and I sat quietly while Victoria cried herself out. Finally, she wiped her streaming eyes and asked, 'What happened? How did Daddy die?'

'He was shot,' Jace said.

'Did he suffer?' The question all loving family members asked.

'No,' Jace said. 'He died in his sleep. He never felt a thing.'

We all say something similar to the victim's family, whether it's true or not. People who knew what really happened to their loved ones suffered even more.

'May I see him?' Though she seemed to be a take-charge person, her question was polite, even tentative.

'I'm afraid not, Victoria. It's best to remember your father the way he was.'

'Oh, no. His death must have been horrible. Poor Daddy.' That sparked another rainfall of tears.

Jace let her cry again, then said, 'That's not the reason, Victoria. You wouldn't want to interfere with a crime scene, would you?'

She sniffled. 'No, of course not.'

'When I first told you your father was dead, you said, "She killed him. I knew she didn't love Daddy. All she wanted was his money." Who were you talking about?'

'Cynthia,' Victoria said. 'My stepmother.'

'Why do you think she killed your father? Was she angry, vengeful, or greedy?'

'Yes,' Victoria said. 'All that and more. Daddy is sixty-six. He's thirty-four years older than Cynthia and he wanted to slow down. Sell the company and retire. He wanted to move to his house in the Ozarks, where he could relax.'

'What would happen to this house?' Jace looked around the vast, over-decorated room.

'Daddy wanted to sell it. The upkeep on this building was horrendous. He also wanted to get rid of his speedboat and the private jet. Cynthia was not happy about those changes.

'Thanks to Daddy, she's becoming a big deal in local society. She's co-chairing the Forest Christmas Ball. That's quite an honor, you know. Especially for someone who grew up in a mobile home.'

I gave Victoria points for saying Cynthia had lived in a mobile home instead of a trailer. She wasn't going to take a cheap shot and call her stepmother 'trailer trash.'

'After her marriage, Cynthia changed. She'd been my father's office manager, but once she tied the knot, she quit working and became quite the party girl. Whenever she and my father flew to the Ozarks or to Telluride, she'd pack the plane with friends and they'd have wild parties – too wild for me, I'm afraid.'

Jace raised an eyebrow. 'Your father participated?'

Victoria blushed and looked down at her manicured hands. 'I never went to those parties – but I heard about them. This was when they were first married and he wasn't quite so . . . uh, Daddy's put on a lot of weight in recent years. I've been trying to get him to eat healthy food. I come over in the morning for coffee and bring him a healthy breakfast. Today it was bran muffins and strawberries.'

'You visit your father every morning?' Jace asked.

'Every weekday morning, before I go to work. I'm an insurance adjustor.'

'How long do you stay with your father?'

'About an hour. It was our time together.'

'Did your stepmother ever threaten your father?'

Victoria looked confused. 'No, never. Cynthia liked to party and she liked pretty clothes, but she never threatened Daddy or anyone else.'

'How do you know?' Jace asked.

'Daddy would have told me.'

'Does your stepmother own any weapons? Does she have a gun for personal protection?'

'No,' Victoria said. 'Daddy has a .22. He keeps it in a drawer by his bed. Cynthia relies on her Malinois, Prince, for protection. About two years ago, a woman who lives in one of these big houses was raped. The rapist came in an open kitchen door during the day, when the alarm system was off. He raped the woman in an upstairs bedroom. The house was so big, the staff couldn't hear her screams. After that, Cynthia kept Prince by her side when she worked alone in her office.'

'Would your stepmother get a big inheritance if your father died?' Jace asked.

'Yes,' Victoria said. 'She'll get everything. The house and the business.'

'How did you feel about this?' Jace asked. 'About Cynthia getting everything.'

Victoria shrugged. 'It's Daddy's money. Also, I married Ashton Du Pres.'

She paused, waiting for us to take in that information. The Du Pres were the richest and most powerful family in the Forest. Victoria was letting us know she didn't need her father's money. 'When Ashton and I married, Daddy settled some money on us and explained that the rest would go to Cynthia. He was very generous.'

'What makes you think that your stepmother killed your father?'

'Her prenup, for one thing. If they divorced, Cynthia would get one hundred thousand dollars – and she's gotten used to high living. If Daddy found out she was having an affair, she would get nothing if they divorced.'

'And was she?' Jace asked. 'Was she having an affair?'

Victoria was silent for a long moment. Then she said, 'My situation with my stepmother is complicated, Detective. She's two years younger than me. She's been married to my father for seven years. I don't like her, but I've tolerated her for my father's sake.'

Jace cut her off, rather rudely, I thought. 'You didn't answer my question, Victoria. Was your stepmother having an affair?'

'I was trying to put it into perspective for you,' she said. 'Yes, Cynthia was having an affair.'

'Who with?' Jace asked.

'Her lawyer, Wesley Desloge.'

'How do you know she was unfaithful?'

'I walked in on them accidentally in her office. She was buttoning her blouse and he was zipping his pants. They looked caught and guilty. The couch was rumpled and there was a wine bottle and two glasses next to it. So yes, they were having an affair.'

'How did you feel about the affair?' Jace asked.

'I was embarrassed and angry for my father's sake. Daddy was trying to help Wesley's career, and he was betrayed by his protégé. I could hardly talk to Wes, I disliked the man so much.'

'Did your stepmother have other affairs?' Jace asked.

'Yes, I think so. At least two that I know about: one with her ski instructor and one with the pool boy. I walked in on her and the ski instructor in the hot tub at Daddy's Telluride home – and both were naked. Cynthia told me not to be a prude. You'd think she'd mend her ways after that, but she didn't. I found men's underwear on the floor at the entrance to the pool house – a bright blue banana sack in a size my father couldn't wear – and Cynthia's bikini, and I heard her giggling with a man in the dressing room. That's not proof, I know. But I had strong suspicions.'

'Did your father know about Cynthia's affairs?' Jace asked.

'I think he didn't want to know,' Victoria said. 'He really loved Cynthia. I didn't have the heart to tell him. That's why I made such an effort to get along with her.'

'When did they start dating?'

'About eight years ago, when she was working at his construction company. She was twenty-four, and Daddy was a lonely widower. Mummy had died five years before.'

For the first time, Victoria's eyes softened. 'My mother had breast cancer. Daddy missed her so much. He threw himself into his work to try to forget his loss.

'Cynthia – she went by Cindy then – was worried Daddy wasn't eating right. He lived mostly off Cokes and snacks from the company vending machine. She started making him home-cooked meals, and soon he asked her out. Next thing I knew, she was planning a big wedding.

'Daddy bought her this great big mansion and let her decorate it.' Victoria tried to keep her voice neutral, but I could hear the suppressed anger.

'How did you get along with Cynthia?' Jace asked.

Victoria paused, and selected her next words carefully. 'I wanted to like her, for Daddy's sake. When Daddy announced he was marrying Cynthia, I thought it would be a golden time for both of us. Ashton and I were engaged, and Daddy had promised us a destination wedding in Paris.

'Instead, Cynthia talked him into giving us a wedding at the Ritz-Carlton in St. Louis – which was lovely, but not the same – and a two-week honeymoon in Paris. I never complained. I knew I'd sound spoiled. Besides, this new plan gave Ashton and me two weeks alone in Paris.'

'What happened to the money that should have gone to your Paris wedding?' Jace asked.

'Cynthia used it to renovate my parents' vacation home at the Lake of the Ozarks into a party place. That's where she introduced Daddy to coke. He never used drugs before he met her.'

'Did he still use drugs?' Jace asked.

She hesitated, then said, 'Yes. I tried to get him to stop, but he said coke made him feel mellow. Mellow!'

'Where does Cynthia buy the drugs?' Jace asked.

'From her trainer. I think she had a fling with him last summer. It's bad enough that coke is illegal, but it's also dangerous – Daddy's already had one heart attack. He's supposed to watch his diet. That's another worry. Instead of serving him healthy meals, Cynthia encouraged him to eat the fattening food that Timmy – Mrs Timmons – cooked. Dinners were fried chicken in cream gravy, or pork roast with gravy, or cheeseburgers with french fries. At night, after dinner, Cynthia would whip up a bowl of sour cream cheese dip and give him a whole bag of potato chips. It was like she was trying to kill Daddy!'

Cynthia might have been hoping her husband would dig his

grave with his teeth, but it wasn't illegal to feed your husband fattening food. Otherwise, half the wives in America would be in jail.

'Sometimes, I felt like Cynthia was in competition with me,' Victoria said.

'For our first anniversary, Ashton bought me a new Beemer. Cynthia insisted Daddy get her a Jaguar. When I got a tennis bracelet from a local jeweler, hers had to be from Tiffany.

'Daddy doesn't work as much in the winter, and Cynthia talked him into buying a condo in Telluride. Then she had to have expensive ski clothes and furs, and parties for her friends. Daddy would fly them out on the company plane.

'Lately, like I've said, Daddy's been talking about retirement. His new office manager, Debbie Carlone, says he's been putting out feelers to sell the business.'

'His office manager talked to you about your father's business?' Jace asked.

'Yes, Debbie and I are old friends,' she said, and smiled. 'I make sure she looks after Daddy and sees that he eats a good lunch.'

Jace asked, 'Where were you between midnight and three a.m. last night, Mrs Du Pres?'

'Where was I?' she repeated.

'That's what I said.'

'I was home. In bed. With my husband.'

'Can you prove that?'

Victoria looked confused for a moment, then said, 'Well, I suppose you could check our home security system. The house alarm was on at eleven p.m., when we went to bed, until six this morning. No doors were opened during that time, and our cars were in the garage all night.'

'How do you benefit from your father's death?'

Victoria's eyes widened in shock. 'Benefit? How can I benefit? I don't benefit at all,' she said. 'My mother's dead and now I've lost my father. I have no one else from my childhood except Timmy.'

She looked at Jace with hurt eyes. 'You don't think I killed Daddy, do you?'

I was thinking the same thing. Jace was being unusually harsh.

'I don't know what to think, Mrs Du Pres. I just want answers.'

SIX

After a weeping Victoria left, Jace and I swept up the broken platter, ruined muffins and spilled strawberries, and went back to work. I hauled my DI case upstairs again to the gold and marble master bath, to finish checking the contents of Tom's medicine cabinet.

On the cherub-infested sink closest to the door, I saw an open prescription bottle with zolpidem, a sleep medication, and next to it a Waterford glass with about two ounces of a clear liquid. It smelled like water. I poured the liquid into a Tupperware container and bagged the glass. The medication, prescribed by Dr Carmen Bartlett, the Forest internist, was for thirty pills, and still contained twenty-three, so Tom had probably not overdosed. If Tom did take those pills, I hoped he was asleep when he was shot.

I stashed all the over-the-counter medications, from corn plasters to calamine lotion, in a container for the ME. These mundane remedies seemed wildly out of place in the ornate bathroom.

Jace stopped by to see how I was doing. 'Almost finished here,' I said. 'I've called the van to take the body to the ME.'

'Do you have everything you need for your DI report?' Jace asked.

'Everything but some demographic information I'll have to get from the decedent's wife. Is she still at Wesley Desloge's house?'

'Yes. After you sign off on the ME's paperwork, we can go over together. I have a few questions for her myself.'

'You had some harsh questions for Victoria.'

'Just doing my job,' Jace said, but his usually genial face was set in a stubborn look.

'Do you think she killed her father?'

'I think she's worth checking out. Why? Do you think she's innocent?'

'I think she was surprisingly honest for a Forest dweller. Most would never admit they disliked their stepmother. She was very straightforward. I liked her.'

Jace shrugged, dismissing my words.

It was ten after ten when I signed off on the paperwork and Tom Lockridge's body was delivered to the ME. I followed Jace to Wesley Desloge's mansion on the other side of the Forest. The up-and-coming lawyer lived in a three-story Beaux-Arts fairytale with towers, spires, and terra cotta leaves and flowers. I wondered if he'd inherited the house.

A trim seventy-something woman with shoulder-length silver hair answered the door. Jace introduced us and we showed our ID. 'I'm Emma Mason, Mr Desloge's house-keeper,' she said. 'How may I help you?'

'We want to talk to Wesley Desloge and Mrs Lockridge,' Jace said.

'I'll inform them that you are here. Please follow me.'

Jace and I tried not to gawk at the entrance hall: It was creamy-white marble with a stunning silver chandelier. Two delicate marble nymphs balancing silver crystal balls on their slender fingers guarded the sweeping staircase. Tiffany stained-glass windows gave the room magical light and color.

Emma showed us to a white sitting room with a pair of antique rosewood sofas upholstered in peach silk. An oval portrait of a nineteenth-century belle smiled coyly over the ornate fireplace. Jace and I sat on a peach sofa. I opened my iPad to Tom Lockridge's case.

'What a difference from the Lockridge place, huh?' Jace whispered.

'This is how to spend money,' I whispered back.

'How does he afford this?' Jace asked. 'Does he have family money?'

'I don't know,' I said. 'I can ask—' I quickly shut up when I heard footsteps in the hallway.

Wesley Desloge was wearing a black silk dressing gown, trousers, embroidered velvet slippers, and the first cravat I'd seen outside of a movie. He was a mid-sized man with a gym-sculpted body and thick black hair. Despite his distinguished reputation, all he needed was a pencil-thin mustache to look like a Victorian villain. I figured I was prejudiced – I hardly knew the man.

Wes escorted Cynthia Lockridge by the elbow. She wore no make-up, which made her pale skin look more beautiful. Her dark hair tumbled down her back. Her blue eyes were red from crying. Cynthia was a tiny woman, barely five feet tall, in a black pantsuit and black heels. Where did she get those clothes? I wondered. She left her home last night wearing black silk lounging pajamas, and she wasn't carrying an overnight bag. Did she keep clothes at her lover's home? Was Wes her lover, or was that just gossip?

Wes steered Cynthia to the peach satin sofa across from us. She sat as far away from the lawyer as she could.

'I want to make it clear that I'm representing Mrs Lockridge.' Wes reached over to pat Cynthia's shoulder. She stiffened and tried to edge away. It was such a small movement, I wondered if I'd imagined it.

'I'm the death investigator for your husband's case, Mrs Lockridge,' I said. 'I need some general information for my report.'

I asked easy, harmless questions: what was her husband's date of birth? Did she know his social security number? She rattled off both facts.

She confirmed that Doc Carmen Bartlett was his internist and that her husband had had a mild heart attack six months ago and had been taking medication.

'Is your husband's daughter, Victoria, his closest living relative?' I asked.

'He has a great-aunt in North Carolina, but they aren't very close. That's about it.'

'When was the last time you saw your husband alive?'

'About eleven thirty last night,' Cynthia said. 'He stopped by my office and said he was going to bed. I told him I'd finish working on the menu for the Christmas ball and then join him. I kissed him goodnight and he scratched Prince's ears. And that's . . . that's the last time I saw Tom alive.' Her voice broke and she began crying. Wes scooted over to put his arm around her and tried to pull her toward him, but she stayed rigid as a statue.

Jace looked at me and raised an eyebrow. I nodded slightly to let him know I had all the information I needed.

'Mrs Lockridge,' Jace said. 'Where were you at the time of the crime?'

Cynthia gave a put-upon sigh. Wes reacted angrily. 'Detective Budewitz! This poor woman has already told you numerous times that she was in her office. How many times does she have to answer this pointless question?'

'As many times as I ask it,' Jace said, 'until Mrs Lockridge answers to my satisfaction.'

Cynthia's voice shook. 'As I told you before, Detective, I was working in my office. My dog Prince was with me.'

'Why didn't Prince react when the burglars broke into the house?'

'I don't know. He was asleep,' Cynthia said.

'Isn't your Malinois a trained guard dog?' Jace said. 'I don't understand how two intruders could enter your house and the dog didn't hear them.'

'My client is not an expert on animal behavior, Detective,' Wes said.

'Was anything missing, Mrs Lockridge?' Jace asked.

'Missing?' She looked bewildered.

'I mean, was anything stolen? Did the Ghost Burglars take silver, jewelry or small works of art?'

'No, I don't think so. My good jewelry is in a safe deposit box at the bank. I keep a few everyday pieces in the jewelry box in my dressing room, and you saw what happened to that: the burglars destroyed my antique jewelry box and ruined my pearls. Ground them to powder! Tom was still wearing his diamond ring, which was appraised for fifty thousand dollars. And none of our art is gone.'

Cynthia wept harder and took a lace-edged handkerchief from her pocket. I hadn't seen one of those in a while.

'How long have you been married, Mrs Lockridge?' Jace asked.

'Seven years,' she said, sniffling.

Seven years? I wondered if Cynthia had the so-called

seven-year itch, or if she'd become disenchanted with her husband earlier in their marriage.

'Have you had any previous marriages?'

'No!' Cynthia said. 'I was twenty-four when I married. I've only been married once.'

'How would you describe your marriage?' Jace asked.

'Happy,' Cynthia said. 'We are – were – very happy. Tom and I had a lovely life. We have our home in the Forest, which I've been decorating, a weekend home at the Lake of the Ozarks, and a winter home in Colorado.'

'So that's how you measure marital happiness?' Jace asked. 'By how many homes you have?'

Wes raised his voice. 'Detective! That's uncalled for.'

Cynthia began crying again. Through her tears she said, 'No, that's not it at all. I just meant that Tom loved me and he catered to my every whim. He's a good man.'

Jace's next question came out of nowhere. 'Are you having an affair?'

Cynthia looked like she'd been punched. 'No! Who would say such an ugly thing?'

'Never mind. Are you having an affair with Wesley Desloge?'

'Of course not!'

'Detective!' shouted Wes. 'That question is inappropriate.'

Jace ignored the lawyer and zeroed in on Cynthia. His eyes were hard, and his voice demanded, 'What's your relationship with Wesley Desloge?'

'He's our family lawyer. He's a friend of mine and my husband's. Wes and Tom were in the same fraternity. Tom hired Wes to help with the money side of my charity work. I deal with a lot of money and Tom wanted Wes to meet the local movers and shakers to help his career.'

'That's all I am, Detective,' Wes said. 'The Lockridge family lawyer.'

'Well, since you're the family lawyer,' Jace said, 'you should know about Mrs Lockridge's prenup. Is it true that if Tom died, Mrs Lockridge inherited her husband's entire estate, but if they divorced, she only got a hundred thousand dollars?'

Cynthia stopped crying. She eyed Jace with a startled expression.

Wes Desloge stood up and practically bellowed. 'This interview is over, Detective! Over! Have you no shame, attacking a grief-stricken widow? I'm asking you to leave my home. Now!'

SEVEN

Jace and I emerged dazed and sun-blinded into the warm spring day. It was almost noon, and the pleasant morning would soon be a scorcher.

My DI case rumbled over the driveway pavers as Jace and I walked to our cars. 'Why do you think the Ghost Burglars suddenly turned into killers?' I asked. 'Did they get frustrated they couldn't find anything to steal? Is that why they shot Tom Lockridge?'

'Couldn't find anything to steal? The victim was wearing a ginormus diamond ring,' Jace said. 'Fifty grand is a nice haul. I tell you, Angela, something is screwy here. I'm wondering if this burglary was a cover-up for another crime.'

He paused to let his words sink in.

'Cynthia killed her husband,' I said, keeping my voice low.

'Exactly,' Jace said. 'But we don't have any proof.'

I clicked open my car trunk and loaded in my DI case. 'Who else could it be?' I said. 'The sweet old housekeeper? The devoted daughter?'

'I'm not sure how devoted the daughter is,' Jace said. 'We don't know enough yet. It could be the ambitious lawyer. With Thomas Lockridge dead, Wes Desloge would have a rich society wife.'

'Were you watching those two?' I said. 'Cynthia practically sat on the sofa's arm to avoid Wes.'

'Could be an act,' Jace said.

'She flinched when Wes touched her.'

'Maybe they had a falling out,' Jace said. 'Crooks do that. Could mean one of them might talk if we apply a little pressure. And we haven't even looked at the construction company and its records. The killer could be someone in Lockridge's office.'

'There's only one person in his office, according to the daughter,' I said. 'Debbie Carlone is the manager.'

'Do you know Debbie?' Jace asked.

'I'm not sure,' I said. 'The name sounds familiar, but I can't put a face to it.'

'Come with me, please,' Jace said. 'You know everyone in the Forest.'

That was an exaggeration, but I did know the Forest ways better than Jace, an outsider from up North. I really wanted to go back to Chris's condo – and his bed. I'd been up since four in the morning, but Jace had been up even earlier. Officially, my job as a death investigator was over as soon as I filed my report. But Jace needed my help. So against my better judgment, I followed him to the office of the Chouteau Forest Construction Company.

Thomas Lockridge's company had graduated from a beat-up trailer to a yellow-brick building in an anonymous office park out by the interstate, but the company's new home wasn't anything to brag about. The name was painted on a glass door. Jace tried the handle, but the door was locked.

'Who's there?' A woman's voice crackled through the speaker by the door.

'Chouteau Forest police,' Jace said.

A buzzer sounded and Jace and I were admitted to the one-room office. A tearful redhead met us at the door.

'I heard about Mr Lockridge,' she said. 'I'm the CFCC's office manager, Debbie Carlone.'

But she wasn't. She was Debbie Martin. I checked her ring finger – no wedding band on her small, pretty hands. I knew another reason why Debbie wasn't going by her old name. I'd have to tell Jace later.

'Angela Richman, Debbie,' I said, deliberately leaving off her last name. 'We went to high school together.'

'Yes, of course,' she said, and gave me a lopsided smile. 'You've changed so much.' My face must have frozen – I'd never be a good poker player – because she quickly added, 'For the better, I mean. I've changed, too.'

So she had. Debbie's once natural red hair was chopped short, dyed carrot orange and looked French-fried. Her voluptuous body had expanded into soft, pillowy curves. Her skin was still smooth and creamy, and her navy pantsuit showed it to best advantage. Her eyes were red from crying and she kept wringing her hands.

'How did you know Mr Lockridge was dead?' Jace asked her.

'His daughter, Victoria, told me. Tom is always here by ten a.m., and when he didn't show by ten thirty, I called his cell and then texted him. No answer. I was worried. That's not like him. He always leaves me his schedule and tells me if he's going to be late. I called Victoria and she was at the hospital with their housekeeper.'

I glanced at Jace. One more point in Victoria's favor.

'How is Mrs Timmons?' Jace was interrupting the natural flow of his interrogation, but sometimes an easy question relaxed the person.

'She's recovering,' Debbie said. 'It was a bad asthma attack, and the doctor wants to keep Mrs Timmons in overnight, mostly for observation. Won't you come over to our sitting area?'

The windowless office was stark white, with the blue CFCC logo painted on the main wall. There were two desks – a small, neat receptionist's desk near the front and a massive oak desk behind a glass divider. File cabinets lined one wall.

Debbie's desk was the one near the door. It looked as if she'd arranged the desktop with a T-square. The computer was precisely in the center. Papers were stacked exactly in IN and OUT boxes on the left. Framed photos of a calico cat were lined up neatly on the right, along with a vase of pink carnations.

'Mr Lockridge gave me those flowers,' she said, and her voice wavered. 'Because this office is windowless, he insisted on brightening my desk with flowers. He was such a good man.' Now Debbie was crying too hard to talk.

The sitting area was in front of the desks. It had a small blue couch, two club chairs and a blue patterned rug. Jace and I each took a club chair. An easel displayed an architect's rendering of a CoffeeTime drive-in building.

'May I get you some coffee?' Debbie nodded at a coffee maker on a table next to a file cabinet. 'I just made a fresh pot.'

'That sounds good,' Jace and I said together.

'We both take it black,' he finished.

Debbie returned with three mugs, emblazoned with sayings by St. Louis artist Mary Engelbreit. She handed Jace one that said, 'Happiness must be grown in one's own garden.' She gave me, 'Walk towards the sunshine, and the shadows will fall behind you.' I took a sip of the coffee – it was hot and strong, just what I needed.

Debbie took 'Bloom where you're planted,' and promptly planted herself on the couch, holding on to the mug like the last life preserver on the Titanic.

'What did Victoria tell you happened to Mr Lockridge?' Jace asked.

'She was crying so hard, I could hardly understand her,' Debbie said. 'She said the Ghost Burglars had broken into the house and . . . and . . . they killed Tom. I couldn't believe it. I know those criminals have been terrorizing the Forest, but they've never killed anyone before. And Tom didn't deserve that. No one does.'

'What is your role at this company?' Jace asked.

'I'm the office manager, receptionist, bookkeeper – you name it.'

'Do you have a business degree?'

Debbie looked uneasy. 'No. I've learned everything on the job. Mr Lockridge hired me right after he married Cynthia. I'd been working as a cashier at the 7-Eleven and he used to stop by for a soda and chat with me. He said I had good people skills and offered me more money than I was making. I was happy to come here. I made it clear that I didn't have any degrees and he said that was fine – I do have a good head for figures.'

'What was your relationship with Mr Lockridge?' Jace asked.

Debbie bristled with outrage. 'Relationship? There is none, Detective. None at all!' She glared at Jace. 'Mr Lockridge is my employer. That's all. He never did or said anything in-appropriate. Never. Not even now, when his marriage is going through a bad time.'

'How do you know his marriage was troubled?' Jace asked.

Debbie blushed and shifted uncomfortably. 'I answer the phone, Detective. When Mrs Lockridge calls the office, I can overhear what Tom is saying. As you can see, there isn't much privacy.'

I glanced around the small white shoe box and saw Tom Lockridge sat ten feet away from Debbie, with only that glass partition between them.

'Did the couple argue?' Jace asked.

'Not exactly, but I could tell Tom was unhappy sometimes. Cynthia – Mrs Lockridge – wanted money constantly. She was determined to turn their Forest mansion into a showcase and Tom wanted to please her. Cynthia is more than thirty years younger than Tom, and like all young people, she wants to have fun. In the spring and summer, she wanted to fly to the Ozarks and party. Or she'd get bored in the winter and want to take her friends to Telluride. On the weekends when they were at home, Cynthia wanted to go to fancy society events and Tom – Mr Lockridge – had to donate thousands of dollars to the charities.

'Tom was trying to run his business. He was getting older and after his heart attack, he wanted to slow down. Cynthia kept pushing him for more: more money, and more fun. I think the poor man wanted to get off the merry-go-round. He told me he'd like to spend more time alone with Cynthia at their house in the Ozarks. He was sending out feelers to sell the company so he could retire. He never got his wish, poor man.'

Debbie sighed, and sipped her coffee, then said, 'When Victoria called and said that Tom was dead, my first thought was that he'd had a heart attack. His health was not good.'

Jace took a long drink of his coffee. 'Did Mr Lockridge want a divorce?'

'Oh, no! He loved Cynthia,' Debbie said, quickly. 'He was so proud of her. He'd always show me the photos of her in the society pages. Here. Look at this one.' She rummaged in the magazines on the table by the couch and found a *Forest Society Magazine*. 'Here she is on the cover, at the Heart Ball.' Tom's bulk was well-disguised in a black dinner jacket. Cynthia wore a glittering red dress designed to show off her perfect figure. Her diamond earrings sparkled. She looked at her husband with an adoring smile.

'Tom called her his Princess Bride,' Debbie said.

'Was Mrs Lockridge having an affair?' Jace asked.

Debbie slowly drank her coffee, as if buying time to organize her thoughts. Finally, she said, 'Victoria told me her stepmother was having an affair, but I never saw Cynthia with any man but Tom. And Tom never mentioned anything like that – not to me and not on the phone to Cynthia. There wasn't a hint. So far as I know, Cynthia was faithful. I like Victoria – we often have lunch together – but I know she's embarrassed to have a stepmother younger than she is. And Cynthia wasn't always kind to her. Victoria's a good daughter, and she never told her father about the games that Cynthia played.'

'What kind of games?' Jace asked.

'Victoria's husband gave her a tennis bracelet from the Forest Jewelers. Cynthia wanted one, too – but hers had to be from Tiffany. She called and called and finally Tom bought it for her. For their anniversary, Victoria's husband gave her the Tiffany T earrings with turquoise. Cynthia insisted on the rose gold and diamond earrings. It was like she was in competition with her stepdaughter.

'I'd take what Victoria says about Cynthia with a grain of salt – no, a boulder.'

'When you and Victoria had your lunches, what did you talk about?' Jace asked.

'Mostly her father. Victoria was worried about his health and she wanted to change his eating habits. It was a hopeless task. You can't turn a meat-and-potatoes man in his sixties into a granola and tofu lover, but Victoria was determined. She wanted me to keep track of his lunches and make sure he ate good food. Well, her idea of good. I told her I would, mostly to make her feel better. But Tom was my boss. I couldn't make him do anything he didn't want to do.'

Jace switched the subject. 'What kind of construction does your company do – residential or commercial?'

'Strictly commercial,' Debbie said.

'Was Mr Lockridge's company successful?'

She smiled brightly and pointed at the architect's rending. 'He just got the contract to build the new CoffeeTime franchise over at the mall. He was very happy about that.'

I noticed she didn't really answer Jace's question. Jace must have too, because he said, 'What are some of your other projects?'

'We built the new First Forest Bank drive-in location on Gravois.' (Six years ago, I thought.)

'And the new Chouteau Forest Doctors Building.' (Four years ago, I mentally added).

'We also built this entire complex,' Debbie said, proudly.

'How old is this office park?' Jace asked.

'Five years old, and seventy-five percent occupied,' she said.

'Anything else besides the CoffeeTime project going on now?' Jace asked.

'Nothing firm,' Debbie said. 'We're talking to several other franchises. We're doing well, even if the market is a little soft right now.'

'I'd like to look at your boss's office and the books,' Jace said.

Debbie shifted uncomfortably on the couch. 'Uh, don't you need a warrant for that?'

'As the office manager, I'd appreciate it if you'd cooperate,' Jace said.

'I'd like to, but what if Victoria gets mad at me? Or Mrs Lockridge?' She finished her coffee and set it on the table. 'I could get fired without a reference. I'll never get a job this good.'

She was pleading now, but politely. 'Would you please get a warrant, Detective, just to cover my tush? I'd really appreciate it.'

'I can do that,' Jace said. 'Angela and I will be back in an hour.'

Once outside, I said to Jace, 'Do you really need a subpoena in a murder case?'

'I'm just being careful,' he said. 'Cops need to follow due process or things can be tossed at trial. If the records belong to the deceased, there's not a big need to worry about a subpoena, but I'm asking for one just to be on the safe side. I'll make the call now.'

He did, then said, 'There's a little Italian place across from here, Luigi's. You want to grab a bite? It's after noon.'

We were seated quickly at the family-run restaurant, decorated with red-checked tablecloths and travel posters of Italy and perfumed with the delicious aroma of garlic and tomato sauce. Jace and I ordered the day's special, homemade ravioli.

When our server left, Jace said, 'You looked like you recognized Debbie Carlone.'

'I did, but she was Debbie Martin when I knew her. I think she's using her grandmother's last name.'

'Why would she do that?' Jace said.

'The summer after high school, Debbie killed her stepfather. He was abusing her – for five years. It was hushed up, but everyone in the Forest knew about it. The police said she was innocent.'

'How did she kill him?'

'Three shots to the head,' I said. 'With a .22. While he was asleep.'

EIGHT

'Does Mr Lockridge have a copy of his will here?' Jace asked.

Now that the detective had the warrant to 'cover my tush,' as Debbie had requested, the office manager was chatty and cooperative. After lunch, Jace and I went back to Tom's office. We were well-fed and reeking of garlic.

Tom's section of the office had been decorated with St. Louis Cardinals' memorabilia, including a Matt Carpenter Stadium Lights bobblehead. A baseball autographed by Stan "The Man" Musial had a special shrine on his desk. Lockridge was clearly a local baseball fan.

Debbie rolled open the top drawer in the file cabinet closest to Tom's desk and said, 'Mr Lockridge keeps most of his personal papers in these two filing cabinets.' She produced a neatly marked 'Last Will and Testament' file. 'The previous will is in there, too. He told me he'd changed his will when he married Cynthia. Before that, everything went to his daughter. Now Mrs Lockridge gets it all – the three houses, the business, and his money.'

'Was Victoria upset that her stepmother would inherit everything?' Jace asked.

'Oh, no,' Debbie said quickly. 'At least, she never mentioned it to me, and she talked to me about Cynthia a lot. Victoria is married to a Du Pres, you see, and well, everyone knows they're loaded. That's why Tom said he wasn't worried about changing his will. He kept most of the other bequests the same in his new will, including one for Mrs Timmons.'

'Is Mrs Lockridge's prenup in that file?' Jace asked.

'No,' Debbie said. 'Mr Lockridge asked me to get that the day before yesterday. It may be in the IN box on his desk.'

It was. Jace added that file to the box he was taking.

In another desk drawer I found more prescription drugs for Tom's heart. He obviously had a serious problem. The drawer was also crammed with various forms of Pepto-Bismol (liquid, tablets and capsules) as well as other drugstore heartburn remedies.

A locked desk drawer revealed a stash of junk food: Snickers candy bars, Ghost Pepper Doritos, an open bag of Hostess glazed mini Donettes, and a nearly empty bag of pork rinds. Judging by his diet, Lockridge's arteries must have been as clogged as Manhattan at rush hour.

'Did Victoria know about her father hiding junk food in his desk?' Jace asked.

'Oh, no,' Debbie said, and managed a watery smile. 'That was our little secret. Like I said, Victoria tried to put him on a healthy diet, but eating that food was just unnatural. He was a grown man! He needed real food. Victoria tried to get him to replace his Doritos with salt-free beet chips. Beets! I mean, who eats those? She gave him lunch meat made out of chickpeas and tofu! Disgusting!

'She'd make Tom these healthy lunches and bring them with her on her morning coffee visits to his home. Victoria would make him promise to take the lunches to work. Tom would, but then he'd toss them in the trash. He felt he'd kept his promise – after all, he did take the lunches to work – but he didn't promise to eat them. No one could. Even the homeless man who slept out by the Dumpsters wouldn't eat those lunches. Tom swore me to secrecy. We both knew that Victoria meant well.'

While Jace was digging around in Tom's desk, Debbie took me aside and whispered, 'Thanks for not mentioning my last name, Angela.'

I felt a guilty twinge when she said that, since I'd told Jace the circumstances surrounding her possible name change.

'I know it's been a while,' Debbie said, 'but could we have lunch sometime and catch up?'

'Will you still be here?' I asked.

'I guess so,' she said. 'If the family has to shut down the office, they'll still need me to do it. I know where everything is. I'm going to hate losing this job. Tom was such a nice boss.' She started crying again, but this time I suspected those tears were for herself.

I agreed to meet Debbie at the Italian restaurant soon. I liked her. I also thought I might learn something useful that could help Jace. I knew the detective would be under intense pressure to solve this case.

A tech arrived, took Lockridge's computer, and copied Debbie's hard drive. It was four p.m. by the time the last files were carried out and the paperwork was signed. A teary Debbie waved goodbye and locked up the office.

I'd been working for twelve hours, and felt woozy from lack of sleep. When I called Chris from the parking lot, he said, 'Come on over. I'll fix you dinner.'

I was too tired to eat dinner, much less see Chris. Plus, I looked like hell. The bags under my eyes could have been branded Samsonite.

'Thanks, but I just want to sleep,' I told him, and stifled a yawn. I hoped he didn't hear me.

'So, you can sleep with me,' he said, then added another incentive. 'I'll make waffles in the morning.'

I was tempted, but I snored like a trucker when I was overly tired, and I didn't want Chris to find that out so early in our relationship.

'Tempting as that is, I still have to say no.'

'Tomorrow night then?' he said. I was pleased to hear the hope in his voice. 'Pizza at my place? Seven o'clock?'

'Deal,' I said. 'I'll bring the wine. Seven sounds good.'

I drove home on autopilot, grateful I didn't encounter any serious traffic problems. At home, I crawled upstairs, dropped my clothes on the floor, plugged my work and personal cell phones in the night stand charger, and fell into bed at five o'clock. I was out cold.

My work cell phone woke me at eight the next morning. I grabbed for it, blinking like an owl in the bright morning light. It was my best friend, Dr Katie Kelly Stern, Chouteau County assistant medical examiner.

'Are you awake?' she asked.

'I am now,' I said.

'I have the results of the Lockridge autopsy. Jace is meeting me here at nine. Come join us. I'll have coffee and doughnuts.'

After a quick shower and an infusion of coffee, I was dressed and at Katie's office a little before nine. Her office is a windowless closet, with barely enough room for a desk, a file cabinet and wire chair from Sadists R Us. Katie had papered the wall behind her desk with an autumn forest scene, which looked peaceful until you saw the grinning plastic skull she'd pasted in the foliage.

When I knocked on her door and squeezed inside, Jace was already chomping on a jelly doughnut. Katie was at her desk, with a cup of coffee and a cinnamon cake doughnut. At first glance, Katie seems rather plain: a trim, forty-something woman with short brown hair, wearing a starched white lab coat, practical pantsuit and sensible shoes. But Katie's brown eyes are bright with intelligence and sparkling with laughter. She'd captured the heart of Montgomery Bryant, the Forest's foremost defense attorney. I knew that Monty called Katie his 'nut-brown maid.' I also knew if I ever repeated that endearment, Katie would autopsy me on the spot.

Katie waited until I'd poured myself some coffee and grabbed a chocolate doughnut before she delivered the results of Tom Lockridge's autopsy.

'As you probably guessed,' she said, 'the victim was shot three times in the head with the .22 registered to him. The first shot left a contact wound and an abrasion ring, a dark circle around the wound. That one probably killed him. I found soot and unburnt powder particles in the wound track. Combined with the other two shots to his head, his brain was oatmeal.

'The victim had sleeping pills in his blood – generic Ambien – so there's a good chance the poor bastard never woke up. At least I hope so.'

'Any sign of poisoning?' Jace said.

'Only what he did to himself,' Katie said. 'If someone wanted to kill this guy, all they had to do was wait a few months. I doubt if he would have made it to the year's end. Tom Lockridge had severe atherosclerosis – hardening and narrowing of the coronary arteries due to the build-up of plaque caused by high levels of cholesterol and fat. There was significant evidence of major heart disease, though it's hard to determine the precise amount.'

Jace whistled. 'So he was a heart attack waiting to happen.'
'You got it,' Katie said. 'With plenty of other problems to
go with it.'
'That goes with what we learned about his eating habits,'
I said. 'He was a junk food junkie.'
Katie shook her head. 'Another one eating himself to death.
Until the shooter ended his life. That's about all I can tell you.'
I reached for another doughnut and asked Jace, 'Any luck
with the files from Lockridge's office?'
'Yes. I just did a quick overview. I'm no forensic accountant,
but it looks like his construction company was teetering on
the edge of bankruptcy. He was barely keeping it going, picking
up small jobs here and there. He was draining his savings
accounts and selling off his assets. His credit cards were maxed
out. I have no idea how he made the payroll every month.
Even I could see he barely made it from month to month.'
'What about the prenup?' I asked.
'Glad we checked that,' Jace said. 'It confirmed what we'd
been told. If Cynthia Lockridge wanted a divorce, she'd get
a hundred thousand dollars. But if Tom Lockridge could prove
she'd been unfaithful, Cynthia wouldn't get a cent.'
I flashed back to the scene at Tom's construction office.
Why did Tom need to review his prenuptial agreement with
Cynthia just before his death? Was there a connection to his
murder? Did he finally realize his young wife was unfaithful
with his protégé?

NINE

For the next two days, Chouteau Forest was peaceful. But it was an uneasy peace. The media reports had everyone panicked: the Ghost Burglars had slaughtered an innocent man in his sleep. Shot him in the head. The one percent were terrified, and I couldn't blame them. One of their own had been murdered in his bed. Gun-toting homeowners patrolled their property with everything from semi-automatic handguns to assault rifles. Granddaddy's World War II souvenir Lugers were dug out of attics. Saturday night specials – cheap, small caliber handguns – were unearthed. Deer rifles were dusted off. Some families even hired armed response teams.

The police patrols were more worried about the untrained armed amateurs than the actual burglars.

We were all waiting for the shooting to start.

And it did. On the third night after the murder of Tom Lockridge.

I was called out at midnight. 'Angela, I need you,' Jace said. 'I can't talk now. Here's the address.' He hung up while I was still slightly dazed by the speedy summons. I dressed quickly, and made myself coffee. Two quick cups and I was awake. The May night was warm enough I didn't need a coat, and the moonlight shimmered on the grass.

I was summoned to the home of Roland Roget III. The real estate mogul lived in a massive marble pile built in the 1890s by his great-grandfather, with all the standard robber baron trimmings: Tiffany windows, crystal chandeliers, sweeping staircases, and a ballroom with potted palms.

Tonight, flashing emergency lights from police vehicles and ambulances gave the mansion the only life and color it had. Across the private road were extra-bright portable lights, and a fleet of official vehicles. Two crime scenes? What was going on here?

Roland Roget was outside on his perfectly trimmed front

lawn, shouting at Jace. Roland – Rolly to his friends – was sixty-something, a Forest regular on the society circuit. Last time I saw him, he was at some charity function, wearing a penguin suit. Rolly had thin white hair, bland features, a rotund body, and a look of smug entitlement. Tonight, he was in starched pale blue pajamas and his face was distorted with rage.

I parked my car alongside the estate's wrought iron fence, pulled out my DI case, and trundled it over to Mike, once again the uniform keeping the scene log book. He gave me the case number and the low-down on the fraught situation.

'Rolly caught the Ghost Burglars breaking into his house,' Mike said. 'He shot both of them.'

I felt a wave of relief at that news. 'It's about time,' I said. 'They've terrorized the Forest for weeks. Are they dead?'

'No such luck,' Mike said. 'One was shot full of holes. He's on his way to the hospital. The paramedics don't know if he's going to make it. Rolly winged the other burglar. Grazed his head. He was bleeding like crazy, but it's not serious. The paramedics patched him up. He's handcuffed in the back of a patrol car.'

'So why am I here?' I asked.

'One of Rolly's shots went wild,' Mike said, 'and he killed the Connellys' live-in assistant, Danny Morton. The poor guy was shot dead while walking the Connellys' golden retriever.'

'That's terrible,' I said. 'Where's his body?'

'Across the road, where those lights are.' He pointed in the direction of the other crime scene.

'Why didn't Danny try to hide when he heard shooting?'

'What good would that do?' Mike asked. 'There's nothing to hide behind, not even a car parked on the street. Here's what we think happened: When Danny heard the shooting, he tried to run, but the dog couldn't. It was old and slow. So he picked up the dog and ran with it, but he couldn't move fast enough. The dog weighed about seventy pounds. Danny caught a bullet – and the dog survived.'

I felt sick. A kind man died trying to save an old dog.

'This Rolly dude insists that shooting Danny Morton was not his fault – the man was "collateral damage in the war on

crime." Those are Rolly's actual words, too. He doesn't think
he should be charged with manslaughter.' Mike rolled his eyes.
  'I bet Jace isn't buying that excuse,' I said.
  'Nope,' Mike said.
  Now I was close enough to see that Rolly's pajamas were
monogrammed. Why does a certain kind of rich person mono-
gram everything – especially pajamas? Does he think someone
will swipe them? Or he'll forget who he is during the night?
  I also saw Rolly was swaying slightly and slurring his words.
'I tell you it wasn't my fault' came out: 'I tell you it washn't
my fault. Beshides, he ishn't even white. Jusht a Toonerville
nobody.'
  'Tell that to his parents, Mr Roget.' Jace's cold voice should
have left Rolly flash-frozen. 'And you've been drinking.'
  'What? A man can't have a drink in his own home?' Now
Rolly was belligerent as well as unrepentant.
  'He can, as long as he doesn't use firearms to kill law-
abiding citizens. Come along, let's go to the station.'
  'Rolly's hammered,' Mike told me. 'He blew .10 on a blood
alcohol test, and .08 is legally drunk. You can see the results
– his balance, reaction time, and judgment are muddled. He's
slurring his words and not thinking straight.'
  As proof of Mike's statement, Rolly waved his arms and
shouted, 'Do you know who I am?'
  Ah, the warning cry of the Forest elite, meant to terrify
underlings.
  Jace wasn't impressed. 'Yeah, you're a rich bozo who killed
an innocent man. Let's go. You've committed a felony:
manslaughter. Criminally negligent homicide to be exact.'
  Rolly had now sobered up enough that he was beginning
to understand his predicament. Jace cuffed the multimillion-
aire's hands behind his back, in the most uncomfortable
position. The prisoner couldn't keep the disbelief out of his
voice. 'You're really taking me to the police station . . . like
a . . . a common criminal.'
  'Yes, I need a statement,' Jace said.
  'Here's my statement,' Rolly said. 'I want a lawyer. I'm a
hero!' Finally, he shut up.
  A uniform drove up in a CFPD patrol car. 'Come along,

hero,' Jace said, handing over the handcuffed Rolly. 'Officer Dunn will process you at the station.'

The patrol officer put Rolly in his car behind the metal screen, and blasted down the winding drive with lights and sirens. If I knew Jace, he was angry enough to insist that Rolly get the full treatment, including a strip search, before he could call his lawyer.

I rolled my DI case over to Jace, and stopped for a minute. The detective was pacing angrily. Finally, Jace quit and noticed me. 'You won't believe this, Angela! A twenty-one-year-old man is dead because of that drunken idiot. Running around here with an assault rifle, shooting off rounds like he's in the damn Wild West. He bought the weapon two days ago at a gun show, after Tom Lockridge was killed. Never been in the military. No experience with guns – especially not assault weapons. They ought to lock him up and throw away the key, but he'll get off scot-free because he's rich.' Jace was bitter – and right.

'What happened?' I asked.

'Two dumb shits – Duke "Spider-Man" Lee' – Jace made a disgusted face at the silly nickname – 'and his sidekick, Alexander "Sandy" Perkins – tried to break into Roland's house.'

Hm. Unlike most cops, Jace rarely used even mild profanity.

'Both of them have records longer than a roll of toilet paper,' he said. 'The so-called Spider-Man bypassed the main alarm, but he didn't know about the silent alarm, which flashed in Roland's study, where the homeowner was downing a bottle of scotch.

'Instead of calling nine-one-one, Roland grabbed his trusty assault rifle and ran down the stairs, spraying bullets. Sandy Perkins was climbing through the kitchen window. The idiot froze when the shooting started, and he caught the brunt of the fire. Sandy was carted off to the hospital unconscious. He's going to need major surgery.

'Spider-Man took off across the lawn, leaving his helpless friend bleeding in the kitchen. Roland fired nearly a full clip – thirty bullets – trying to bring down the fleeing burglar. All Spider-Man got was a small graze by his ear. But one of

Roland's wild shots hit Danny Morton, who was minding his own business, walking a dog. Danny died instantly. Roland thinks it's no big deal. He expected me to pin a medal on him. Instead, I've hauled his worthless ass off to jail for felony murder.'

'Why didn't Spider-Man keep on running if his injury was minor?' I asked.

'Because it was a head wound, and you know how those bleed. He was terrified he was going to die. That's how we finally caught the bastard. Too bad it's at the cost of another innocent life, but I'll be able to charge him with Danny Morton's murder, since the death occurred during the commission of a crime.'

'What can you tell me about the victim?' I asked.

'Danny Morton, age twenty-one. African-American. Working his way through college as a live-in assistant for Muriel and Robert Connelly.'

The Connellys were one of the few wealthy people of color in the Forest. Muriel was a renowned plastic surgeon. Bob had invented a part for a bread slicer that brought in tons of dough.

'They're at the scene now,' Jace said. 'They'll have Danny's contact information.'

'Have they notified his family yet?'

'No, they want to do it in person. His father died of a heart attack. Danny has a mother, who teaches special needs children, and two grown sisters. The Connellys don't want his widowed mother to see her boy with his chest blown apart.'

'Do you have the weapon?' I asked.

'Nitpicker is over there, packing it up,' he said. 'It's a Colt AR-15. The same kind of semi-automatic rifle that killed the kids at Sandy Hook Elementary School, the Las Vegas Harvest Festival and other mass shootings.' He radiated anger and contempt.

I opened the Firearm Fatalities Form on my iPad and headed over to Nitpicker.

The CFPD tech was on her knees in the dew-drenched grass, packing the fatal firearm into a long cardboard box. I approached the weapon as if it was a dangerous snake. It was a collection of sharp angles, and looked like it had been made from spare parts.

'That's an ugly beast,' I told Nitpicker. Her hair was a vibrant blueberry today.

She snorted. 'Why this asshole needs a military weapon is beyond me. He could have chased off the thieves with a plain old shotgun. This is cheap by automatic weapons standards – sells for less than a thousand dollars.'

I filled in the details on my form. The semi-automatic was a Colt XM177E2 Commando Retro Carbine. I measured the total length of the rifle (32.5 inches from the muzzle to the end) and the length of the barrel, from the muzzle to the end (ten inches). The magazine could hold ten rounds of .223 caliber Remington ammunition.

'You should see how he sprayed those bullets around his property,' Nitpicker said. 'He put major holes in the kitchen walls and floor, blew apart the dishwasher, shattered at least four windows, destroyed the kitchen door and nearly took down a privacy fence.'

By now, I'd filled out my form. It was time for the body identification.

I dreaded having to meet the victim's grieving employers.

But I knew the death investigation for Danny Morton, the promising young man who'd been brutally cut down, would be infinitely worse.

TEN

I hurried down the driveway to the scene across the street, dread seizing my stomach. Now I was close enough to hear the Connellys weeping as they knelt by the body of a tall, thin young man. Rick, the new uniform, kept reminding the couple to avoid touching or cradling the body. 'I'm really sorry,' he said gently, 'but you can't contaminate the crime scene.'

'Danny's not a crime scene,' Muriel said through her tears. 'He's a young man who died before his time. It's such a terrible waste.'

'I understand, ma'am,' Rick said. 'And I'm sorry. But we want to make sure he gets justice, don't we?'

'Danny was brilliant.' Robert Connelly's rich baritone sounded like a final judgment.

The power couple looked impressive, even in the harsh glow of the portable lights. Muriel wore jeans, a crisp white shirt and white sneakers. She was about forty, with close-cropped hair. She wore no make-up. With her caramel skin and high cheekbones, she didn't need it. Her husband Robert was in the Forest uniform for successful men at home: khakis and a polo shirt, Top-Siders and no socks.

They both stood when they saw me approach. I introduced myself and asked who'd found the body.

'I did,' Muriel said, still sniffling back tears. 'I went looking for him. Danny lived with us and helped out. He was working his way through City University. He was walking our old dog, Sally. She's a twelve-year-old golden. She has arthritis and is slow, so a short walk takes about fifteen or twenty minutes. But when Danny didn't come back after an hour, Robert and I went looking for them in my car. That's when I heard the commotion caused by that cracker fool next door.' Anger sizzled in her voice.

'I found Danny,' Muriel said. 'On the sidewalk. Sally was

whimpering and licking the blood off his face. It was heart-breaking. We had a hard time pulling Sally away, but we finally got her into the car. Robert took her home and came back. I stayed with Danny.'

'Was there any attempt at resuscitation?' I asked.

Muriel shook her head and her dark brown eyes filled with tears. 'I'm a surgeon,' she said. 'There was no point. Look at his chest. Looks like a grenade went off in there.' Her husband put his arm around her to comfort her, and she wept harder. 'Danny was killed by that worthless racist shit-bag.'

'There's no reason for language like that,' Robert's deep voice rumbled. 'Don't stoop to his level.'

Danny looked younger than twenty-one. His skin was a light tan and his brown hair was cut short. He wore khaki cargo shorts and a blue T-shirt with some sort of saying on it. I couldn't tell what it said – Danny's chest really did look like it had exploded. When I got a closer look at the chest wound, the bile rose in my throat and I felt dizzy. This was far worse than a shotgun wound – his chest was destroyed.

I took several deep breaths to try to calm myself, and began the familiar ritual of the body examination. The routine was soothing. I opened my Death Scene Investigation form, wrote the case number, the date, the time (1:25 a.m.) and the ambient temperature (58 degrees). The weather was clear and there was a light wind. He was lying on the grass and his head was pointing northwest.

Now I started on the demographic information. Muriel gave me Danny's full name (Daniel Langston Morton). 'His middle name was for Langston Hughes, the poet.' Muriel's statement launched more tears. She struggled to answer my other questions about Danny's marital state (single) and age without crying. 'Danny would have been twenty-two on July seventh. I bought Danny his first legal drink on his last birthday.'

By this time, I was having trouble holding back my own tears. I bit my lip – hard – and told myself to woman up. I couldn't help Danny if I indulged in melodrama.

The victim was lying face-up on his back. 'I picked him up and held him,' Muriel said, 'but I tried to put him back the way he fell.'

The blood smears on her white shirt, shoes, and jeans, and the drag marks in the blood, attested to her statement. I photographed and measured them, and noted that Danny's body had been moved when it was discovered. Danny was six-feet-one-inch tall and weighed about one-hundred-eighty pounds. The ME would get his exact weight during the autopsy.

The decedent was lying in a pool of blood. It painted his hair, neck, upper body and face – except where the faithful Sally had licked it off his right cheek. I felt the tears well up in my eyes and blinked them away.

Danny had been a handsome man. I could see that from the side of his face that Sally had cleaned in a futile effort to revive her fallen friend. Danny had a beautiful bone structure – high cheekbones, a strong jaw, and full lips. His nose a little too large, but it gave his face distinction. It was the sort of face he would grow into. I paused and the sorrow hit me again. No, Danny would never grow into that face.

I took out my point-and-shoot camera and photographed the decedent, taking long shots, medium shots and close-ups, especially close-ups of that dreadful chest wound. The camera lens put a screen between me and that awful reality, and that helped steady me.

The blood pool around his upper body was crisscrossed with shoe prints and paw prints. I measured and photographed the blood pool and then did the same to the blood on his head, neck, arms and upper body, and noted the paw prints in the blood on his neck and shoulders.

Danny had been shot in the back, and the bullet literally blew out his chest, leaving a nasty, jagged crater the size of a man's fist. The bullet looked like it had destroyed everything in its path. From the splinters of bone in his chest, his ribs seemed to have disintegrated.

'I'm sure he died instantly,' Muriel said. 'Even if I'd been here, I couldn't have saved him. There was just too much damage. I hate automatic weapons. Hate them.' Fury burned in her dark eyes. 'Handguns kill, too. But they're not as destructive as assault weapons.'

I silently agreed and went back to work, patiently noting

and measuring the details. Danny wore no jewelry. A set of
keys and his cell phone were in the right pocket in his bloody
cargo shorts. Danny's black-framed geek chic glasses lay near
his body, blood spattered, lenses shattered. They would also
go with the body to the ME's office. I saw no defensive wounds
on his blood-smeared hands, but I bagged his glasses and
sealed the paper bags with evidence tape.

At last, I finished the meticulous work on the front of the
body. I brought out a clean, sterilized white sheet, and asked
Rick the uniform to help me turn the body. The fatal wound
was two inches below his right shoulder. The entrance
wound was surprisingly small – about the size of a quarter
– for all the damage it did exiting the body. There was more
blood on Danny's head, neck and back. I measured it.
Otherwise, there wasn't a scratch or a bruise on the young
man. That made his death worse, somehow.

It was nearly six in the morning by the time I finished and
the van came to take Danny to the ME's. I signed the paperwork for the chain of custody. It was time to inform his mother,
Susannah Morton. The Connellys offered to come with me
for the notification, and I accepted their offer. I would make
the formal notification, and the Connellys would stay and
grieve with Danny's mother. Jace, who usually accompanied
me on a notification, approved of this plan. He was still working
the scene and wouldn't have to go with me.

Muriel Connelly changed out of her bloody clothes. The
sun was coming up as I followed the Connellys' Lexus to Mrs
Morton's house in the working part of town, which had the
sneery nickname of Toonerville. Poor Susannah Morton. This
had been her last night of peaceful sleep.

We were there all too quickly. Mrs Morton lived in a
two-bedroom ranch house, white siding with black shutters
and a red door. Tulips bloomed in the flower beds. It was
picture-perfect.

I followed the Connellys to the front door and rang the
doorbell. Mrs Morton answered, dressed for work in a black
skirt, pink silk blouse and pearl earrings. She had the same
sculpted good looks and light brown skin as her son. Her face
paled when she saw us.

'Wha-what happened?' she stuttered. 'What's wrong with my son?'

'Let's go inside, Mrs Morton,' I said, and led the bewildered woman to the couch in her living room. Once she was seated, I broke the news. It was as horrible as I'd expected. Susannah screamed as if her heart had been ripped from her body, and began rocking back and forth. I gave her the basic details. The Connellys sat on either side of Susannah. Muriel held her hand while she cried and Robert rubbed her back. There was hot coffee in the kitchen – Susannah had expected to leave for school in thirty minutes – and I poured three cups. I promised Susannah that her son did not suffer. I did not tell her how his chest had been blown open, and I hoped she'd never find out. She did not have to formally ID his body. The Connellys had done that.

Finally, my dreadful duties were done. I left Susannah with the Connellys, and walked outside into the sunshine. I'd held it together for seven difficult hours, and now I was wiped out. I was so exhausted, I could barely walk to my car. All I wanted to do was go home to bed and pull the covers over my head.

But that didn't happen. I was surprised to see Chris in his uniform, leaning against the door of my black Charger.

He ran forward as soon as he saw me. 'Angela!' He held me in his arms, and I leaned into him and breathed in his scent – coffee and Old Spice.

'How did you know I was here?' I asked.

'I heard there was a particularly brutal assault rifle killing and you were the DI. Jace said you were here to notify the family. How are you?'

'I'm fine,' I said, determined to tough it out. 'I'm used to gruesome deaths. I've worked decomposed bodies, headless accident victims, bloody stabbings, and shotgun deaths. I'm a professional. I handled it.' A vision of Danny's exploded chest appeared in my mind's eye as I was talking. 'I did just . . .' and then I burst into tears.

Chris held me tighter and rocked me gently. 'Sh,' he said. 'You did fine. And it's OK to cry. Assault rifle deaths are the worst. My first one was a gang shooting. An AR-15 literally blew the poor kid's leg off and he died before the ambulance could get there. I was so shaken I could hardly call it in. These are war wounds, Angela, and they take their toll on the bystanders as well as the victims.'

He brought out a clean pocket handkerchief and dried my tears. 'Hey, now,' he said, softly. 'I'm off work now and so are you. Come home with me and I'll make you breakfast.'

The morning sun gilded the pink and purple clouds. Chris and I rode east into a glorious new day.

ELEVEN

spent the entire day with Chris, and he helped me recover from the horrors of my first assault weapon death investigation. He was easy to be around. He understood when I wanted to be alone – as long as I wasn't moping. He was a skillful lover and a good cook. He made me laugh. He was almost perfect. I felt myself growing closer to him, but I was wary. I'd fallen in love before, and then lost my husband. That pain never went away, but I was finally learning to live with it. Could I risk falling for Chris, a man in a job where he could be killed during a routine traffic stop? I pushed those thoughts away and tried to enjoy my time with Chris.

The next morning, I was back on duty, and thanks to Chris, ready to return to work. I guess I should explain my odd work situation. Death investigators work for the ME. We're not medical professionals or law enforcement agents. We're a fairly new profession, started in 1978, and we take care of people who die unexpectedly, suspiciously, or violently.

Right now, Chouteau County has two other death investigators. We were squeezed into a room that was OK, as long as none of us tried indoor cat swinging. But Evarts Evans, the Forest ME, wanted a Swedish shower for his office, and the only way he could get it was to expand into the death investigators' territory. Since I was the least politically connected, he took my space. We had an unspoken agreement – I could work from home, as long as the detectives could reach me, and I turned in my work on time. That was fine with me.

The next morning, Katie summoned Jace and me to the ME's office at noon for Danny Morton's autopsy. After what she'd found in that autopsy, she'd worked herself into a fiery rage.

I stopped for three coffees from Supreme Bean, the local coffee shop, on the way to the ME's office at SOS. I knocked on her door. Katie looked tired, and I could almost hear her nerves jangling with pent-up fury. Jace was already perched on the corner of Katie's desk. She accepted the coffee gratefully, gulped down half a cup, then launched into her rant.

'I did Danny Morton's autopsy this morning.' Katie's voice was shaking with anger. 'Nobody should have to suffer what that young man did. Nobody!'

'The wounds were terrible,' I said.

'Terrible? Terrible?' Her voice was almost a shriek. 'That doesn't begin to describe it. That young man's bones exploded! Exploded! As for the organs and soft tissue, they were shredded. The bullet that fathead used was three times as fast as one from your average Saturday Night Special – Lord knows I've autopsied enough of those victims.' Katie threw out her arms in frustration and Jace ducked to avoid getting hit.

'It looked like Rolly Roget's weapon started to overheat – that happens with cheap assault weapons – and the bullet was unstable,' Katie said. 'It didn't go through the victim – it rolled around and tore up his insides. The bullet hit him in the back, then went into his body, destroying the tissue and organs in its path. His heart? Gone! Six ribs? Splintered! Arteries? Exploded! The bullet finally ricocheted off a remaining rib and took out his left lung, before it lodged between his vertebrae. That's where I got it.'

Katie held up a long, thin brass bullet in a plastic evidence bag. I studied the evil object. 'This is the son of a bitch that killed that young man,' Katie said. 'No, wait. It's not the bullet's fault. It was fired by Rolly Roget. He's the SOB who belongs behind bars.'

'I have him in jail,' Jace said. 'For now. I'm not sure he'll stay there.'

'Of course not,' Katie said, her pale face once more contorted with anger. 'He's a premier member of the Forest idiocracy.'

'He used military rounds,' Jace said, examining the bullet. 'They're designed to be one shot, one kill.'

'Yes, they are,' Katie said. 'No wonder the rest of the world thinks this gun-happy country is nuts.' She paused for a sip of coffee, then said, 'Tell me something good. What's happened to the jackasses who triggered this mess, Jace?'

'Ouch,' I said. 'Did you mean that pun?'

'Of course not!' she snapped, and glared at me. Wow. Katie really was on edge. I hunched down like a guilty schoolgirl.

'I was talking about the burglars,' Katie said. 'Jace, talk some sense, will you?'

'I finally have news. I've been working on this for hours,' he said. 'The two burglars have been caught, as you know. Sandy Perkins is still in a coma after he was shot. He's at SOS, handcuffed to his bed. His partner, Spider-Man Lee . . .' Jace stopped, made a face and said, 'Damn, I hate using that stupid nickname.'

'Is it any worse than calling Roland "Rolly" like he's in some English drawing room comedy?' Katie asked.

'I guess not,' Jace said. 'But I hate glorifying that killer. Anyway, Spider-Man wanted to make a deal. He says he knows who killed Thomas Lockridge. He wants immunity for the murder.'

'Immunity?' Katie said. 'You've got to be kidding. When he's responsible for the murder of Danny Morton and Lockridge? I can't believe it.' I thought the same thing, but kept quiet. Spider-Man would be charged with felony murder during the commission of a crime for Danny's death.

'I talked with the Chouteau County Prosecutor,' Jace said. 'He laughed at Spider-Man's request. He didn't say no – he said hell no!'

'Good!' Katie said. 'That man's got some sense.'

'He reminded Spider-Man that Missouri is a death penalty state, and he'll get the needle.' I winced. Lethal injections had a gruesome history in the US.

'Spider-Man was smart enough to know that lethal injections can go badly wrong,' Jace said.

'Yep, they get botched all the time,' Katie said. She sounded almost cheerful. 'Remember the Oklahoma killer injected with the wrong drug? He was given potassium acetate instead of potassium chloride. Potassium chloride would have stopped his heart. Potassium acetate is used for mummification. He was mummified alive for seven minutes before he died. His last words were "my body is on fire." Sometimes the botched executions are so bad, the witnesses faint.'

'Spider-Man knew enough stories about bungled lethal injections that they scared the stuffing out him,' Jace said. 'The county prosecutor told Spider-Man he'd get one deal – and one deal only – he'd have to tell everything, and testify. Then, if he's lucky, he'll get LWOP.' Jace pronounced it 'El-wop.'

I knew that meant Life Without Parole. In other words, Spider-Man would die in an overcrowded state prison.

'Did he take the deal?' I finally felt brave enough to say something after Katie had slapped me down.

'Yes. He didn't even stop to think about it.'

'So who killed Tom Lockridge?' I asked.

'Spider-Man says he was hired by Cynthia to kill her husband.'

I wasn't surprised by that revelation. In fact, I'd expected it.

'Where did Cynthia meet the likes of Spider-Man?' I said. 'He isn't exactly on the society circuit.'

'Spider-Man says he lived in the same trailer park as Cynthia Lockridge – he called her Cindy – before she married Tom Lockridge, and that's how he knew her,' Jace said. 'Here's his story: Spider-Man says Mrs Lockridge wanted rid of her rich old husband. She was going to pay him twenty thousand dollars – half before the killing and the rest after the estate was settled.

'He says she drew him a map of her Forest mansion and marked the upstairs bedroom with an X. The map showed him the route there using the service staircase, and also where her husband kept his loaded weapon. Mrs Lockridge said she'd leave the kitchen door open and the alarm system off. She would be on the other side of the house in her office, and keep the dog with her.

'On the night of the murder, Spider-Man broke the basement window to make it look like that's how the two burglars entered the house, but he was too stupid to check that the door leading upstairs was locked.'

'And he did all this with the promise of the rest of the money later?' Katie asked. 'It will be months before the estate is settled.'

'Spider-Man said Mrs Lockridge told him her husband wore a big diamond ring and the killer could take that as a down payment until he got the rest.'

'Then why didn't he take it?' I asked. 'The ring was still on Tom Lockridge's finger when I did the death investigation.'

'Spider-Man said he panicked after he shot Tom Lockridge,' Jace said. 'He told me, "I'm not used to killing people. I'm a burglar. I don't even own a gun. I don't carry one, in case I get caught. I don't want them to get me for felony murder."'

Jace laughed, but there was no humor in it. 'As it is, we've got him for felony murder anyway, because Danny Morton was killed during the commission of the crime.

'Spider-Man says after he shot Tom Lockridge in the head, he threw the gun out the bedroom window and didn't take the ring. He was shaken by the blood from the shooting – and the noise.

'He says he was wearing gloves and didn't leave prints,' Jace said.

'We already know that,' I said. 'How did Spider-Man survive even a graze by that powerful ammunition?'

'The paramedic who patched him up had been in the Gulf War. He figured Spider-Man had been grazed by a bullet fragment. That's why he survived,' Jace said. 'But his reign of terror in the Forest is over.'

'How did he get in all those fancy houses in the first place?' I asked. 'It had to be an inside job.'

'It was,' Jace said. 'Most of the mansions in the Forest used a Jamaican woman to do the heavy work – scrubbing the floors and stairs, things like that. Her name was Chandice Burton. Her first name means "one who is talented and smart." Chandice was a hard worker, and she was definitely smart. The families who employed her treated Chandice as if she was invisible. While she worked, she silently made a list of valuables in each house, the codes to the security systems and safes, the dates when the families went on vacation and how long they would be gone.

'After years of laboring in the Forest, she asked for a raise of a dollar an hour. The homeowners banded together and refused this outrageous request. Chandice was forty now, and her knees were hurting. She was still pretty, and she wanted to go back home to Jamaica, but she needed fifty thousand dollars.

'She sold Spider-Man this wealth of information she'd collected. His first haul was his biggest – uninsured diamonds in a cheap home safe. He fenced the diamonds, gave Chandice her money, and she left town.'

'Can you track her down in Jamaica?'

'Maybe,' Jace said. 'But I doubt that she's using her own name there, or that the Chouteau Forest PD would pay to send me to Jamaica. We're going to have to make do with Spider-Man.'

'Are you going to arrest Cynthia?' I asked.

'I can't,' he said. 'I don't have any evidence.'

'What about the map she drew?'

'Spider-Man doesn't have it.'

'Then how did you know he was telling the truth?' Katie asked.

'I had him describe the interior of the house in detail, so I know he was in there. Despite the confession, I can't arrest Cynthia. There are no cell phone or email connections to the killer. Yes, she has a motive – the death of her rich old husband – but there's no proof she hired someone to kill him.'

'What do you need to go to trial?' Katie asked.

'A lot more. There's no money trail or cash withdrawal. No cell phone calls or cell phone locations that put the two together. Spider-Man says he met Cynthia at the mobile home park but her phone records show she was never there and there are no witnesses.'

'So even though we know she did it, we have no evidence,' I said.

'And don't forget,' Jace said. 'Once we arrest Cynthia, the "speedy trial" time clock starts ticking.'

'Are you under a lot of pressure to make an arrest?' Katie asked.

'Unbelievable.' Suddenly, Jace looked tired. He wiped his face with his pocket handkerchief, and I could see the dark bags under his eyes.

'What can I do to help?' I asked.

'Will you go to Cynthia's mobile home park with me, Angela? You'd be better talking to the locals.'

I knew it was risky – officially, my job ended when I'd turned in my report – but Danny Morton was dead. A terrible, wasteful death. I wanted to track down the person who'd triggered his murder.

TWELVE

Cynthia Lockridge grew up in a down-at-heels mobile home park on the outskirts of Festus. Jace and I drove there in about thirty-five minutes. Festus was only thirty miles from Chouteau Forest, but economically the two towns were thousands of miles apart. Festus was pretty, but nowhere near as rich as the Forest.

The sign for Cynthia's former mobile home park was so old and faded only the letters ALE had survived. Whether the actual name was Sunnydale, Springvale, or Beyond the Pale, I had no idea. The place had a cool green canopy of shade trees and two rows of mobile homes. Most were rusty old-fashioned single-wides, but four were newer, shining double-wides. Down the center of the park was a white gravel drive.

Jace and I parked in front of the first mobile home, which had a small "Manager" sign on the door. It was one of the best-kept on the lot, surrounded by pink flamingos and a family of plastic ducks, fronted by petunias in blue-painted tire planters.

Jace had never seen those DIY planters before. 'Are they really made out of car tires?' he asked.

'Yes. This is the deluxe version – the tires have been turned inside out, the edges are scalloped and they're painted. There are many versions of tire culture.'

'Tire culture?'

'Look it up on the Net, city boy,' I said, and smiled.

Jace knocked on the aluminum screen door and a tiny woman in a pink-flowered housecoat answered. I estimated her age and her weight to be about the same – eighty-five. She had luxuriant chin-length gray hair, which I suspected was a wig. I thought back to my own mother, who wore an Eva Gabor wig when she'd lost her hair during her cancer treatment.

Jace identified us and showed his badge, and the woman said, 'I'm the manager and the owner. My name is Mrs Rawlins. Shirley Rawlins. Are you here to talk about that terrible man, the one who calls himself Spider-Man? I saw his picture in today's paper. He used to live here.'

'That's one thing,' Jace said.

Mrs Rawlins invited us in. The mobile home was narrow and neat. Collections of china figurines covered nearly every free surface. 'Would you like to sit in the living room?' she asked.

We followed her through a tiny kitchen. Sure enough, the medicine bottles lined up above the kitchen sink told me Mrs Rawlins was being treated for breast cancer and its symptoms. In the living room, Jace and I sat on the green couch.

'Can I get you something to drink?' Mrs Rawlins asked. 'Tea, coffee, water?'

Jace and I both asked for ice water. While Mrs Rawlins fussed around in the kitchen, I looked at the local newspaper on the coffee table, near a pack of china poodles. The front page headline screamed: 'Ghost Burglars Caught!' Spider-Man's old mug shot was the first photo of him I'd seen – I'd only caught a glimpse of the killer the night of his capture. Spider-Man's hair was in long, greasy ringlets, surrounding an acne-scarred, chinless face. His teeth were crooked and his eyes were mean slits. I shuddered when I examined those dead eyes. Goat's eyes. As for Danny Morton, his death barely rated a mention in the story, and no photo.

'Here you go.' Mrs Rawlins brought us two glasses of ice water and the coasters to put them on. She sat in the matching green upholstered chair beside the couch, and settled her liver-spotted hands in her lap. 'Now, Detective, what can I tell you?'

'When did this Spider-Man live here?' Jace asked.

'About fifteen years ago. Only for a short time, maybe two years or so. Lee – that's what I called him, none of that silly Spider-Man business – spent most of his time drinking and smoking pot. Probably dealing, too. His whole trailer was in a marijuana fog – and he had some rough-looking friends. Trash, all of them. We had the police here nearly every night.'

'What about Cynthia Lockridge?' Jace asked. 'Did she live here then?'

'Oh, yes. She was in high school at the time.'

'Was she one of Spider-Man's friends?'

Mrs Rawlins laughed. 'No! She wouldn't have anything to do with him. Naturally, he tried to ask her out. She was a pretty little thing. I heard him inviting her to his home to party – drugs, no doubt – and she was afraid of him. She ran to me and knocked on my door and I let her in and told Lee to get lost. Cindy wouldn't even talk to him.

'Lee was here the year the tornado hit this park. Took his mobile home and crushed it like a beer can. Insurance replaced it with one of the nice, new double-wides. Once he was living in the new mobile home, Lee's behavior got even wilder. He had loud, all-night parties, and half-naked women smoking weed and drinking on the steps. One of his party friends even fired off a weapon. And his pursuit of Cindy was relentless.

'Cindy was one of the reasons my husband Ron decided to evict Lee.'

'Could your husband evict him if Lee owned his mobile home?' Jace asked.

'Darn right he could. He leased this land from us. He was engaging in illegal activities. That's in the terms of the lease. He sold his home and left. I was glad to see the last of that bum. He was nothing but trouble. I don't know where he went after that. May have moved to Crystal City.'

'Crystal City's only eight miles away,' I said.

'Didn't matter,' Mrs Rawlins said. 'It was far enough. He never came around here again, and good riddance!'

So how did Cynthia Lockridge overcome her fear of Spider-Man and hire this lowlife to kill her husband? I wondered. Where did she even find him?

'We're also interested in learning more about Cynthia Lockridge,' Jace said. 'It sounds like you knew her.'

Mrs Rawlins's face broke into a smile. 'Oh, yes, I know her well. She was Cindy back then, and she practically lived here with me and my husband. At least for a while. She's our local success story. We're real proud of her. She's quite the lady now.'

'What was she like when she lived here?' Jace asked.

'Cindy was a nice girl. A real nice girl. And no thanks to her mother, Lee-Ann. That woman never married, not even Cindy's father. Cindy wanted to know who her father was. She thought I'd know because her mother lived here before Cindy was born.

'That poor girl would pester me with questions: "Did my mother have a special boyfriend? Was he handsome? Do you think he was rich?" You know young girls. They have such romantic ideas. I had no idea who her father was, and I told her so, but Cindy really wanted to know. I didn't have the heart to tell her that her father was probably a customer, and a low-life drunk, besides.

'I won't say the word for what Lee-Ann was, but my husband made her take the red light out of her home. He should have tossed her out – men coming in here every night until all hours! But my Ron felt sorry for Cindy, and that poor girl would have been homeless if her worthless mother was forced to move.'

Mrs Rawlins absently rubbed the wedding ring on her blue-veined hand, and glanced at the wedding photo on the end table before she resumed her story.

'Many a night Cindy spent here in our home, doing her schoolwork, while her mother "entertained," if you know what I mean. Cindy usually ate dinner with us. I taught her how to cook. Just simple things – meat loaf, pot roast, beef stew. She had a real knack for plain cooking. I didn't mind having her here. She was smart, well-behaved and hard-working. I didn't want that girl going down her mother's path. Cindy was always quiet, no trouble at all.'

I was touched by Mrs Rawlins's story. I glanced over at Jace. He wasn't buying the story of Saint Cindy.

'You're telling me that a girl who looked like Cindy didn't date at all?' Jace asked. I could hear the disbelief in his voice. Mrs Rawlins did not.

'Oh, yes, detective. She was a good girl. A very good girl. She concentrated on getting good grades in school. It was a miracle.'

'It certainly was,' Jace said. Again, Mrs Rawlins missed the sarcasm.

'I figure Cindy's mother turned her off men. The things that poor girl must have seen: drunken fights and worse.'

'And yet Cindy came out pure as the driven snow,' Jace said. I glared at him. Really! What was wrong with that man?

'Yes, she did, Detective,' Mrs Rawlins said. Now I heard defiance in her voice. 'She didn't have time to be bad. In high school, Cindy worked part-time at the McDonald's. The same manager still works there. You can stop by and ask him yourself, if you don't believe me. His name is Bates. Nelson Bates.'

Jace wrote down the name. 'Thank you, Mrs Rawlins,' Jace said. 'I will.'

'When Cindy was in high school, that's when she sort of lived with us. She was so pretty with that long black hair of hers, and many nights she was afraid to go home, what with her mother's "friends" being in their home. She slept right on that couch where you're sitting.'

Poor Cindy, I thought. This couch is harder than a bill collector's heart. No wonder she surrounds herself with luxury now.

'That's when Cindy started feeding us,' Mrs Rawlins said. 'She'd bring home burgers and fries from work, and those little apple pies. I liked those pies.' Another brief smile.

'Her mother died of a drug overdose right after Cindy graduated from high school. If you ask me, it was a blessing. By then, Cindy had a scholarship to secretarial school. Ron and I didn't charge her to keep her home here. We even paid the utilities. She finished, with high marks. We went to her graduation. She wore a real cap and gown. That's her picture there, next to my wedding photo.'

The color photo showed that young Cindy was definitely a beauty, with silky black hair, a soft, clear complexion, and a bright smile – so different from her practiced smile in the society pages.

'She's wearing a string of pearls,' I said. 'The Ghost Burglars ruined a pearl necklace.'

'We gave her that necklace,' Mrs Rawling said. 'Ronnie and me. Real cultured pearls. She told me she cried when those burglars tore up her pearls. Said she should have put them in the safe with her diamonds.

'After Cindy graduated, that's when her luck changed,' Mrs Rawlins said. 'And if you ask me, it was about time. That girl had been through enough. She was hired right after graduation as office manager for the Chouteau Forest Construction Company. That's the area's largest construction company, you know. Thomas Lockridge was the owner. Cindy told me Mr Lockridge worked long hours and was a kind, fair boss. I read the papers. I knew he was a widower with a grown daughter. I figured he had to be lonely. I know I was after my Ron died.'

She glanced at the wedding photo again. My heart hurt to see her studying the petite blonde bride in the 1940s satin dress, and the smiling, dark-haired groom.

'Your husband was tall and handsome,' I said.

'Yes, he was.' I heard a wistful note. 'We were very happy.'

She shook her head, and continued. 'I knew Mr Lockridge was way older than Cindy, but I thought he'd make a good husband. I wanted to help things along a bit.'

I studied the old woman. She was taking credit for engineering Cindy's marriage. Jace looked at her stone-faced.

'I knew how men thought,' she said. 'I asked Cindy what her boss ate at the office and she said nothing but junk food. It was me who suggested that Cindy start cooking meals for Mr Lockridge, and take them to her job. I knew the way to a man's heart was through his stomach. 'Course it didn't hurt that Cindy was drop-dead gorgeous.' She grinned at us. Jace refused to return her smile. What a grump.

'It wasn't long before nature took its course and Cindy was going out with Mr Lockridge, and then she was engaged to be married. She stopped by to show me her ring. That girl was so excited. And that ring cost more than her home!

'Well, you know the rest.' Mrs Rawlins gave me a smile and avoided looking at Jace. 'Cindy had a big wedding, and she became a big deal in society. She asked me to start calling her Cynthia – society people like names like that, and I didn't mind.'

Then she looked Jace right in the eye. 'And Detective, if you have any doubts about what kind of person Cindy was, after her marriage, she gave me her mobile home. Deeded it to me flat out, as a gift. She said she wanted to repay me for all those years I took care of her. It was in bad shape, but she gave me five hundred dollars to fix it up, and I did. She said I could have the income if I rented it out. Except I'm not getting any income these days, not after that worthless Cody Ellis moved in. He just laughs at me when I ask for the rent. I'm sure he's dealing drugs, too.'

'I'll have a talk with him, Mrs Rawlins, when I get ready to leave.' There. That was the Jace I knew. I smiled at him.

'Thank you, Detective,' Mrs Rawlins said. 'I'm old, but I'm not stupid. I can tell by your face you don't believe that Cindy was a good girl, but she was. Don't go outsmarting yourself. Sometimes, there are good people in the world, you know.

'Cindy – I mean, Cynthia – met her Prince Charming, and she's been living happily ever after in a palace. Until poor Mr Lockridge died.'

Until poor Mr Lockridge was murdered, I thought. Maybe by Cinderella.

THIRTEEN

'Angela, where the hell are you?' I recognized that rude, impatient voice – Ray Greiman, my least favorite detective on the Chouteau Forest PD. I couldn't tell him I was with Jace Budewitz – fire and brimstone would rain down on my head.

'Are you calling for a death investigation?' I asked.

'Yes,' he said. 'Pedestrian was run over at the corner of Gravois and Windsor Road.'

'Is that by the Forest bank?' I asked.

'You know it is. Get your ass over here.'

To take this call, I'd stepped outside Mrs Rawlins's mobile home. Now I poked my head inside the door, said goodbye, and ran for my car. On the way to the scene, my phone rang again. It was Chris. I put my cell phone on speaker to talk to him. 'Angela, are you on your way to the pedestrian death by the bank?' Chris's voice was unusually low and cautious.

'Yes. What's wrong? Why are you whispering?'

'Problems,' he said. 'Greiman. He's on the phone right now.'

'Probably trying to make a date with some badge bunny,' I said. 'So what's the problem?'

'I was the first one at the scene. The driver who killed the pedestrian was intoxicated.' Chris was still whispering.

'Who is he?'

'She. Mrs Cordelia Du Pres Wellington.'

'Oh, no.' My heart sank. Cordelia could make major trouble for Chris, a by-the-book guy. 'You know she's Reggie Du Pres's sister. The old guy who runs the Forest.'

'I figured she was a big deal by the way Greiman is acting,' Chris said. 'She blew through a stop sign going about seventy and hit a bank teller coming back from lunch. Knocked the poor woman right out of her shoes.'

'Oh, jeez. Seventy? Is there anything left of the victim?'

'That woman was destroyed, Angela! Destroyed! You're going to have trouble documenting all the injuries. Broken ribs, multiple fractures, internal injuries and head trauma. I think the head injuries killed her, but that's for the ME to decide.'

'Who was the victim?' I asked.

'Rose McClaren,' he said. 'Do you know her?'

'No,' I said.

'She's fifty-nine,' Chris said, and he sounded sad. 'Her co-workers at the bank told me Rose is the mother of two children, one still in high school. Her daughter is married, and Rose has three grandchildren. She's been married to William McClaren for thirty-five years. She's also a church volunteer and bakes amazing double-chocolate brownies.'

A picture of the victim was emerging – a hard-working woman, ordinary in the best sense of the word.

'I'm going to hate to break the news to her family,' I said.

'You won't have to,' Chris said. 'Her co-workers called her husband, Bill. He's a maintenance man for some apartment buildings. Bill identified her at the scene, so you don't have to go through notifying him.'

'But Bill saw his wife dead at the scene,' I said. 'That poor man must be shattered.'

'He is. I called his grown daughter, Tina. She's with him, but he won't leave the scene until his wife is taken to the morgue.'

'I'll get there as fast as I can,' I said. 'What about the driver, Cordelia? Was she injured?'

'Airbag deployed. Not a scratch,' Chris said. 'She wasn't a bit sorry, either. She looked at the victim and said, "I don't know her. She must live in Toonerville," as if it was OK to run down people from that part of town.'

'Talk about entitlement,' I said.

'Cordelia makes Marie Antoinette seem like Mother Teresa. She was more upset about the damage to her car: the right front fender and the hood are dented and the windshield is broken and spider-webbed. Cordelia informed me that her car was a top-of-the-line Mercedes S 450 sedan, and it cost more than a hundred thousand dollars.'

'Did she even see the victim when she was crossing the street?' I asked.

'I think Cordelia saw double. She was hammered. She's not some careless kid, either. Her driver's license says she's seventy.'

'She wishes she was that young!' I said. 'Cordelia is eighty if she's a day.'

'She definitely looks old. She's kinda scrawny and wore an old pink suit and neckful of gold chains, like a rapper.'

I smothered a laugh. 'That's probably a Chanel suit, Chris. It may be old, but if you live in the Forest, it's called a classic. It's what rich ladies wear to lunch. The long gold-and-pearl chains are part of the Chanel look. And she's fashionably thin, not scrawny.'

'You sound bitter,' Chris said.

'I am. I hate the idea that a productive life was ended by a useless old woman who spends her days lunching and playing bridge at the Forest Country Club. Her lunch is mostly the three olives in her martinis.'

'That's right,' Chris whispered. 'Cordelia Wellington told me she'd just come from "luncheon" – not lunch – and she'd had "a few drinky-poos" – her words, not mine. She was definitely drunk. She slurred her words so bad I could hardly understand her, and I smelled alcohol on her breath. Cordelia refused to do the standard roadside sobriety tests. She wouldn't walk heel-to-toe along a straight line, or try a one-leg stand. She said the tests were undignified. All she had to do was stand on one foot. What's undignified about that? She also refused to take a Breathalyzer test.'

'Can't she lose her license for that?'

'In sensible states, yes. But we're talking about Missouri. Here she may get her license revoked for a year. I took her license and gave her a notice of revocation. She'll have thirty days to challenge that.'

'I bet she was livid,' I said.

'Livid doesn't begin to describe it,' Chris said. 'Cordelia drew herself up to her full five feet nothing and glared at me. "Young man," she said, "do you know who I am?"

'"Yes, ma'am," I said. "You are a drunk who doesn't belong behind the wheel."'

'Oh, Chris, you didn't!'

'I did. And then I booked her for DUI.'

'I admire your courage, but there's going to be hell to pay.'

'There will be hell to pay if another innocent person is run down by that drunken woman. I had to put a stop to it.'

'I hope you did. She doesn't belong on the road.'

'That's not what Greiman said. When he showed up, he started giving me a hard time. He said I didn't understand local customs: when a solid citizen like Cordelia had "a few too many" the Forest police, as a courtesy, stopped her, took away her keys and called her housekeeper, who hops in a cab and drives the old lush home in the car. I gathered this wasn't the first time Cordelia had been stopped for a DUI, but there's nothing on her record. If she'd had any DUI priors – a suspension, revocation or conviction, she would need an ignition interlock device. She couldn't start her car if she was "tipsy." That's what Greiman called her – "tipsy."

'If he and the other courteous members of the Forest PD had done their job, Rose McClaren might still be at her teller window this afternoon instead of dead in the street.'

'Oh, Chris, I'm sorry. But that's the way things work here,' I said.

'I hate small town politics, Angela! Hate them.'

'Chris, you're shouting! Lower your voice, please!' Of course he was angry. Any person with a conscience would be. But it wouldn't help anyone if Chris was fired.

Now he spat out each word in a low, angry voice. 'In normal towns, a Crimes Against Persons unit would not investigate a traffic accident, unless it was intentional. The sheriff should be doing traffic fatalities.'

'It's not right,' I said.

'Of course not,' Chris said. 'But how else can the city serve the one percent? I'm not going to let that happen. I'm getting a warrant for the car's EDR.'

'The black box?' I knew EDR stood for event data recorder, and was similar to the device that told airplane crash investigators what had happened.

'That's right. It's going to show the driver's speed. Her airbag was deployed, so that would probably show when the brakes were applied – if she even tried to stop before she plowed into the victim.

'How far away are you, Angela?' he asked. 'When will you get here?'

'In about two minutes,' I said.

'Hell, Greiman's getting off the phone. Expect to see us arguing when you get here, Angela.'

And that's exactly what I saw. Chris had blocked off the street, and Patrick, another uniform, was rerouting traffic. Pat recognized me and let me through. Someone had erected a screen around the body, but curious passersby were gawking anyway, staring at the skid marks and blood. There was no sign of Cordelia Du Pres Wellington, though her wrecked car was still blocking the intersection. The car was long and black as a hearse. The broken windshield was crisscrossed with cracks and there was a head-sized break in the glass, rimmed and spattered with blood. The hood had a dent as big as a basketball, and the driver's side headlight was broken. The driver's door hung open.

Chris stood by the car, shouting, 'And I'm telling you I'm placing a "hold" on this car at the tow yard so it won't be turned over to the owner or the repair shop.'

'The hell you are!' Greiman, red-faced, eyes bulging, shouted back. His silk tie was flapping like his lips, and spittle leaked down his chin.

I pulled my DI kit out of my car and rolled it over. I wanted to stop the fight before a bystander reported them.

'Ray!' I said.

The detective turned his ire on me. 'Where the hell have you been – running around with that lame-ass detective from Chicago? You're not supposed to be helping him.'

I kept my voice level. 'I'm here to do my job.'

He looked at Chris and said, 'I thought you were here to do him. You're fucking him, aren't you?'

'That's it!' Chris punched Greiman in the face. Now the detective's nose was bleeding on his blue monogrammed shirt. As much as I'd wanted to punch Greiman, I figured I'd better step between them. I lowered my voice to a whispering hiss. 'Hey, you two. Pull yourselves together. Show some respect. There's a dead woman on the other side of that screen.'

Chris looked ashamed. Greiman didn't stop threatening. 'If you were helping that Jace Budewitz, Angela, I'll have your job. And I'm getting numb nuts here fired, too.'

'You can't,' Chris said. 'I followed procedure. I went by the manual for a motor vehicle fatality.'

'So what?' Greiman said. 'You irritate the shit out of the chain of command. They'll find a way to get rid of you.'

Greiman understood the situation better than Chris, but I still had to break this up.

'Officer Ferretti,' I said. 'Don't you have a long fatal crash report to do? As I recall, it's darn near a booklet.'

Chris recovered himself enough to look sheepish. He retired to his patrol car.

Still sounding like Medusa in a black pantsuit, I hissed, 'And you, Detective Greiman. You're not reporting anyone for anything. Mention one word, you sneaky SOB, and I'll file a sexual harassment lawsuit against you for the way you talked about Chris and me. And you're smart enough to know that's a career killer.'

At last, Greiman shut up.

FOURTEEN

'Excuse me, miss. I am mean, ma'am. Are you the uh, the uh . . .?' Bill McClaren's question trailed off. I knew he was the victim's husband because his name was embroidered on his navy coveralls. Bill couldn't bring himself to say the word 'death' in my title.

Not with his newly dead wife's broken body ten feet away. Bill was a big man, about six feet two, going a little soft around the middle. His dark hair was tinged with gray. His sunburned face might have been handsome if he wasn't so distraught.

I helped him out and introduced myself, saying the word he couldn't. 'I'm Angela Richman, Chouteau County Death Investigator.'

'Are you taking photos of my Rosie?'

'Yes, sir.' I chose my words carefully, hoping I was picking the least distressing. 'At the start of my investigation, I take long shots, medium and close-up photos. It's just routine.'

Rose McClaren was on her back in the street, her clothes in disarray, her brown hair framed with a dark halo of blood. She wore a pale yellow striped blouse and black skirt. Her black leather heels were about six feet away from her body.

'Could you do me a favor and pull her blouse down, please?' her husband asked. 'It rode up, along with her brassiere. She'd be so embarrassed.' Tears were shining in his eyes.

I gulped back my own and sternly reminded myself that I was a professional. I wanted to tell him: The dead can't be embarrassed, sir. And they have no dignity. It doesn't matter to them any more. They are free of our concerns.

Instead, I said, 'I'm sorry, Mr McClaren, but I have to document what happened. Your Rosie wants to tell us exactly what happened to her, and these photos will help.'

I hated how I sounded. I wanted to put the poor woman's

clothes back on her properly, so her pale, middle-aged breasts wouldn't be exposed to the harsh afternoon sun, but I couldn't. I couldn't put her shoes on, either, even though I could see her naked feet through her shredded nylons. Rose McClaren had suffered from bunions and corns. Standing all day at her teller window in those heels must have been torture.

I knew the rules, and they were harsh but necessary: I couldn't touch the body before it was photographed. I wanted to shout, 'Screw the rules,' and make Rose McClaren look like the proud woman she was, but I couldn't. Not with Ray Greiman watching my every move. Even if he wasn't here, I couldn't. This was one part of the death investigator's code I hated following.

A brunette in her early thirties came over and said, 'Come on, Daddy, the lady has to do her job. Mama would understand. Let's go in the bank and sit down.'

'I'm sorry,' I said to them. 'Mrs McClaren seemed like a good, hard-working woman.'

'She was,' the brunette said. 'I'm her daughter, Tina Nicholas. This is so unfair. Mama wasn't doing anything wrong. Just walking back from lunch when that drunk killed her.'

I lowered my voice and said, 'You didn't hear this from me, but you need to talk to a good lawyer. About a civil suit.'

Bill interrupted us. 'I don't want money. I just want my Rosie.' He was crying now, harsh, inconsolable tears. For some reason, men's tears hit me worse than women's.

'I know, Mr McClaren, and I'm so sorry,' I said. 'But that's not possible. And the only way you're going to stop someone like this driver is to hit her in the wallet – hard.'

'I don't want money,' he repeated. Now he sounded angry. 'Money won't do me any good. All I want is Rosie.'

'Money can't bring back your wife, but don't you want your grandchildren to go to college?'

Tina stepped between us. 'It's OK, Daddy,' she said.

'It's not,' he said. 'Your mother's dead. It's never going to be OK again.'

Tina wrapped her arms around her grief-stricken father to comfort him and patted his back. She turned to me and said in a low voice, 'What's the name of that lawyer? Daddy is too shocked to handle anything right now.'

'Montgomery Bryant,' I said. 'He's the best.'

Tina repeated the name, nodded her thanks, and steered her father across the street to the bank.

Chris's prediction was right. This death investigation did take longer. Almost twice as long, by the time I noted all of Rose McClaren's injuries, down to the last contusion, scrape and cut-like defect. Her daughter, Tina, came back out to give me her mother's demographic information, leaving her father in the care of two bank employees.

The death investigation paperwork on a vehicular-related death went on for pages – from the color of the decedent's clothes to the type of roadway (concrete) and its condition (dry, no debris, and no visual obstructions at the location). That last question was important to document. I was sure Cordelia Du Pres Wellington's lawyer would claim something had obstructed her vision, besides multiple martinis. The techs had videoed and photographed the fatal site, and I photographed it, too, just in case something disappeared. I also noted the time and temperature and how clear and sunny the day was.

It was almost dark – eight o'clock – by the time I called the service to take Rose McClaren's body to the morgue and signed the chain of custody paperwork. By then, Tina Nicholas had taken her grieving father to her home, hoping her three children would help comfort their grandfather.

At last I was finished. I went straight home and took a shower, but I was too restless to settle in. I kept seeing Rose McClaren and hearing her husband crying. Finally, I called Chris, and invited myself over for dinner. I picked up Chinese takeout – extra spicy General Tso's chicken for Chris and ginger shrimp for me – and drove to his place. He kissed me at the door and poured me a cold white wine.

We ate a quiet dinner on the couch in his living room, our feet up on the coffee table, while I listened to him rail against Ray Greiman.

'He threatened you today, Angela,' Chris said. 'What are you going to do about that?'

'Ignore him. Continue to help Jace,' I said, and stabbed a fat shrimp with my fork, wishing it was Greiman's eye. 'Tomorrow I have a hair appointment with Mario at Killer Cuts. I'll ask him for information about Cindy Lockridge. Jace is sure she's the one behind the killing, but he needs proof she hired Spider-Man.'

'And you,' Chris said. 'Who do you think killed Thomas Lockridge?'

'Either Cynthia or her lawyer. Maybe both of them were in it together.'

I watched Chris expertly manipulate a chunk of chicken with his chopsticks and pop it into his mouth. I admired his skill. For me, chopsticks were like crutches – something else to trip me up.

'Ray will try to make trouble for you, you know that,' Chris said.

'I do. But he's really going to make your life miserable, Chris, after you popped him on the nose. I think he bled all over his favorite shirt.' I paused to savor that memory, along with another shrimp.

Chris looked at me seriously. 'So what? He was wrong. And if the chief won't do anything, I'm prepared to take this issue to the county prosecutor, or even the press, if I have to. That woman does not deserve special treatment. It's not right.'

'I know that, but what if you lose your job?'

He shrugged. 'Then I'll live off my pension. I'll be OK. I own this condo free and clear and my car is paid for. That Cordelia Whatever Wellington—'

'Du Pres,' I interrupted. 'It's a name you should know.'

'She killed an innocent woman, and she's going to pay,' Jace said. 'If it costs me my job, then it's still worth it. We have to get her off the road. Next time, she could hit you.

'And I'm worried about you, too, Angela,' Chris said.

'Why? I handled the case just fine.'

'I was watching you. You nearly started crying at least once. You're taking these deaths too hard, Angela. You need to talk them out.'

'I am. Right now. With you.'

'No, you're not. You're avoiding the subject. Tell me what had you so upset.'

So I did. I told him I was angry and sad all rolled into one and it wasn't fair what happened to Rose McClaren or her heartbroken husband. I said I was frustrated by the Forest bigshots who got away with – well, in this case – murder. I talked and drank wine and finally, I burst out crying.

'I'm glad you're crying, Angela,' he said. 'You needed to do that.'

'But it's not professional.'

'You're not working now,' he said. 'And learning how to deal with grief is part of your profession. Otherwise, you'll burn out.'

I kissed his right hand, the one he'd hit Greiman with, and said, 'Thank you for punching Greiman in the nose. I can't tell you how much I've wanted to do that.'

'Really,' he said, kissing me back. 'I can think of better ways to thank me.'

'So can I.'

And soon we forgot about Ray Greiman and Rose McClaren, and the rest of that long, sad day.

FIFTEEN

Mario Garcia's hair salon, Killer Cuts, was the American Dream in stylish chrome and glass. Mario had left Cuba in 1980 as a Marielito – a refugee in the dangerous Mariel Boatlift. Castro's thugs were shooting gay people, and Mario figured it was only a matter of time before they killed him. He left his home country with only the clothes on his back.

Now he owned the finest salon in Chouteau County – maybe all the Midwest. Today, the place was humming: every stylists' chair was filled, scissors were snipping, hair dryers were whirring and manicurists were painting. When I changed into a robe in the dressing room, there was barely a hanger left. I was happy to see the salon so busy.

I had an appointment with Mario himself, in his orchid-filled alcove. With the palms and flowers, his styling station felt like a bit of the tropics transplanted to Missouri.

Mario was remarkably handsome, with high cheekbones and thick black hair. As always, he was dressed in black, with a Spanish silver belt. He looked like a gunfighter.

Mario finished scolding me for waiting so long between haircuts, and I made my usual excuse about being busy. This ritual always ended the same way: Mario gave me a thimbleful of cafecito, sweet, thick Cuban coffee, which was twice as strong as American coffee.

Next he sent me to his assistant so she could wash my hair. Finally, with my damp head wrapped in a towel, I was seated back in his chair. He began sectioning and snipping my hair.

Only then did I ask my question: 'Was Cynthia Lockridge one of your clients?'

'Isn't she the woman whose husband was murdered by the Ghost Burglars?' Mario still spoke with a slight accent.

'Yes. I need your help, Mario.'

His answer was very serious. 'You know I never discuss

my clients, Angela. Never. No matter how much I like you.
You have your code and I have mine.'

'I understand,' I said. 'But you must know someone who
does. I need information to help a good guy.'

'When Cynthia came here, Dante did her hair. One reason
I fired him was that Dante liked to give the *Chouteau Forest
Gazette* gossip about his clients. Also, he wasn't very good.
He's started his own shop out by the highway. And Cynthia
no longer comes here. So you can ask Dante about her.'

Mario was pulling on both sides of my wet hair to make
sure they were even. He trimmed a minuscule amount off
the left side. Before he fired up his hair dryer to blow out
my hair, I asked, 'What excuse should I use to see him? If
Dante's not very good, I sure don't want him touching my
hair.'

'Make an appointment for a consultation,' Mario said. 'I
think he charges fifty dollars. Get him talking and he'll say
anything. But whatever you do, don't let him near your hair.
He'd love to chop it off. He gives everyone the same haircut.
It's the only one he knows.'

Half an hour later, Mario's magic had turned my dark unruly
hair into a shining shoulder-length mane. He was the only
stylist I knew who could tame it.

Back in my car, I called Dante's Stylistics for a consultation. The receptionist said Dante 'was finishing up with a
customer, but he can see you in about forty-five minutes.'
Thirty minutes later, I was at his salon, in a strip mall store-
front squeezed between a tattoo parlor and a consignment
shop.

Inside, Dante's Stylistics looked like an old-fashioned
beauty parlor: scuffed tile, two stylists' chairs and one mani-
curist. The walls were plastered with posters of pouty-lipped
beauties with impossibly silky hair. In the waiting area, two
women were sitting on hard plastic chairs, reading magazines.
Both seemed to be somewhere in their sixties and had identical
hairstyles: heavily sprayed helmets, one blonde and the other
orange red. Joanie, the pale twenty-something receptionist,
had the same style, except in hot pink. When she greeted me,

Joanie sounded like she had a cold – she kept sneezing and blowing her nose. I wanted to send her home and tuck her into bed with a hot drink.

'May I get you some water or coffee?' Joanie asked, and gave a juicy sneeze. I said thanks, but no thanks.

There was only one stylist at work. Dante, I presumed. He had a cute geeky vibe: a navy windowpane-check waistcoat over a light-blue dress shirt rolled up at the sleeves, and dress pants. Black-framed nerd glasses and brown oxfords completed the ensemble. I liked it.

He was spraying another sixty-something woman, completing the finishing touches on a gray helmet. I'd thought Mario was being a touch snide when he described Dante's talent, but maybe not.

After I was seated at his station, Dante said, 'Now, what can I do for you?'

'I'm tired of my hair,' I said. 'I wanted to consult you about a new look.'

He examined my freshly coiffed hair from several angles, turned me around in his chair, and made *hmm* sounds. Finally, he asked, 'Are you married or single, Ms Richman? That might help me decide.'

'I'm a widow,' I said.

'Oh, so you don't have to dress up for anyone.'

'Except myself,' I said.

'Wouldn't your life be easier without all that hair?' He pulled my hair back, so I could see myself with shorter hair. I looked like a nun.

'I'm not sure,' I said.

'I could dye it a fun color like Joanie's.' He nodded at the sneezing receptionist, whose nose matched her hair.

'Her hair is nice,' I said. 'But I'm not sure it would do for my work.'

'What exactly is your job?'

'I'm a death investigator for Chouteau County,' I said.

'Really?' Now I had his interest. 'Work any cases I might know about?'

'The death of Thomas Lockridge.'

'I heard he was killed by those Ghost Burglars.' Dante was breathless with excitement. He'd forgotten all about cutting my hair, and that was fine with me.

'He was,' I said. Knowing Dante's reputation as a gossip monger, I was careful to only tell him news that was public knowledge.

'Did you see his mansion? What did you think?' I saw the hope in Dante's eyes. He wanted me to dish, but I wasn't going to knock Cynthia's taste.

'It was amazing,' I said. That was the truth. 'I also met Mrs Lockridge. Cynthia. Do you know her?'

'Oh, yes,' Dante said. 'And she wasn't always so grand. She was plain old Cindy when I first knew her.'

He dropped his voice to a whisper. 'You'd never guess, but she used to be trailer trash.' I hated that condescending phrase, but I kept my mouth shut and nodded.

'What did she look like when you first knew her, in the beginning?' I asked.

He shuddered. 'You wouldn't believe it: She had big hair and ruffly dresses. Ruffles! She wore polyester.'

'You say that like polyester is a crime,' I said.

Dante laughed, a short, sneery laugh. 'It is. A crime against fashion. Cindy asked me to style her hair. I wanted to cut it short, but she insisted on long hair – she said her future husband liked it that way.

'After she got married, she quit working at the construction company and didn't want to dress like a secretary any more. Now she wanted to learn how to look like a society wife. I offered to help her. And she used me. Used me brutally.' He sounded like a betrayed lover.

'What did you do for her?'

'Everything! I transformed that woman. *Transformed* her. First, I sent her to Chouteau Forest Pilates, where simply everyone goes. You go there, don't you?'

'I've seen it,' I said. I passed it on the way to the bakery.

'Well, Pilates knocked the country pudge off her, and soon Cindy was fashionably thin. She also needed elocution lessons. You wouldn't believe the way she talked! She actually said she wanted to drive a "Jag-wire" instead of a "Jag-u-ar."'

He stretched the word into three syllables, in the British manner. 'Her teacher also helped her speak properly. Cindy needed so much help. The words she used!' Dante shook his head.

'Like what?' I asked.

'She said "drapes" instead of "curtains." And "I'm done with my dinner" instead of "I'm finished." She'd ask "Can I get a drink?" instead of "May I have a drink?" And she dropped her G's. Constantly!' He shuddered delicately.

'In other words, U and non-U speech,' I said.

'Yes, exactly. I had to tell her that secretarial school wasn't higher education. I also told her she needed to go to church, even if she wasn't a believer. The right church could be good for her socially and for her husband's business. Thanks to me, she started attending the Forest Episcopal Church.' Dante sounded triumphant.

'Where the elite meet God,' I said. Dante did not smile.

'Once she started mixing with the right people, she became easier to work with. She saw how they dressed and wanted to look like them. I took Cindy clothes shopping, and introduced her to the right salespeople, who made sure she was well dressed. I toned down her Dolly Parton hair to a chic style. I showed her how to do her make-up and convinced her to ditch that awful orange lipstick. I persuaded her to cut her red dagger nails for a simpler, shorter French manicure.

'We had fun. We went everywhere together – lunch, dinner, society events when her husband couldn't escort her.' And I bet Cindy paid for them all, I thought.

'Thanks to me, Cindy was transformed,' Dante said. 'Now she was not just country pretty but glamorous, and her husband loved to show her off. When she asked me to call her Cynthia instead of Cindy, I knew I had succeeded. Apparently, I succeeded too well.'

I heard the bitterness in his voice. 'What happened?'

'She developed a taste for champagne and high living. That was fine. But then Cynthia became greedy and turned into a party girl, spending her husband's money on expensive clothes and coke.

'Cynthia even got old straight-arrow Thomas to try coke. At first, Tom was reluctant, but then he enjoyed it. Cindy reconnected with some of her trailer park friends, who worked in the Ozarks. One was her cocaine connection.'

'Was he someone named Spider-Man?' I asked.

Dante looked puzzled. 'No, I never heard her mention that name, but if you need some blow . . .'

'No, thanks,' I said. 'That was just a name of someone she might have hung around.'

'Not when I knew her. As I was saying, Cindy became a party girl. Thomas didn't like that life. He tired quickly and went to bed early, but Cindy could stay up all night, and frequently came home at dawn.

'Cocaine changed her,' Dante said. 'She became mean and bitchy. She was bored. She told me her husband was too old and too dull and couldn't get it up any more. She said she hadn't had sex in almost a year and put her hand on my knee. I told her, "Don't look at me, honey. I'm batting for the other team."

'That's when she began her affair with Wesley, her lawyer. It didn't bother Wes that he betrayed his patron by screwing his pretty young wife.'

'How did you know that? Did you see them?'

Dante frowned. I'd interrupted his dish session. 'No,' he said. 'But I could tell by the way Cynthia talked about Wes they had something going. She did tell me that Wes wanted to marry her. She turned him down, of course. Sensible girl. Wes saw her as his shortcut to Chouteau Forest society.'

'What do you think of Wes?'

'He's a rising star, but he has a dubious reputation.'

Now I was curious. 'What kind of reputation?'

'Well, he takes any kind of case, no matter how sleazy the client. His firm uses him for the cases they don't normally represent: a client's kid gets arrested for possession, or a wife has been shoplifting. And – don't quote me' – he lowered his voice – 'but I hear Wes has sticky fingers.'

'What sticks to them?' I asked.

'His clients' money.' Suddenly Dante looked alarmed. He said, 'You can't quote me. I can't prove that last rumor.'

'It's OK,' I said. 'I won't spread it. Thank you for the information about Cynthia.'

'Most people don't know Cynthia,' Dante said. 'They only see the glittery surface. They see her as a society lady who goes to church every Sunday, supports worthy causes, and dresses like a fashion plate. She and Thomas went to all the right parties. He was an adoring husband. For her birthday, he gave her a new red Jaguar convertible.'

'When was this?' I asked.

'I last talked to her about a year ago. That's when she was getting so high and mighty. She dropped me and went to a big-deal hair stylist in St. Louis. Just because he charged more didn't make him better. Suddenly, she didn't have time for me any more. She was too busy to go to lunch or dinner with me. She said she wasn't getting any party invitations that I could escort her to, but I knew that was a lie. I saw her photos in the paper.' Dante sounded angry and hostile – and hurt. Very hurt.

So Saint Cynthia was smart and calculating, I thought. She knew when it was time to drop Dante. She couldn't keep running around with a gay hairdresser if she was going to succeed in Forest society. Dante had cleaned her up, showed her where her new friends shopped, and now she could rely on the right saleswomen to dress her properly. She didn't need a Henry Higgins any more.

I decided to test Dante with one more question:

'Do you think Cynthia killed her husband so she could marry Wes?' I asked.

Dante laughed – a loud bray. 'Marry him? Why should she? She had a doting husband who turned a blind eye to her affair, and showered her with gifts.

'Wes is just starting his career and he doesn't have nearly as much money as her husband. Tom had a long-standing reputation as a generous donor. He far outranked a shyster lawyer. Cynthia could get all the nooky she wanted from Wes. She used him, just like she used me.'

SIXTEEN

I wasn't surprised that Katie was assigned Rose McClaren's autopsy. Our boss, the crafty Evarts Evans, knew that Mrs McClaren's death would create a tangle of civil and criminal court cases. Evarts deftly passed that political football to his assistant ME. He knew Katie would make meticulous notes and spend the long hours in court, waiting to testify.

One thing you could say about Evarts – he'd never die of overwork.

Usually, Katie accepted her lot with good humor: she understood her lazy boss and he gave her a great deal of freedom. But this time, Katie seemed different.

Two days after the fatal accident, she called Chris and me into her office to talk about Rose's case. She'd also invited Greiman, but we all knew he wouldn't bother showing up.

It was eight in the morning, when I wasn't at my brightest. I was relieved that Katie had brought coffee and a platter of homemade cookies. Chris was chomping a chocolate chip cookie when I arrived. I was a little shy around him in the company of Katie. I gave him a smile, then chose a snickerdoodle, the cinnamon sugar cookie with the funny name, and perched on the edge of her desk. Chris sat next to me on the desk, and reached for my hand. I squeezed his hand, but I was distracted.

I was worried about Katie. The assistant ME looked tired – her hair needed a wash and she had suspicious smears on her lab coat that I hoped were from yesterday's lunch. I wondered what was wrong.

'First, I have news,' she said. 'Sandy Perkins, Spider-Man's sidekick, died of his injuries.'

'Good,' I said.

OK, that was harsh, but the pointless burglary by Sandy and his colorfully named partner in crime had caused the wasteful death of a fine young man, Danny Morton. I kept seeing Danny's bleeding, shattered body in my dreams. Somehow, my cookie had disappeared. I helped myself to a healthy cranberry oatmeal and took another sip of the strong black coffee.

'Did Sandy ever regain consciousness?' Chris asked.

'No,' Katie said. 'He never woke up from the coma. His sister came down from Peoria, Illinois to be with him. She's a teacher and his closest relative. She consented to have his organs harvested.

'That's probably the only good to come out of that man's useless life,' she said. 'Sandy Perkins: a petty thief, a burglar, and a pot dealer. Gone and quickly forgotten.'

'What an epitaph,' I said.

'Perkins's sister said she was glad their poor mother was dead,' Katie said, 'so she would never know about the family's shame.'

'And speaking of shame,' I said. 'What's the word on Rose McClaren?'

'About what you'd expect,' Katie said. 'I did the autopsy. The victim was struck from the side at a high rate of speed. The cause of death was massive head injuries. The bumper hit her legs, her head hit the hood, and then the windshield. You both were at the scene. You probably know that already.'

Chris and I nodded like a pair of bobblehead dolls.

'So what killed the poor woman?' Chris asked.

'Blunt force trauma,' Katie said. 'Also known as traumatic brain injuries. I found thirteen pieces of tempered windshield glass imbedded in her scalp. You want to hear the rest of this sad story?' She sounded angry, as if she was accusing us. Chris and I both said yes. I reached for a chocolate swirl cookie, just in case the healthy cranberry-oatmeal would shock my system.

'Mrs McClaren also had hip and pelvis fractures,' Katie said. 'And numerous abrasions – Angela and I counted fifty-three – plus torn ligaments in her left knee, injuries to her rib cage, liver, and lungs. Both hands and wrists were fractured.

'Her body followed the classic trajectory for a pedestrian accident: Rose's lower body was thrown forward, her head hit the hood and the windshield, and she was launched into the air. Her body slid about seventy feet. I believe she was dead by then. At least, I hope so.'

I winced as Katie recounted Rose's injuries, even though I'd seen them the other day. Enumerating them all again somehow made them worse.

'Angela, I heard the victim's husband asked you not to photograph his wife with her blouse up and her breasts showing.' That was unusually delicate phrasing for Katie. I wondered if it was out of deference for Rose McClaren.

'Yes,' I said. 'I had to tell that poor man I couldn't pull his wife's blouse and bra down. I felt like a jerk.'

'You did the right thing,' Katie said. 'I'm glad you stuck to your guns. If this goes to a jury, every woman there will see the photos and think, "That could be me, flapping in the breeze for the whole world to see." The men will look at Rose's battered body and think, "That could be my poor wife, exposed like that for strangers to stare at." How Rose looks won't make one bit of difference to the victim, but the shock value might help the lawyer who sues Cordelia.'

'I gave Monty's name to the victim's daughter,' I said.

'Good,' Katie said. 'He'd love to go after the rich bitch who did this.' I waited, expecting Katie to sing the praises of her lover the way she usually did, but this time she was silent. Was there a problem with her romance?

'Is the driver still in jail, Chris?' Katie asked.

'No,' he said. 'Cordelia's lawyers got her out and bundled her off to a fancy rehab place. Instead of eating baloney sandwiches in jail, she's eating four-star meals at some spa for loaded lushes. If that wasn't bad enough, Chief Buttkiss invited me in for a "little talk" about Cordelia's arrest.'

I caught the snark in Chris's voice. 'I gather Chief Lawrence Butkus was living up to his nickname?'

'Oh, yeah,' Chris said. 'And his motto to protect and serve – the Forest's one percent.' His arm snaked out and he grabbed the last chocolate chip. I told myself I'd had enough, then realized I was in the county morgue. Life is short. I took another chocolate swirl.

'The chief said I shouldn't have been so rough on poor Mrs

Wellington,' Chris said, 'because "that poor lady has been having problems coping since her husband died two years ago." The chief said the couple had been married sixty-one years and Cordelia had "bravely lived through many sorrows." She only started drinking heavily after her husband's death. Buttkiss said the Forest PD was well aware of her "little problem" and generally made arrangements to drive her home.'

'They couldn't drive her home this time,' Katie said. 'Not after she killed a woman.'

'The chief said if I'd consulted him first after the accident, Mrs Wellington's "problem wouldn't have been so public."'

'In other words,' Katie said, 'Buttkiss would have covered it up.'

'That's my guess,' Chris said, 'though he was too savvy to spell it out. And how he could cover up a fatal accident that happened downtown in broad daylight is beyond me.' He crunched the cookie viciously, as if biting off the chief's head, then continued talking.

'I didn't score any points when I told the chief that was why Cordelia was drunk when she ran over Mrs McClaren. Thanks to all the enablers in the Forest, she didn't have to face facts. Maybe if the CFPD had arrested Cordelia – or even given her a warning – for a DUI earlier and she'd had to go to some AA meetings, she would have gotten a grip and stopped drinking.'

'I bet he loved that,' I said.

'Buttkiss said I couldn't expect a lady like Mrs Cordelia Wellington to go to AA meetings, where everyone would know her. I said, "Why not? The group's name is Alcoholics Anonymous, after all. Hollywood is full of AA meetings with people far more famous than a Forest bigwig."'

'Oh, Chris,' I said. 'Tell me you didn't.'

'I did,' he said, and rewarded himself with another cookie. 'The chief was also unhappy that I got a warrant for her EDR. That bit of technology really fried her bacon.' He reached into his shirt pocket and triumphantly produced the probable cause affidavit.

The 'Complaint Affidavit' was part of the arrest form. Katie read the stilted officialese out loud:

'By using published mathematical formulas, it was calculated the Suspect's vehicle was traveling at approximately seventy mph when the crash occurred. After obtaining a search warrant and utilizing the Bosch Crash Data Retrieval (CDR) system, the Airbag Control Module (ACM) was removed from the vehicle and imaged. The ACM recorded an impact speed of approximately seventy-four mph. It was also recorded that the Suspect's vehicle was traveling at approximately eighty mph just prior to the crash while approaching the intersection.'"

'Good lord. Cordelia was going eighty through downtown!' I said.

Katie glared at me, and continued reading: "'The posted speed limit where the crash occurred is thirty-five mph.'"

I whistled.

Katie said, 'Here's the good part: "Based on this information, probable cause exists to believe that the Suspect operated the vehicle in a reckless manner, likely to cause death or great bodily harm of another, and the Suspect did cause the death of the Victim."

'This is pure gold,' Katie said. 'The lawyers are going to love this. You've served them their wrongful death case on a platter.' She handed the affidavit back to Chris, and he tucked it in his pocket.

'Good,' he said. 'I hope they sue that woman for every last nickel, so she has to take the bus.'

Katie shook her head. 'Chris, I admire your courage, but you've called a heap of trouble down on your head. Be careful, will you? Chief Butkus will be looking for ways to get rid of you. Sneaky ways. If you have any problems, you have Monty's phone number, right? Call him right away.'

'He's on speed dial,' Chris said.

'Good,' Katie said. 'The chief will have his spies watching every move you make.'

'They already are,' Chris said. 'That's why I wanted to warn you, Angela. Don't do any more digging around for Jace Budewitz. You could lose your job.'

'I could,' I said. 'But I can afford to lose it. I don't have any children. Jace has a family.'

'Why are you being so stubborn?' Chris said. 'Why do you care? You don't know any of those people.'

I thoughtfully crunched another cookie. That was a good question. Why was I risking everything?

'Because I am stubborn,' I said. 'You're right. And Tom Lockridge's murder set off a chain reaction that resulted in the death of an innocent man – and Danny Morton's death didn't even rate a photo in the local paper. I want to see the killer punished, and I know the people here better than you do, Chris. That's why I want to help find the killer.'

Katie looked at her watch and began shooing us out. 'Sorry, folks, it's time for you to go. I have a meeting soon. Take some cookies with you.' She handed us plastic zip-lock bags, and Chris and I stuffed them with our favorites. He thanked Katie for the cookies and left.

I lingered and asked, 'Are you OK?'

'Why wouldn't I be?' Katie was sitting on the other edge of her desk. We were perched there like birds on a wire.

'That's not an answer,' I said. 'Come by my house tonight after work. I'll have dinner, wine and chocolate. I know something's bugging you. Did you really spend the night baking cookies?' Why weren't you with Monty? was my unspoken question.

'I woke up about three a.m. and couldn't go back to sleep.' Katie ran her hands through her hair and looked even more frazzled. 'Thought I might do something useful.'

I looked at her carefully: the oily hair, the dark circles under her eyes, and the nervous way her fingers impatiently tapped her desk top.

'Really?' I said. 'You expect me to believe you had an attack of domestic divahood at three in the morning?'

Katie sighed. 'It's the Forest. I think I've been here too long. I'm starting to hate the place. Everyone tiptoes around a rich woman like Cordelia Du Pres Wellington, and they don't give a damn about Rose McClaren's family. What could Cordelia have suffered that would turn her into a drunk?'

'She lost her husband,' I said. 'After being married sixty-one years, that must feel like an amputation.'

'So? You lost your husband, and you didn't start hitting the bottle.'

'No, but I have some idea how much it must hurt. And I had good friends to make me straighten up and fly right.' I looked her in the eye. 'You, for instance. You dragged me out of my funk by the scruff of my neck.'

She wasn't gentle about it, either. Katie had cursed, prodded and cajoled me back to life, and for months I fought her every step of the way. 'I'm grateful you did that, Katie. But pain isn't a contest. It can't be measured.'

Katie's phone rang. Time for me to leave. I grabbed my bag of cookies and waved goodbye.

'See you at seven tonight,' I said, right before she answered the phone.

SEVENTEEN

'**W**hat could Cordelia have suffered that would turn her into a drunk?'

Katie's question about the alcoholic who killed Rose McClaren haunted me. Chief Butkus said the poor woman had suffered many sorrows. What were they? Like a lot of people who had to work for a living, I believed a cold cash compress solved most problems – and Cordelia was born an heiress and married more money.

All morning long, while I shopped for the dinner with Katie, I pondered that question. I stopped at the supermarket for a fat roast chicken, salad fixings and fresh asparagus. I went to the bakery (averting my eyes when I passed Chouteau Forest Pilates) for crusty French bread and a triple-chocolate torte. I bought two bottles of a good merlot at the wine shop.

I was home by noon. Then I looked up Cordelia Du Pres Wellington in the *Forest Gazette* online files. The computerized records went back to 1920 – more than enough time to explore Cordelia's life.

The first mention was when she made her debut at the Chouteau Forest Cotillion in 1956. Back then, most young women were about eighteen when they debuted, so Cordelia was born in 1938 or 1937, making her at least eighty-one. Her photo was a picture of fifties perfection: Cordelia's silky blonde hair was worn in a Grace Kelly French twist. The deb wore a strapless ball gown that set off her creamy shoulders. Her dress was 'made of the finest satin silk and thousands of seed pearls,' according to the breathless description by the society writer.

Nothing sad there, I thought, and kept searching. The following year I saw an obituary for her mother, who died at age eighty-one 'after a long illness.' That was probably code for cancer, and yes, when a young woman lost her mother, that could knock her world sideways. It did mine.

Two years later, in 1958, Cordelia married Alister Robert Wellington III. No photo of the groom, though I did know he would become the CEO of his family's successful company, Wellington Sprocket Industries in St. Louis. But the bride, Cordelia Du Pres, was stunning in yards of tulle and Alencon lace. Her bouquet was made of roses and rare orchids. Nothing but the best for a Du Pres.

In 1965, Alister Robert Wellington IV was born. Two years later Lucas Du Pres Wellington grabbed his silver spoon and showed up at SOS. Cordelia had produced an heir and a spare, and her childbearing duties seemed to be over.

The next years chronicled her success as a fundraiser for the library and the Sisters of Sorrow Hospital, both worthy causes. In 1985, she was Chouteau County Woman of the Year. That photo was in color, and she wore a smile and a pink Chanel suit with long gold and pearl necklaces. I wondered if it was the same suit she was arrested in after running down Rose McClaren.

Five years later, Cordelia's sorrows started. First, her oldest son was killed in the Gulf War in 1990. He looked heartbreakingly handsome in his photo as a second lieutenant. And so young. He was only twenty-five. The obituary also mentioned that Alister had graduated from the Harvard School of Business.

Two years later, her second son, Lucas, died at age twenty-six. His obituary was strangely uninformative for such a prominent family. It simply said he'd graduated from North Dakota State University with a degree in Business Administration and was a vice-president at the Wellington Sprocket Industries. North Dakota? When his older brother went to Harvard? Neither son married nor had children.

Two dead sons, and Cordelia was now in her early fifties. After that, Cordelia disappeared from the files. Her husband retired from Wellington Sprocket at age seventy-five and sold the company in 2012. He died of a heart attack in 2020. And his grieving widow took to drink and killed a bank teller.

Chief Butkus was right. Cordelia did have a life of sorrow, and her vast fortune could not bring back her sons or her husband. I felt sorry for the woman.

I hurried around my house, putting it in order for Katie's visit – dusting, vacuuming, and cleaning the guest bathroom. Then I picked flowers for the table – my mother's lilacs were blooming and they smelled sweet. I set the table, prepared the salad, and drizzled the olive oil on the asparagus and set the oven temperature, then opened the wine so it could breathe. I pulled out two wine glasses and made sure they sparkled. It was six thirty when I rushed upstairs, showered, and changed.

When Katie rang the doorbell, I was ready. She looked a little better this evening. She was wearing fresh clothes – jeans and a blue striped shirt – and her brown hair was still damp from the shower. Despite these improvements, I still saw the dark circles under her eyes, like bruises. Katie brought the same brand of merlot I was serving. We knew each other well.

We sat on the big leather couch in the living room, chomping salted cashews and working on the first bottle of merlot. I poured us both a generous glass.

After we got through the opening chitchat, I told Katie what I'd found out about Cordelia and her sad life, and showed her the newspaper articles I'd printed out, from Cordelia's debut and wedding to her sons' and husband's obituaries.

'Imagine, Katie,' I said, helping myself to a big handful of cashews. 'Cordelia lost both sons when they were in their twenties. That must have been unbearable.'

'I don't want to imagine it.' Katie took a big gulp of wine, as if to wash away the awful idea.

I handed her the printout of Alister's obituary with the photo of the slim young officer in his dress uniform. 'Why do you think Cordelia's son Alister went into the military?' I was trying to slow my alcohol intake, so I kept my drinking to sips. For now.

'He wasn't drafted,' I said, 'and rich kids don't usually serve in the military – not in the US, anyway. I don't think this was his chosen career. I'd bet my last nickel Alister planned to run his family's business. He had a Harvard degree.'

Katie grabbed another handful of cashews and said, 'Alister was the oldest, wasn't he? By the looks of him, he was the family golden boy, expected to take over the reins of their multinational business. Could be that Alister joining the military was a business decision by his father. Look at this photo.' She held up the young man's obit picture. 'It would look perfect in a company brochure. It's good business to have a war hero running the show. That works in politics, too. Look what John F. Kenney's PT-109 adventures did for his career. Made him Senator and then President Kennedy.'

It did, I thought, but President Kennedy and his Senator brother, Robert, were both assassinated. Katie was on a roll, and I didn't interrupt. She was so enthusiastic about her explanation, I expected her to pull out a blackboard and a pointer as she gave her lecture.

'Old man Wellington was no dummy,' Katie said. 'Like Joe Kennedy, he could have been grooming his son for a Senate run. Only war wasn't like the movies – his son got killed. A terrible miscalculation – and something an entitled family never expected.'

Katie finished her second glass and I poured her another. And one for myself, while I was at it. There seemed to be a leak in my glass. The merlot was vanishing quickly.

'What about the second son, Lucas?' I asked. 'He was dead within two years of his brother. We don't even know what killed him.' I showed her Lucas's brief, almost anonymous obit. 'And why did he go to North Dakota when his older brother went to Harvard? This death notice doesn't even have a photo of the dead man. Why was his death so mysterious?'

'Nothing mysterious about it,' Katie said. 'I heard about that kid. The previous assistant ME was involved in the cover-up, and he was rewarded handsomely to make sure word didn't get out to the press. So handsomely he retired at fifty.'

'Then how did you find out?' I asked.

'You know what hospitals are like. They love gossip.' Katie grinned, then popped a cashew in her mouth. 'This time, the SOS rumor mill was accurate. I was told that Lucas was found in his bedroom with a spike in his arm, and I saw the photo.'

'Why was Lucas using needles?' I asked. 'What was he injecting: coke, meth, Ecstasy?'

'Nope, heroin,' Katie said. 'Nearly ten years before white people started using it. At the time Lucas died, heroin was thought to be a drug for poor people, mostly black and brown ones. It wasn't until the opioid crisis of the late 1990s that suburbanites switched to heroin. It was stronger, cheaper, and easier to score than prescription opioids. Nice white people using heroin was called a "crisis." Before, when people of color used heroin, it was a "war on drugs."

'Lucas's death was a double shame for his family. He not only OD'ed and failed to carry on the family work – and its name – but he died using a so-called ghetto drug. No wonder his family didn't want any photo with his obituary. They did their best to hush up his death.'

'But why did he turn into a junkie, Katie?' I felt ridiculous asking that question as I poured us our third glass of wine, but I asked anyway.

'I think he had a fatal case of second son syndrome,' Katie said.

'What's that?'

'How's your British history?' she asked.

I shrugged to let her know my knowledge was so-so and swallowed more wine.

'Excuse the lecture, but it's the only way I can explain it. You've heard of George VI, Queen Elizabeth's father?'

I nodded. I had a mouth full of cashews. I'd seen the photos of the grave dark-haired man with the aristocratic features and a uniform with a chest full of medals.

Katie grabbed the last handful of cashews and said, 'George wasn't supposed to be king. He didn't want the job. He was a nice, shy fellow with a bad stammer. His popular brother Edward, the Prince of Wales, was groomed for the job. Except Edward fell for that spavined, middle-aged temptress, Wallis Simpson, and abdicated. George was stuck with the job he didn't want and wasn't trained for. He was crowned king.

'In a small way, that's what happened to Lucas Wellington. He was the second son, a charming slacker with a nice trust fund. He skated through a fourth-tier college, and after graduation, lived at home with his parents. He wasn't a bad kid. But he was useless.

'Daddy gave the young screw-up a pointless job in the family firm. Lucas rarely showed up at his office. He was busy running up an impressive bar tab at the country club.'

'Maybe he got his taste for booze from his mother,' I said.

Katie ignored my interruption and kept talking. 'Nobody much cared what Lucas did. His golden older brother was supposed to run the company. Then his brother died in the war.

'Suddenly, Lucas was under terrific pressure to take his brother's place. He had to run a multinational company and, just as important, marry well. Gossip said Lucas had a secret vice – at least a vice by Forest standards – he was gay. He didn't want to marry.

'And he sure didn't have the guts of King George, who led his country through World War II. Lucas cracked under the pressure, and started using heroin. He was dead two years later and his family quietly buried him.'

Katie's story made me shiver. It felt like the Wellington family had realized Lucas was a mistake and quickly shoved him underground. 'But you have to admit, Katie,' I said, 'that these sad stories about her sons gave Cordelia a reason to drink.'

'Not a reason,' Katie said. 'An excuse. Alcoholism is now classed as a disease. Cordelia could – and should – have gotten treatment. Instead she crawled into a bottle. Her friends could have helped, but no one would dare tell a Du Pres she was drinking too much. Her family enabled her. I heard when Cordelia was falling down drunk and couldn't attend an event, her family would say she had the flu. The wine flu.

'I don't want to sound harsh,' Katie said, 'but if Cordelia wanted to remember her sons, she could have done any number of things: Set up scholarships in their names. Start a foundation. Endow a hospital wing. Instead, she tried to wipe out their memories, one martini at a time.'

Katie reached for the wine bottle, and discovered it was empty. That seemed the perfect end to her lecture. We both laughed, and I said, 'How about dinner?'

Though I'm not much of a cook, my salad, asparagus and roast chicken dinner was tasty. We polished off another bottle and were working on the third over the chocolate torte. Katie asked, 'How's that hunky cop of yours? He sure looked good in my office today.'

Suddenly, I was on high alert. I realized I was slightly sloshed – well, more than slightly – and Katie had the ability to prize secrets out of me.

'Chris is fine,' I said. Katie was smart enough to pick up my cautious tone.

She took a sip of wine and said, 'Better than fine, would be my guess. I hear you're at his house four or five nights a week.'

'Says who?' I stuffed my mouth with chocolate torte.

'This is the Forest,' Katie said. 'Everyone knows everyone else's business. I also heard Chris has never slept over here, in your house. Why is that?'

She waited for me to swallow my torte, which bought me time to think. 'I like his bed,' I said. 'It's nice and big.'

'And not crowded with memories of your late husband, Donegan.'

Bull's eye. I had to change the subject. 'How are things going with you and Monty?' I asked. 'Any trouble in paradise?'

'Why would you think that?' Katie said, and gulped down nearly half a glass. I'd hit my target.

'Because earlier today, when I said Rose McClaren's family needed a good lawyer and suggested Monty, you usually spend at least twenty minutes singing his praises. This time, silence. Something's wrong. What is it?'

Katie took a long sip of wine. Finally, she spoke. 'He's pressuring me to get married.'

'What's wrong with that?'

'I'm not the marrying kind,' she said. 'I don't want to be the little woman, keeping the home fires burning for the great lawyer.'

'But you wouldn't be. You're not that now.'

'Exactly. Marriage changes everything,' she said. 'Why ruin a great relationship?'

'Why would marriage do that?' I asked.

Katie yawned and looked at her empty glass. I tried to pour her more, but she said, 'I'm really tired. I need to get home.'

'We've had nearly three bottles of wine. Do you want to sleep in my guest room?' I asked.

'The truck knows the way,' she said. 'Thank you for the dinner.'

'You can't drive in that condition. You're drunk – and considering who we've been talking about, you shouldn't be behind the wheel. I'm calling an Uber.'

Katie didn't fight me, but she also didn't say anything else about the touchy subject of marriage. In fact, she seemed to nod off. But as soon as the Uber was in my driveway, she jumped up, alert and ready to leave.

'Katie Kelly Stern,' I said. 'Have you been avoiding me?'

'Yes,' she said, and was out the door.

EIGHTEEN

My work cell phone rang at nine thirty the next morning, the sound splitting my head open like a dull ax. I'd been too tired – OK, too drunk – to make it upstairs to my bedroom after Katie left last night. Instead, I'd fallen asleep on my living room couch. Good thing I'd left my cell phone on the coffee table. It still had enough juice left to work – and I was on call today.

Detective Jace Budewitz sounded like a kid at Christmas. 'Angela, the judge finally granted me a subpoena and two search warrants.'

'How did you get them?' My tongue felt like an old carpet – thick, dry and dusty. I could hardly form those five words. I sat up carefully on the couch so my head wouldn't roll off my shoulders.

'Cynthia Lockridge's lawyer, Wesley Desloge, has been fighting me every step of the way. The judge denied the first subpoena. I wanted Mrs Lockridge's office records and the judge said I didn't have a good reason why those records would contain information pertaining to her husband's murder. Wes argued that Cynthia's office contained personal records and charity records, and had nothing to do with Tom's murder. But we got new information and now I can search Cynthia Lockridge's office – and search her mobile home.'

'What mobile home?' I said. 'She lives in a mansion.' Coffee. The word echoed in my hung-over brain. That organ sluggishly delivered a new thought: must have coffee.

'This new information,' Jace said, 'is based on what our informant, Duke Spider-Man Lee says. He claims that Cynthia rents a mobile home from Mrs Shirley Rawlins in the same place where Cynthia grew up. Number 221. One of the new mobile homes. He says that's where he met Cynthia to discuss her husband's murder. Spider-Man says the rental payments would be in her office records. He also said Cynthia has a burner phone either in her mobile home or her office that has information on it. I want to look for that, too. So I got a search warrant for the mobile home, too.

'Meanwhile, I also got a subpoena from her cell provider for an itemized list of her phone calls for the six months prior to her husband's death. Same for her emails.'

I stood up slowly, and grabbed the edge of the couch until the room stopped spinning.

'Do you think she's been destroying anything incriminating while you were getting the subpoena?'

'I doubt it. She's too arrogant. So is her lawyer. He thinks he can outsmart everyone.'

'Where are you now, Jace?' I asked, speaking slowly and carefully.

'On my way to Cynthia's house to execute the search warrant. But first, I'm going to ask her if she hired Spider-Man to kill her husband. This is going to be doubly fun.'

I was glad to hear him sounding gleeful. Lately, he'd been so discouraged. 'I'll join you shortly,' I said.

'Angela . . .'

'Don't waste your breath warning me, or telling me what I should be doing, Jace. I'll be there in half an hour.'

'Then I'll meet you at Cynthia's main gate. I'm about thirty minutes out.'

I ran to the kitchen, my roiling stomach shooting rebellious geysers of acid. First, I put on the coffee and popped a piece of bread in the toaster. Then I drank a tall glass of water to rehydrate. Next, I forced myself to drink a full bottle of fruit punch Gatorade. Nasty stuff, but it did replace the electrolytes and carbohydrates. It also punished me for my sins, and boozers needed to be punished before we began to recover.

By that time, the coffee maker gave its death rattle. I poured myself a mug, ate the toast dry, poured a second cup and hurried upstairs, where I showered, pulled my damp hair into a ponytail and put on my sensible black DI suit and shoes. Today, with my bilious stomach and pale skin, black made me look like a sickly undertaker. I was dressed and coffeed in ten minutes flat.

Outside, I was relieved to see Katie's truck wasn't in my

driveway. She must have found a ride over here early this morning and driven it to work. I made it to Cynthia's front gate in thirty-one minutes.

I was still patting myself on the back when Jace rolled up, with Nitpicker Byrne and two cop cars equipped with four officers. Jace pressed the button on the gate's call box and Cynthia let us in. The lawyer's shiny black Beemer was parked in front of the mansion.

We all parked right behind the lawyer's car. Today, Nitpicker's hair was a dramatic peacock blue. I gave her a thumb's up in greeting and she grinned. I pulled out my DI case, just in case I needed it. The cops unloaded boxes and evidence tape. The whole crowd marched defiantly up the marble front steps – no servants' entrance for us – and Jace rang the doorbell.

Wesley Desloge opened the door, looking like a mob lawyer in a silver gray Brioni suit. (And how could he afford so many luxuries: that mansion, a Beemer and a six-thousand-dollar suit? Where was his money coming from?) Cynthia, dressed in widow's black, was behind him, weeping noisily. She glared at us with murderous eyes.

'I'm here to ask you some questions about Spider-Man,' Jace said.

The weeping stopped. Cynthia looked at him in surprise. 'The burglar? Why would I know him?'

'You tell me,' Jace said.

Wesley stepped between them. 'My client doesn't have to answer any questions.'

'She can answer them here or I can take her to the station. In handcuffs,' Jace said.

Cynthia erupted into more tears. When she finally turned off the waterworks, she said, 'We can sit in the breakfast room and discuss this.'

We followed the widow to the cheerful chintz room, her widow's weeds rustling softly. It was the same room where Jace had conducted his interviews the day of Tom Lockridge's murder.

When everyone was seated, Jace's question was swift – and brutal.

'Did you hire Duke Spider-Man Lee to kill your husband?'

'Don't answer that!' Wesley was shouting. The lawyer rose and put one hand protectively on Cynthia's shoulder. She flinched when he touched her.

'I will answer it,' she said. 'No! I did not hire him.'

'Did you know Spider-Man?' Jace said.

'Keep quiet!' Wes said, but Cynthia ignored him.

'Yes,' she said. 'For a short time we both lived at Fairdale Manor Mobile Home Park.'

'Did you pay him ten thousand dollars to kill your husband?'

Cynthia hesitated for a long moment. What was that about? Finally she said, 'No! Of course not. I loved my husband!' Now she was crying too hard to say any more.

Wes stepped in. 'This interrogation is over, Detective. Over! I'm asking you to leave.'

'Not yet,' Jace said. 'I'm not finished. I'm here to execute a search warrant.'

Cynthia's tears magically dried up. In a steady voice, she said. 'I want to see it.'

'That's your right,' Jace said, and handed it to her.

'You want to search my office and take my computer?' she said, her voice rising to a shriek. 'You can't. I'm co-chair of the Forest Christmas Ball.'

'Lady, I don't care if you're the Sugar Plum Fairy,' Jace said. 'I have the legal right to search your office.'

Cynthia turned to her lawyer. 'Wes, can this person' – she made a sour face – 'do this? Can't you stop him?'

'No,' Wes said. 'I can't stop Detective Jace Budewitz.' He emphasized Jace's name, as if that would earn him extra points. 'Not while the warrant is being executed.' He reached over and patted Cynthia's hand. 'Why don't you have a nice cup of tea and wait this out?'

'I don't want to.' Cynthia stamped her foot like a spoiled child. 'Why am I paying you?'

'Good question, Mrs Lockridge,' Jace said. 'There's no reason to have your lawyer here. He can't walk around in your office while we box things up. He can't tell us what we can or cannot take. He can't be involved in the search in any way.

'There is one thing he can do, though.' Jace had a wicked gleam in his eye.

'What?' Cynthia asked, sniffling.

'He can run up a nice fat fee hanging around here. That's fine with me, if you and Wes want to drink tea together for seven hundred bucks an hour. Your tea party might cost you' – he checked his watch – 'about twenty-eight hundred dollars. But it's your money. Don't worry, though, Mrs Lockridge. Once the warrant is executed, I'll have ten days to give you an inventory of the property we've seized. Oh, and you can keep that copy of the search warrant for your scrapbook.'

Cynthia looked outraged. Wes whispered in her ear, but I didn't think it was sweet nothings. She glared at him, shook her head, and then stomped off toward the living room.

'Detective,' Wes said, 'could I have Mrs Timmons, the housekeeper, make you and your personnel hot coffee while you conduct the search?' Wes was trying to win points by appearing cooperative – and volunteering someone else to do the work.

'No, thanks.' Jace started for the staircase.

'How is Mrs Timmons?' I asked. 'Did she recover from her asthma attack?'

'Yes,' Wes said. 'Now if you'll excuse me, Miss—'

'It's Ms. I'm Death Investigator Angela Richman.'

'Fine. Ms Richman. I have to be with my client. You've upset her terribly.' Wes turned his back on me and marched after Cynthia. I hauled my DI case back up those endless marble stairs, cursing myself for bringing it inside in the first place.

Cynthia's office was a hive of activity. Uniforms were rooting through file cabinets, packing neatly labeled file folders into boxes and sealing them with evidence tape. A tech was removing the hard drive from Cynthia's computer.

Nitpicker was examining the office couch. 'There's definitely body fluids on the couch,' she said. 'My guess is they're semen. Do you want me to take samples so we can show that Mrs Lockridge was having sex with her lawyer?'

One of the uniforms sniggered and said, 'The lawyer could always claim he was spanking the old monkey.'

'That's enough, Rick,' Jace said, and frowned at the culprit. Jokes like that – and worse – were part of many crime scenes, but Jace didn't permit them. A lot of the uniforms thought he was a tight-ass. Jace didn't care. He said he'd once had a grieving husband overhear the cops investigating a murder scene with a nearly naked young woman, the man's wife of three months. The cops were making rude jokes about the dead wife's breast implants. The tech taping the scene stupidly had the sound on, and caught the whole ugly exchange. The man's lawyer subpoenaed the tape and the husband sued for mental anguish. The department settled out of court, rather than have a jury hear the officers saying things like, 'Look at those knockers. What a waste. Man, I'd tap that. If she was alive.' The conversation devolved quickly into necrophilia jokes.

Jace went back to searching Cynthia's desk. 'Well, well. Angela, look at this.' He waited while the tech photographed the contents of the top desk drawer.

First, he pointed to a cheap black flip phone. Nitpicker dusted it for prints and reported, 'Only one set. They belong to Mrs Lockridge.'

Jace turned on the phone. It contained only one number, and about twenty calls. Jace dialed the number and got the recording, the cracked voice of an older woman: 'You've reached the manager of Fairdale Manor Mobile Home Park. Please leave a message.'

'That sounds like Mrs Rawlins,' I said.

'Wait till you see this,' Jace said. He pulled out a rubber-banded stack of handwritten receipts, the kind sold in books at office supply stores.

He held them up in a gloved hand. I read them.

'Cynthia is paying fifteen hundred dollars a month to rent a mobile home from Mrs Rawlins?' I said. 'Why would she need one, with all this room?'

'Beats me,' he said. 'But when we finish here, I want to have a little talk with the sweet old manager of that mobile home park. Could be that Saint Cindy wasn't quite so perfect after all.'

Nearly four hours later, the cops had carried out enough boxes to fill a police van. My work cell phone had stayed blissfully silent. The Forest's citizens were staying alive – good news for all of us.

By the time Jace was finished with Cynthia's office, he'd worked himself into a first-class rage. He was so angry I could almost see steam coming out of his ears. He was furious at Cynthia and Mrs Rawlins. He wanted to see the manager of the mobile home park next.

'Are you going to talk to Cynthia again?' I asked him.

'Nope, I'm going to see what I can get out of Mrs Rawlins first.' By his tight, angry face, I guessed Jace wanted to scare the old woman into saying something useful.

'Then I'll come back here,' he said. 'When I get information from both of them, I'll compare notes and see if I can catch one – or both – lying.'

He marched into the kitchen and told Mrs Lockridge, 'I'll have your inventory list within ten days, like I said. I have to file it with the court.' Cynthia glared at him, but didn't say anything. I didn't see Wes the lawyer anywhere, and his Beemer wasn't parked in the circle.

Jace was so angry, he didn't bother stopping for lunch. On the way to the mobile home park, I ate a stale energy bar I dug out of the glove box. My mouth was dryer than the Sahara by the time we got to Fairdale Manor.

Mrs Rawlins was outside, digging in her painted tire flower bed by the front stairs. She wore a pink flowered housecoat and that luxuriant gray wig. The frail old woman looked up when she saw Jace and me get out of our cars.

'Detective,' she said, smiling at him. 'I never thanked you for talking to that horrible Cody Ellis, the drug dealer who wasn't paying his rent. He moved out in the middle of the night. He didn't pay his back rent, but he left behind a nice big TV, a sixty-inch. I'm keeping it until he pays me. I'm glad to see him gone. I've been cleaning out his home and I'll be able to rent it next week.'

Jace gave her a hard-eyed stare until the smile faded from the manager's face.

'Detective? Is something wrong?' Her voice quavered.

Jace pulled out the evidence bag with the receipts for number 221. 'You're damn right something's wrong. You didn't tell me that Mrs Lockridge was renting a mobile home here.'

'Oh. Oh, yes, she is, Detective.' She fluttered like a wounded bird. 'I didn't realize it was important.'

'In a murder investigation, everything is important,' he said. I stood there like a lump. I couldn't talk. My mouth felt like it was filled with sand.

'Oh. Oh, dear. I meant no harm. Would you like to come in and talk about it?'

'You're damn right,' Jace said, and we followed the small, terrified woman up the stairs and into her home.

NINETEEN

nside her home, old Mrs Rawlins was shaking so badly she had to hold on to the kitchen counter. Finally, she asked, 'Can I get you water or coffee?' Her voice was thin and high.

'Water,' I said, as if I'd just walked across Death Valley. Jace glared at me, but I didn't care.

Mrs Rawlins held up a can of potted meat. 'I was just about to make myself a sandwich,' she said. 'Would you like one?'

'No,' Jace said.

'Yes,' I said. This time, his glare could have fried my hair, but I needed food. Besides, once she started fussing with my sandwich, Mrs Rawlins calmed considerably. 'I fix it with mayonnaise and pickle relish,' she said.

'That's how my mother made it,' I said.

'I only have white bread. I'm going to toast it,' she said. 'OK?'

'That's fine.' Jace gave a little impatient growl.

'Would you like the crusts cut off, Ms Richman?' she asked.

I was surprised she'd remembered my name. Shirley Rawlins was sharp. Her 'oh, I forgot' excuse wouldn't go far with Jace. He was getting more irritated by the second.

'No, thanks,' I said.

While Shirley fixed my ice water and sandwich, I avoided looking at Jace and studied her china figurine collection on a what-not in the living room. One shelf was devoted to Dresden shepherdesses, another to angels, and a third to statues of a white, blond Jesus. These told me Shirley was probably religious, a little sentimental and conventional, none of which were bad.

'Here you are, dear.' Shirley had cut my sandwich in half and put it on a dainty blue plate. She gave me a folded paper napkin and a coaster for my water. I drank nearly the whole glass and tried not to wolf down my sandwich. Jace and I were seated on the green couch.

Mrs Rawlins perched on the edge of the matching green chair, with her plate on her lap. She nibbled at her sandwich while Jace said, 'Now, Mrs Rawlins, why didn't you mention that Cynthia Lockridge still rents a mobile home here?'

'I didn't think it was important,' she said.

'Well, it is!' His forceful, furious voice frightened Mrs Rawlins. She dropped her sandwich in her lap.

Now Jace switched from bad cop to good cop. His voice was soft and soothing as honey on a sore throat. 'I didn't mean to scare you, Mrs Rawlins, but this is serious. Cynthia is a person of interest in her husband's murder investigation.'

'Murder!' Mrs Rawlins voice rose to almost a shriek. 'Cindy would never kill anyone. Never! She's a good girl!'

'Then it's important you tell me the truth so we can clear her name,' Jace said.

Mrs Rawlins put her sandwich back on her plate and set it on the coffee table. Then she sat up straight, blinking like an alert robin. 'I want to help. Mr Lockridge was a nice man. He didn't deserve what happened to him. But let me repeat – Cindy would never kill him. Or anyone else.'

'Fine,' Jace said. 'Let's take it from the beginning. When did Mrs Lockridge rent that mobile home from you?'

'About a year after her marriage,' she said. 'We stayed in touch. She would drop by once in a while to see me. She checked on me after the tornado hit this park. When one of the new double-wides I got with the insurance money was available, she wanted it.' She dipped her napkin in her water glass and dabbed at the spot of potted meat on her housedress.

'Fifteen hundred dollars is rather stiff rent for a friend,' Jace said. 'Especially one who gave you her old mobile home.'

'Cindy insisted on paying the market rate,' Mrs Rawlins said. 'She said she had plenty of money. Normally, a deluxe mobile home like that would rent for eighteen hundred. I gave her a little bit of a break, but not enough that Cindy would notice. I didn't want to take advantage of her.'

'How often does she visit her mobile home?'

'No set pattern,' Mrs Rawlins said. 'Sometimes once a
month, other times once or twice a week.'

'When was the last time you saw her?'

'The day her husband died.'

'Thomas Lockridge was murdered, Mrs Rawlins.'

'I'm aware of that, Detective. She invited me over for coffee
and cupcakes. The good ones, from the Forest Bakery. We
talked about what everyone did then – those Ghost Burglars.
Cindy said she was scared in her home – the mansion, not
here. She said it was so big no one could hear her if she was
attacked. That's why she kept Prince with her all the time, for
protection, even though the dog . . .' She paused and looked
embarrassed. 'The dog . . .' Her voice trailed off.

'The dog what?' Jace asked.

Mrs Rawlins gathered her courage and spoke quickly.
'Cindy says Prince passes gas something terrible. She changed
his food and everything, but she has to use a lot of air
freshener.'

I bit back a smile. Jace was too angry to think a farting dog
was funny.

'What else did she talk about?' Jace asked.

'That Christmas ball she's co-chairing. It's a great honor
but a lot of work. She talked about the menu with me and
how the price of steak was too high for the budget. That was
darn near driving her crazy.'

That dovetailed with what Cynthia had told Jace.

'She also said she's having trouble handling all the money,'
Mrs Rawlins said.

Jace was suddenly alert. 'All what money?' he said.

'I didn't understand this before Cindy told me,' she said.
'There are thousands of dollars in those fancy society balls. The
Christmas ball brings in more than a million dollars for
the hospital each year.'

I knew the Christmas ball brought in major money, but I
had no idea they were dealing with that amount. 'It's definitely not like putting five dollars in the church collection
plate,' I said.

'No, indeed,' Mrs Rawlins said. 'Cindy told me her
committee has to deal with all levels of sponsorships. If a

business gives ten thousand dollars, they get ten tickets to the ball, their name in the program, and special gifts. The levels go down from there, ending in just buying a plain old ticket for two-hundred-fifty dollars.

'Well, for that kind of money, you can understand why Cindy wanted to give them steak. People expect it. But she was also under pressure to make at least one-point-four million dollars – the amount the ball made last year.

'She told me she's not good with figures, and that's why she was glad to have that Wes lawyer handle the money for her. Mr Lockridge knew how worried Cindy was about this ball, and that's why he hired that Wes Desloge and paid him out of his own pocket to help her.'

I couldn't look at Jace. Tom Lockridge's good deed made him a cuckold.

'Are you sure Mrs Lockridge never brought that lawyer here, to her mobile home?' Jace asked.

'Never.' Mrs Rawlins's denial was firm and final. 'She came here to get away from that. She came here to talk to me about her worries, and that's what she did.'

'What time did she leave that day?' Jace asked. 'The night Tom Lockridge was murdered?'

'About three o'clock in the afternoon. She usually stays an hour or so longer, but she said she wanted to do her committee work at home and it was going to take all night.'

'What does Mrs Lockridge usually do when she's here?'

'Nothing much. It's her little getaway. She's under a great deal of pressure in her new life, Detective, and she has to meet a lot of muckety-mucks who are important to her husband's business – senators and representatives from Washington DC, Missouri politicians, the governor and various mayors. Also, she deals with society ladies, who look down on her because she grew up here. Cindy knows they laugh at her behind her back.'

I noticed Mrs Rawlins had reverted to calling her Cindy instead of Cynthia, the name for her new identity.

'Cindy has to make sure she dresses right and talks right and uses the right fork or she will embarrass herself,' Mrs Rawlins said. 'So she comes here some afternoons and reads books and drinks coffee. Often she calls me and we have coffee and cake together. She doesn't have to worry what she says or does around me, Detective. I won't judge her.'

I felt sorry for Cynthia, the mobile home park girl who'd risen to great heights. Her new life must be frightening, and very lonely.

I didn't think Jace was buying this explanation, or that he had any sympathy for Cynthia. He began machine-gunning more questions:

'Does Mrs Lockridge ever spend the night here?'

'No. She always goes home just before dinner.'

'Does she ever have her lawyer, Wesley Desloge, meet her in her mobile home?'

'No. I already told you that.'

'What about other men?'

'No!' Mrs Rawlins was almost shouting now. 'Just what are you implying? I don't run that kind of establishment. I'm a respectable married woman. And so is Cindy.'

'But you did run that kind of establishment when Mrs Lockridge's mother was here. Didn't you say the lady made her living on her back?'

'Yes. Not in those words, but yes, her mother was a prostitute. I also told you my husband and I decided that her mother could stay, despite her profession, so that Cindy would have a home and not have to go into the foster system. And it worked, Detective. Our plan worked. Cindy finished school, got a job and made a good marriage.'

Mrs Rawlins was defiant now, determined to defend her friend and protégé.

She turned to Jace and looked him in the eye. 'Why don't you want to believe that Cindy is a good, decent person, Detective?' Her voice was soft but firm.

I was glad Mrs Rawlins asked that question. I'd wanted to, but couldn't. Jace looked uncomfortable. Finally, he answered, 'I'm trying to find out the truth, Mrs Rawlins. And you haven't been entirely forthcoming. I had to find out about this mobile home rental from a confidential informant.'

'Yes, but—'

'No excuses, Mrs Rawlins.' Jace held up his hand to stop
her. 'I have here a search warrant for Mrs Lockridge's mobile
home.' He handed her the warrant.

Mrs Rawlins looks stunned. 'Does Cindy know about this?'
she asked. 'Should I call her?'

'You can, but she knows. A police tech and a uniformed
officer are here to help with the search.' I heard the sound of
tires on the gravel drive. I peeked outside. Nitpicker and one
uniform, Mike, had arrived. Jace asked Mrs Rawlins if Nitpicker
could take her prints 'for the process of elimination.'

After that, Mrs Rawlins led us to number 221, a long beige
mobile home with black shutters on the windows and white-
painted wooden stairs up to the front door. Mrs Rawlins
unlocked the door. We all put on booties, even Mrs Rawlins,
and then followed her inside.

'This is a big home, bigger than mine,' Mrs Rawlins said.
'Sixteen hundred square feet, two bedrooms, and two
bathrooms.'

The mobile home was spotless and sterile, almost like a
showroom. The white front door opened on to a living room
painted a pale, fashionable light gray, with a nubby oatmeal
carpet and a soft, inviting white sofa. There was a dark coffee
table and two matching white chairs. Bright orange pillows
added what decorators call 'pops of color.' An orange-and-gray
abstract brightened the main living room wall.

Most of the personal touches were books: a bookshelf under
the painting was stuffed with hardcovers. I checked out some
titles: three Miss Manners's etiquette books, Agatha Christie's
Death on the Nile, Sue Grafton's mysteries, and Charlaine
Harris's Southern Vampire series. More hardcovers were piled
on the coffee table. A worn brown teddy bear sat on the bookshelf. There were no photos.

What a contrast to Cynthia's gaudy gilt and marble mansion.
'Her mobile home seems so . . . uh' – I skidded to a stop
before I blurted 'tasteful' and managed a quick save – 'different
from her other house. Did she decorate it herself?'

'Oh, no,' Mrs Rawlins said. 'It came furnished this way.
That old teddy bear is hers, about the only thing she brought
from her old life. And like I told you, she loves books. She

says it's nice to read hardcovers and not have to return them to the library.'

'This place is very clean,' Jace said, running a gloved finger along the coffee table. 'Hardly any dust.'

'It's dustier than usual,' Mrs Rawlins said. 'I usually clean Cindy's home every two weeks, but I wasn't feeling so well last time.'

A bad reaction after a chemo treatment? I wondered, but said nothing. 'So you haven't cleaned this mobile home since when?' Jace asked.

'Since a week before the trouble started.' Mrs Rawlins looked at him defiantly.

'You mean, a week before Mr Lockridge was murdered,' Jace said.

'If you want to put it that way.' I admired the tiny woman's spine, as she stood up to a glaring Jace. I also wondered why he had a burr under his saddle about the subject.

Cynthia's mobile home kitchen was newer and better than mine. She had expensive white cabinets and an orange-and-gray backsplash. 'All the latest appliances,' said Mrs Rawlins, 'including a dishwasher. And that door there leads to a laundry room with a washer and dryer.'

On the kitchen counter was a Keurig coffee maker and a rack with assorted coffee pods. Jace opened up the fridge. Empty, except for half a loaf of wheat bread, cheddar cheese, a stick of butter and bottled water. In the freezer were half a dozen cupcakes from the Forest Bakery. The kitchen cabinets had a set of cookware, white dishes and flatware and a few staples, including sugar and peanut butter. All perfectly ordinary.

'We can take it from here, Mrs Rawlins,' Jace said. 'Why don't you rest up in your home?' It wasn't a suggestion, it was a command. Mrs Rawlins left us.

Jace instructed Ken, the older uniform, to go through the books, looking for papers.

'Nitpicker, fingerprint everything. I want proof that Mrs Lockridge had someone else in this place besides Mrs Rawlins.'

'Angela, put on your gloves. You can help me search the bedrooms.'

Once again, the master bedroom looked like a high-end hotel room, except this time the colors were off-white and pale blue. There was a forty-inch TV on the bureau across from the bed.

'Nothing in the nightstand drawers but a sleep mask,' I said. 'No condoms or anything that says she had sex here.' I pulled back the sheets and examined them carefully. They were clean. 'No one has slept in this bed. I think her sheets are ironed.'

The dresser drawers had a few faded T-shirts, old jeans, socks and underwear. The closet had one business suit, a cocktail dress and a black evening gown, and four pairs of shoes. 'Jace, do you think she kept these here in case she had to dress for a special event?'

Jace shrugged. I photographed everything, then got up the courage to ask, 'Why were you so rough on Mrs Rawlins? That poor lady has cancer.'

'That poor lady withheld important information, Angela. Let me give you a tip that may save your life. Never under-estimate an old person – especially cute little old ladies. Nine times out of ten, they're playing you when they pull that "I'm old and harmless" act. I found that out the hard way when an eighty-year-old woman pulled a weapon out of her knitting basket and nearly blew my head off. And I know a thirtysomething nurse who was raped by a ninety-year-old man.'

He must have seen my astonished face because he said, 'That's right. Raped. In a nursing home. So don't you be ageist, no matter how sweet or helpless old people seem. Remember this: The older they get, the more dangerous they are. And the less they have to lose. Life in prison? When you're ninety? Who cares?'

He was right, and I knew it. Jace and I worked in silence after that. The master bath had make-up, hair spray and brushes, and common over-the-counter drugs like aspirin and cough syrup. The shower was clean and fluffy blue towels hung on the rack.

The second bedroom and bath looked like no one had ever set foot in them. We found no computer, desk, papers or receipts. Ken the uniform found four bookmarks and a coupon for a local restaurant.

By now, the rooms looked like they were covered with fine dark snow – fingerprint powder was everywhere. Nitpicker took prints off everything, including the TV remote. 'If there was a man in here, his prints will be on that remote,' she said. 'No man can let a woman handle one alone.'

It was six o'clock when we finally left, and though all the prints hadn't been run yet, we knew this search was a failure. So did Mrs Rawlins. She met us when we came out. 'Well?' she said. 'You didn't find anything, did you? And you won't. Mark my words, Detective. Cindy is clean as a whistle.'

TWENTY

I n the soft light of dusk, Fairdale Manor looked at its best. The rust spots and dings in the aging mobile homes were hidden in the lengthening shadows. A sweet breeze rustled the old shade trees and made the flowers dance.

Jace walked me to my car, parked under a tree. As we crunched across the white gravel, I noticed that Jace's hands were in his pockets, and his shoulders were slumped. The day must have really gotten to him – he looked so down.

'Thanks for your help, Angela,' he said.

'No problem. I want to catch the killer, too.'

'Which killer?' he asked.

'Both of them. Tom Lockridge didn't deserve to die, but at least he had a full life. Danny Morton's senseless murder is what really gets me. That young man didn't have a chance to live.'

'His killer, Rolly Roget,' Jace said his name like it left a bad taste, 'is out on bail, still insisting he's innocent.'

'He was actually charged? I thought his lawyer would get it dismissed.'

'Yep. Involuntary manslaughter. A felony. Rolly's looking at three to ten years in the state pen.'

I raised an eyebrow in surprise. 'This isn't how things work in the Forest. Rolly's indiscretion should have been swept under the rug.'

'That new county prosecutor is slick. He tipped off the press to Rolly's bail hearing. The lawyers stupidly used Rolly's argument that Danny's death was "collateral damage in the war on crime." That didn't go over well with the judge. Not in front of muckraking reporters from St. Louis. Rolly's bail was set at fifty million dollars.'

I whistled. 'That's a serious chunk of change, even for a rich guy.'

'Yep. Rolly is wearing an ankle bracelet and confined to

his house. The judge didn't buy the argument that golf at the country club is necessary exercise.'

'Good,' I said. 'So what's next? How can I help?'

'The next work is on me,' Jace said. 'I'm going over Cynthia Lockridge's records with a fine-tooth comb. Until we talked to Mrs Rawlins, I didn't realize that much money was involved in that Christmas charity ball. She has to make more than a million dollars. How much more money does Cynthia need to take in to reach that goal?'

'Beats me,' I said. 'Forgive me, Saint Gloria Steinem, but I thought charity balls were run by dimwits in designer dresses.'

'That may be, but those women are dealing with seven figures,' Jace said. 'That much money is bound to attract trouble. And Wesley Desloge is betraying the man who hired him by screwing his wife, so I wouldn't put it past the little weasel to be skimming from a charity.'

'How are your money skills?' I asked. 'Can you spot fraud in Cynthia's records?'

Jace shrugged. 'I took a night school course in accounting. I may be able to see that something is off.'

He stopped walking and looked me in the eye. That's when I saw how sad and tired he was. 'Time is running out for me, Angela. Chief Butkus says I have one week to solve this murder. After that, well, Greiman takes over this case, and I'm transferred to midnight patrol.'

I felt sick. 'Oh, no, Jace. What a waste. You'll be doing convenience-store robberies, domestics, and burglaries.'

'Don't forget late-night traffic stops,' he said. 'A good way to get my head blown off.'

I shuddered, even in the warm evening breeze. 'That's terrible.'

It was. For Jace. Me, too. I was selfishly calculating what this change would mean for me. I'd be stuck with Detective Ray Greiman. I hated his sloppy work and snide attitude. Pretty soon I'd be arrested for murder – Greiman's.

'Can the department demote you like that?' I asked.

'According to our officers' bill of rights, technically, it's not a demotion,' Jace said. 'The chief calls it a "lateral transfer." Since there's no loss of pay, I'm not entitled to a full-blown hearing.'

There was no point in saying it was unfair. We both knew that.

'The CFPD is clever, Angela. Chief Butkus has a lot of noble reasons for this move. He told me that working patrol is the "backbone of the department." Also, patrol lets me "share my valuable experience and train other officers." Oh, and last but not least, I'm "helping new recruits to learn and move up."'

'So even though being a detective isn't a promotion,' I said, 'you're being knocked back to patrol to help promote other officers?'

'You got it,' he said. His dusty shoe traced a line in the gravel.

'So how will going through Cynthia's charity records help solve Tom Lockridge's murder? If you do find something, are you going to blackmail Wes into talking?'

'Blackmail?' Jace grinned at me. 'Don't you mean "encourage"?' Then he laughed – an angry, bitter laugh.

'Besides, Angela, who says Wes is in this alone? Could be Cynthia and Wes are both helping themselves to all that moolah.'

'Why would Cynthia do that?'

Jace snapped his fingers at me, as if he was waking me up. 'Angela! Get real! You're so sure Cynthia is innocent, you're overlooking what's right in front of you. Spider-Man says she paid him to kill her husband.'

'He could be lying,' I said.

'He could. But he was right that she was renting a mobile home at Fairdale Manor.'

'Where you found nothing to tie Cynthia to the murder,' I said.

'This whole case is about nothing,' Jace said. 'If her husband divorced her for adultery, she'd get nothing – zero. Fortunately, he just happened to die first. What if she was preparing for the day when Tom found out about her escapades?

'A little polite skimming from a million dollars could give her a nice nest egg. And if her husband was catching on to her infidelity, Cynthia would have a good reason to kill him, wouldn't she?'

I chirped open my car. 'Yeah, you're right.' I still didn't believe Cynthia would kill her husband. 'Didn't she say she wasn't good with numbers?'

'She said that, Angela, but is it true? The new office manager – Debbie Carlone, the one who has Cynthia's former job – said she has to have a good head for numbers. So wouldn't Cynthia need math skills, too? Playing dumb is a good cover. Lots of smart women use it.'

I couldn't argue with that.

'Time to sharpen my red pencil,' Jace said. 'I have to catch a killer.'

I waved goodbye and was almost out of Fairdale when my cell phone rang. It was Chris. I put my car in park and answered. I felt better hearing my lover's voice.

'Angela,' he said. 'Can I make dinner for you tonight? Or do you have other plans?'

'Yes. I'm planning to go home and make scrambled eggs. I also have half a loaf of slightly stale bread. I hear that makes the best toast.' I hoped Chris heard the smile in my voice. I was happy he'd called.

'All I have is pork loin chops in apple brandy sauce, mashed sweet potatoes, and asparagus.'

'Well—' I said.

'What if I throw in a chocolate strawberry cake for dessert?'

'Sounds tempting. What can I bring? Wine?'

'I have a nice Malbec,' he said. 'Three bottles. And home-made yeast rolls.'

'So what should I bring?' I asked again.

'Yourself,' he said. 'And that half-loaf of stale bread. We can have French toast in the morning. Are you on call tomorrow?'

'Not until midnight – of the next day. I have tomorrow free.'

'The weather is supposed to be good. We could spend the day in old St. Charles – if that isn't too touristy.'

'I'd love to,' I said. 'Let me go home and change. What time do you want me?'

'Any time,' he said. 'Day or night.'

I giggled like a schoolgirl. 'What time should I show up at your place tonight?'

'Eight o'clock,' he said.

At home, I showered and changed, packed a small bag, and was at Chris's door with my stale bread and a bouquet of flowers from my garden. Chris welcomed me with a kiss. I saw our dinner table was on his balcony, with candlelight and a single red rose in a vase.

'Want some wine? It's decanted and ready to drink.' Chris handed me a glass of the deep red wine.

I sipped it. 'Mm. This is delicious. It has a chocolaty taste.'

'With top notes of coffee, leather, and hints of blackberry.' He grinned at me. 'I read that in the online reviews. This is an Argentine Malbec.'

I dragged out my one Malbec fact. 'Argentina produces the best Malbec in the world. Better than France's.'

He kissed me again and we alternated kisses and sips until he said, 'Would you like to go upstairs?'

'Yes. But will the delay ruin your dinner?' I asked between kisses.

'No. But I can always make scrambled eggs and toast,' he said.

We ran upstairs, shedding our clothes along the way, and didn't come back until we were groggy with love, an hour later. I leaned against the kitchen wall in Chris's robe, drinking wine while I watched him plate our dinner.

I don't remember what we talked about that night, but I felt happy and content during dinner. We were still hungry for each other, and took the strawberry chocolate cake upstairs to bed and spent hours making love.

The next day was as beautiful as promised. Chris made French toast, and we sat on his balcony and admired the morning, and his neighbors' gardens. The air was bright with sunshine and fragrant with May flowers – sweet honeysuckle, purple irises, waxy pink magnolia flowers and carpets of bluebells.

After breakfast, we drove to St. Charles, an old town – well, old by US standards – on the Missouri River. The streets, sidewalks, and most of the buildings were red brick in the Main Street historical district. We blended in with the other tourists – families with small children, older people, and young students of history.

Soon our heads were stuffed with historic dates: The town was founded by fur trader Louis Blanchette in 1769, before the United States was born. The Boone's Lick Trail was blazed by old Daniel himself.

We admired both the pretty white George Sibley house – and the Sibleys's courage. They saved radical publisher Elijah P. Lovejoy when a mob tried to lynch him. Lovejoy's radical idea? He wanted to end slavery.

I was intrigued by the business acumen of J.J. Dozier, owner of the once popular Farmers Tavern. By 1821, St. Charles was the temporary capitol of the new state of Missouri, and Dozier invited the legislators to board there with this ad: 'Lodging, 2 bits a night. I specialize in good food. Corn Bread and Common fixings 2 bits a meal. White bread with Chicken Fixings 3 bits.'

When we tired of soaking up the history, we explored the small shops selling tea, spices, coffee, books, art and antiques. Lots of antiques. Chris bought me an exquisite antique cameo, carved from a delicate shell. I got him a vintage shaving mug with a big brown dog on it. After an hour or so, I wanted to get away from the antique shops. No matter how pretty the antiques were, I began to feel the weight of the former owners' lives.

Chris seemed to sense my melancholy mood. I cheered up when we tried the beer at the microbrewery. Then we ate a long, leisurely lunch on the brick patio of a small, charming restaurant. After lunch, we strolled along the banks of the Missouri River in Frontier Park. That's when we had our only serious conversation of the day.

'You know the chief is trying to demote Jace Budewitz,' Chris said.

We passed a couple walking a frisky yellow Labrador pup, and I stopped to pet the little dog. After the pup's ear had been scratched, and the couple moved on, I said, 'Jace told me. He's worried.'

'He should be,' Chris said. 'The local bigwigs are upset that he arrested good old Rolly Roget, who gunned down an innocent dog walker, and Greiman is doing his best to pour gasoline on the fire.'

We stared at the wide, brown expanse of the river. A cottonwood tree, roots and all, floated downstream. Even its massive size was no protection against the powerful forces.

I told Chris about Jace's plans to burrow into Cynthia Lockridge's charity records, and added, 'I really don't want to have to work more cases with Greiman. What can I do to help Jace?'

'Can you think of anyone who could give you more information?'

'Maybe Debbie,' I said. 'Debbie Carlone. The office manager. I promised to have lunch with her. Yes, that's what I'll do. I'll call Debbie.'

A family passed us: Mom, Dad and two little kids, all licking ice cream cones.

'Want some ice cream?' Chris asked.

I did. We got chocolate-chip cones, sat on a bench and people-watched, the sun warming our faces. I yawned sleepily.

'Ready to go home?' he asked.

I was. We both were. We made two more stops. We bought a bag of barbecue sandwiches for dinner, and freshly made cinnamon buns.

On the drive home, I fell asleep on Chris's shoulder, and he kissed me awake when we got to his place. We carried our food upstairs to his bed, along with the rest of the wine. About eleven o'clock, I plugged in my office cell phone, and kissed Chris goodnight.

'Thank you,' I said, 'This has been a perfect day. I'm on call after midnight, but I hope tomorrow will be just as good.'

My hopes were dashed at 2:47 that morning, when my ringing office cell phone dragged me out of a sound sleep. It was Jace.

'Angela.' I could hear the stress in the detective's voice.

'What's wrong, Jace?'

'It's Mrs Rawlins. She's dead.'

I felt like someone had kicked me in the gut. No, not Mrs Rawlins – that small, tough, smart woman couldn't be dead.

'What was it?' I asked. 'A heart attack? A stroke?'

'No, Angela. She was murdered.'

TWENTY-ONE

Twenty minutes after Jace called, I was showered, dressed and ready to leave Chris's home. He kissed me goodbye – a long, lingering kiss that made me wish I could stay – and handed me an insulated mug of hot coffee and a microwaved cinnamon bun. The warm, sticky treat was wrapped in waxed paper and a napkin. Chris thought of everything.

The early May morning smelled fresh and clean, the start of a new day. A day that Mrs Shirley Rawlins would not be enjoying. I stood outside my car for a moment, drinking that wake-up cup of coffee, before I started my car.

All the way to the Fairdale, I thought of Mrs Rawlins and wondered who had murdered the harmless older woman. What did she know? Was she killed to stop her from telling Jace something? Was she harboring an illegal activity in one of those mobile homes: prostitution? Illegal drugs? It couldn't have been someone cooking meth. We would have noticed its distinctive odor.

Or was Mrs Rawlins blackmailing her protégé, Cynthia Lockridge? I didn't think so, but there was Cynthia's supposed lover, Wesley. Did Mrs Rawlins know something damning about the lawyer? I could see Wes killing the poor woman – he was slick and ambitious and she was small and helpless.

I finished the last of my cinnamon bun at a long red light, and wiped my fingers on the napkin. I thought again of our touristy date in St. Charles. Chris was an easy man to be with. So easy, I might be falling in love with him, and I was afraid. I still loved Donegan, and I wasn't ready to let go of my late husband. Donegan didn't follow along on my dates with Chris, but he was still in the background. Many of Chris's gestures and sweet ways reminded me of my lost husband – the single red rose, the courtesy, the pampering, the way we laughed at nothing – and those joys also gave me a pang of sorrow. What would I do if Chris said he loved me? Or asked me to move in with him?

What about marriage? whispered a small, fearful voice, but that was unthinkable. I quickly shut it up.

I was grateful when I saw the faded sign for Fairdale Manor in the flashing emergency lights. Now I no longer had to debate those tricky questions about Chris. I could do my job.

Jace had cordoned off a wide perimeter around Mrs Rawlins's home. There were too many official vehicles for me to park in the gravel drive, so I left my car by the park's sign, dragged out my DI case and trundled it up the gravel drive. I checked in with Mike, the uniform in charge of the scene log, and he gave me the case number.

As I approached Mrs Rawlins's home, the glare of the portable lights revealed a sizeable crowd gathered outside the yellow crime scene tape. I guessed they were residents of Fairdale. Most were in various states of undress – gaping bathrobes, pajama bottoms, boxer shorts, or T-shirts that stopped too soon. Flip-flops, pink curlers, and assorted beards completed these ensembles. Jace had erected a screen to hide Mrs Rawlins's body, so the curious crowd couldn't see her.

I stepped inside the screened area, and greeted Jace. He looked washed-out and exhausted in the harsh lights. He needed a shave. 'Mrs Rawlins is there, at the bottom of her stairs,' he said.

Shirley Rawlins looked pitifully small and scrawny, crumpled at the foot of her front stairs. Her pink nightgown and robe had ridden up, revealing bare, varicose-veined legs. One of her pink plush bedroom slippers had come off. Saddest of all, her luxuriant wig sat in the flower bed like a small, mischievous pet, leaving her chemo-bald head exposed.

Five wooden stairs led down from a tiny porch to a small concrete pad. That's where Mrs Rawlins had landed.

I knew from sad experience that falls were the number one cause of accidental death for people over seventy-five, and most of these deaths happened at home. 'How do you know Mrs Rawlins's death was murder and not an accident?' I asked.

'Look at this.' Jace pointed to the top step. It was broken – snapped in two. On closer inspection, I saw the step wasn't broken – it had been sawn through, except for a patch the size of a postage stamp. Even a footstep by someone as light as Mrs Rawlins would have broken that stair.

The untreated wood was dry, rough, and cracked. 'Can you get a fingerprint off that wood?' I asked.

'No way,' Jace said. 'But the wood was full of splinters, and one bit back. The killer left a small drop of blood on a splinter, and Nitpicker says there's probably enough for DNA.

'Also, we got lucky. The killer used a hacksaw to cut through the step, and a label from the blade fell on the ground under the stairs. No useable fingerprint, but it had a store price tag, the Dollar General out by the highway. We'll see if the store has a video of the killer buying the saw blade.

'Nitpicker also found sawdust, so when we catch the killer, we can look for sawdust in his shoes or pants cuffs and match it to the sawdust at the scene.'

'Do men's pants have cuffs any more?' I asked.

'I guess so,' Jace said, and shrugged. 'I hate clothes shopping. My wife buys mine, and she never buys me pants with cuffs.'

'Why didn't Mrs Rawlins hear the killer sawing apart her front step?'

'Nitpicker found a bottle of sleeping pills by her bedside. And you were right. She did have cancer. The drugs were on her window sill and on the bathroom sink. We're going to get this creep, Angela. He screwed up.'

'Then I'd better get to work.'

I unzipped my DI case, and got out my point-and-shoot camera. I dreaded this part of the job the most. Yesterday, Mrs Rawlins had fixed me a potted meat sandwich and now she was broken and bleeding on a concrete slab.

It was easier to look at her battered body when I took my photos, with the lens as a screen in front of the sad sight. I took my shots – long, medium, and close-up. Mrs Rawlins had been bleeding from the ears, nose and mouth, which suggested a possible fracture at the base of the skull. Her back was twisted, and I wondered if her spine was broken. Her hands were bent at an awkward angle, and so were both

ankles. Were they broken, too? The ME would have to determine that.

I put on multiple pairs of gloves, and called up the death
investigation form on my iPad. The terse, bureaucratic language
helped me focus. I noted my arrival time, the location of the
deceased at the scene, and the direction of the body: Mrs
Rawlins was lying in the fetal position with her head pointing
east and her feet southwest. I brought out my thermometer to
record the ambient temperature – 62 degrees, and recorded
the time: 3:19 a.m.

The decedent's height was four-feet-eleven inches, and her
estimated weight was eighty-five pounds. I noted the dried
blood on her ears, nose, and mouth, plus her broken hands,
and the old contusions (bruises) and cut-like defects on her
arms. Her hands had twelve small cut-like defects – shallow
scratches, really. I wondered if they were caused by her
gardening. On the third finger of her left hand she wore two
yellow metal rings. One band was thin and plain, and the other
had a small clear stone. Her wedding ring set.

The neck of Mrs Rawlins's nightclothes revealed a chemo
port on the upper right side of her chest, covered with a clear
bandage. The port was about the size of a half-dollar, and
attached to a catheter threaded into the large jugular vein
above the right side of the heart. A closer inspection of the
inside of her arms at the antecubital fossa, the elbow pit,
showed the tiny scars in the skin. Mrs Rawlins's frail veins
were played out from all the needle sticks, and the doctors
had given her a port for her chemo.

I described her clothing next. The victim wore a long pink
cotton nightgown and pink polyester robe. One pink plush
slipper was on her left foot, and the second slipper was twelve
inches from the body, in the painted tire flower bed. I bagged
it. The slipper would go with the body to the ME's office. Her
right foot – the bare one – had a deep cut-like defect four
inches long at the shin, possibly from when her foot went
through the broken stair. I counted six splinters at her ankle.

I brought out a clean white sheet, spread it on the ground,
and Jace helped me turn the small body. There were two
healing contusions on the back of her right leg, each less than

one inch, a cut-like defect on her right leg on her knee, and another on the back of her ankle.

I described and photographed the blood at the scene: A ten-inch puddle where the decedent's head had fallen.

Next, I called up the Investigation of Falls on Stairs Form and answered the questions.

'History of recent alcoholic intake?' No. And I couldn't smell any alcohol on the decedent.

I answered questions about the door handle, and whether the door opened away from or into the staircase.

The questions about the stairs were incredibly detailed.

'The number of steps in the staircase?' Five.

'The material?' Untreated wood.

'Any coverings or safety treads on the stairs?' No.

'Type of surface covering at the TOP of the stairs.' A Welcome mat made from coconut fiber.

'Type of surface covering bottom of stairs.' Concrete.

The questions about the staircase were even more thorough. It was not enclosed. It had handrails on both sides. The rail was six feet long and forty-two inches high.

The stairs were in good repair and had no objects on them that could have caused Mrs Rawlins's fall.

'Was the light good? Was it on at the time of death?' I asked Jace. 'Yes,' he said. 'The porch light is on a timer from dusk to dawn.'

'Any witnesses?'

'One,' Jace said. 'The woman who found the body. She's sitting in the lawn chair by that tree over there.' Jace used his chin to indicate a fifty-something woman with a pale lavender chenille bathrobe and a head bristling with curlers. 'Her name is Peggy Nolan. The man with her is her husband, Bob. I'm going to talk to her. Want to come along?'

I followed Jace over to the woman in the lavender robe. Peggy Nolan was clutching a wad of tissues. Her eyes were red and she'd obviously been crying. A heavyset man about her age in jeans and a T-shirt was standing beside her, patting her hand.

'Mrs Nolan,' Jace said. 'Thank you for helping. We want to find the person who killed Mrs Rawlins.'

'That poor little thing,' Mrs Nolan said. 'She was so sweet. That Cody Ellis is evil, I tell you. Just evil. Killing that harmless woman.'

Cody Ellis. Why did that name sound familiar? Jace knew.

'Mr Ellis is the drug dealer who wasn't paying his rent,' Jace said.

'That's him,' Peggy said. 'A police officer – wait, it was you, wasn't it? You're the one who talked to him and told him to pay up or leave. We were so happy to see him gone. He moved out that very same night, and didn't pay a cent of his back rent. But he left behind a great big TV, and Mrs Rawlins kept it. Because he owed her money. More than three thousand dollars.

'He came back tonight about eleven o'clock, beating on Mrs Rawlins's door and demanding she give him back his TV. He was yelling so loud we could hear him and we live in 220.' She pointed to a newish mobile home two units away.

'I poked my head out, to see if he was going to be trouble, but Mrs Rawlins told him to quit making so much noise or he'd wake up the whole place. She invited him inside. Everything was quiet for about ten minutes, and then Cody came out, screaming and cursing. "I want my TV back!" He used the B-word and the C-word. "Pay me my rent and you can have it," Mrs Rawlins shouted at him. He gave her the finger and drove off in his pickup.

'I went over there to see if Mrs Rawlins was OK. She was, just good and mad. I asked if she wanted to call the police, in case Cody came back. "He won't dare," she said. "I'm not afraid of trash like him!" She was a feisty little thing.

'Bob and I went back to bed – and I'd just fallen asleep about two o'clock, when I was awakened by a funny noise – like a scream and some thuds. I wasn't sure what it was. I went outside to check, and found Mrs Rawlins at the foot of her steps. I called nine-one-one, but it was too late.' Mrs Nolan burst into noisy tears, and the man patted her hand.

'Did you see anyone push Mrs Rawlins down the stairs?' Jace asked.

'No.'

'Did you hear anyone come back after Cody Ellis left?'

'No. But it was him. I know it was.' Mrs Nolan was crying harder.

'Did Mrs Rawlins have any family?'

'No, she was all alone after her husband died.'

'What about you, Mr Nolan?' Jace asked. 'Did you see or hear anything?'

'No. It happened just like Peggy said. I take my hearing aid off at bedtime. She's better at noticing things.'

I left Bob Nolan comforting his wife, and climbed the backstairs to Mrs Rawlins's home. I put on booties at the door. The inside was neat and tidy. All the lights were blazing. Jace had told me the police had turned them on. When they entered the home, only the bedroom and the living room lights were on.

I bagged the chemo medicines on the kitchen window sill, then checked the fridge. Inside were four brown eggs, half a stick of butter, a quarter loaf of white bread, jars of mayo, pickle relish, catsup, and half a cupcake. No wonder Mrs Rawlins was so tiny.

The bathroom was spotless. The medicine cabinet held six different remedies for an upset stomach, plus corn plasters, aspirin and cold remedies.

In her bedroom, Mrs Rawlins had tossed her underwear and housedress in the clothes hamper. The covers on her double bed had been thrown back as if she'd awakened quickly. What was that on the pillow next to the crumpled one with the indent of her head?

I leaned over for a better look. It was an old black-and-white photo of a blond young man in a tux, a carnation in his button-hole and a smile on his handsome face. On the back was written: 'My Ronnie. On our wedding day.'

I hoped Mrs Rawlins was with her Ronnie now. I wiped away a tear. Crying was so unprofessional.

TWENTY-TWO

I t wasn't until seven o'clock that morning that I finally signed the paperwork for the morgue van. Mrs Rawlins's small, battered remains were transported to the ME's office. I went home – to my house. I didn't want to see Chris right now. I wanted our overheated romance to cool down. I needed to think, but I was too tired right now.

I went straight to bed, and didn't wake up until four in the afternoon. I was grateful for the uninterrupted sleep. I didn't want to deal with any more death investigations that day. I checked my work cell phone, just in case. Nothing. Katie had texted me that she'd autopsied Mrs Rawlins and Jace and I should report to her office at nine tomorrow. *Bring doughnuts or something for breakfast, Angela*, she wrote. *Jace will haul in the coffee.*

I took out one of the blueberry pound cakes I'd stashed in the freezer. I'd bought six at the school bake sale. They were homemade baked goods. Just not made in my home.

I was hungry, and scrambled some eggs, my default meal. When I finished, I took a favorite comfort read, Agatha Christie's *And Then There Were None*, out to the garden, and sat in a lawn chair near my mother's honeysuckle trellis. The sweet smell of the curly yellow flowers and the soft buzz of the bees lulled me to sleep in the warm sun. I woke up when the book fell off my lap with a thud. Sun-warmed and still sleepy, I gave up and went to bed. I was too ashamed to check the time, but it was early. Like old-people-early.

The next morning, as instructed, Jace and I were in Katie's closet-sized office. The detective needed a shave and his clothes were rumpled. Jace looked sad and tired, and I suspected I didn't look much better. Mrs Rawlins's death weighed on both of us.

Meanwhile, Katie looked fresh and chipper. She wore one of her plain brown suits and a fresh white lab coat. She had a manic buzz to her. I figured we were in for a bumpy ride.

As instructed, Jace had brought the hot coffee, and I had the pound cake. We all cut ourselves thick slices. Jace looked so tired, I took that mini torture device, the wire chair, and let Jace sit on the edge of the desk.

Katie paced in the cramped floor space while she gave her report. 'Not many surprises here,' she said. 'Shirley Rawlins died of injuries from the fall down her stairs. She had the classic injuries from a stairs' fall: fractures to her face and hands, wrists and ankles, along with spinal cord damage, and deep lacerations on her face and ankles.'

I shuddered, even though I'd seen those brutal injuries close up. 'Did she feel any pain?' I knew family members asked that question all the time, and we rarely gave them the truth. But I needed reassurance.

'I doubt it,' Katie said. 'Shirley Rawlins fell head-first down the stairs and died almost instantly. She might have felt a few seconds of fear when her foot went through the top step, but it was over quickly.'

'You sound angry,' Jace said.

'I am,' Katie said, eyes flashing. 'That woman had breast cancer. Cancer! Shirley Rawlins had had a double mastectomy, and the cancer came back. She fought it every step of the way for five years. The cancer had spread to her bones. She must have been in pain, but she kept on going. Doc Bartlett said she was a good patient and a good woman. Shirley wanted to live. Her life was simple. She went to church. She liked to garden and sit outside in her yard. And some . . . some . . . shit-stain killed her. For what? A friggin' television! I hope he gets the death penalty.'

'Oh, he will,' Jace said. Now he sounded triumphant. He sat up straighter as he announced, 'I caught the worthless son of a bitch.'

I blinked. That was harsh language for Jace.

'A neighbor lady heard Cody Ellis fighting with Mrs Rawlins,' he said, 'and she put us on his trail. It was a stupid murder – Cody left behind DNA, sawdust, and the dip-wipe virtually told us where he bought the saw blade. Once I got confirmation the killer was Cody, I tracked him down in the early morning hours.' Jace reached over and rewarded himself with another hefty slice of cake.

'Where was Cody?' I didn't like the ugly feeling of glee dancing through me, but I felt it any way.

'Cody was roosting on a barstool in a redneck bar out by the highway,' Jace said, 'eating a pickled egg.'

'Ugh,' I said. 'Disgusting.' Pickled eggs made me gag. The sickly white peeled hard-boiled eggs floating in vinegar brine looked like medical specimens. 'I've seen jars of those eggs in low-rent bars,' I said, 'next to the beef jerky and stale peanuts, but I was never tempted to eat one.'

'I couldn't get drunk enough to eat one,' Katie said.

'How did you know Cody would be at that bar, Jace?' I asked.

'I got a tip from the bartender,' Jace said. 'He wants to stay in my good graces. I overlook an occasional violation, and he lets me know when a serious felon shows up. The bartender said Cody had been drinking boiler makers since midnight. He told me Cody was trouble, and he wanted him out of there before he picked a fight. I called for back-up, but I didn't need it. When I walked into the bar at four this morning, Cody's so-called friends ran like rats. He was sloppy drunk, slamming back shots of cheap whiskey, then knocking off cheaper beer. He must have really been out of it to start eating pickled eggs. I caught him with egg on his face.'

I groaned. 'Really, Jace, did you have to say that?' I asked. He grinned at me.

'Did Cody put up a fight?' Katie asked.

'He was too drunk,' Jace said. 'He'd reached the fighting stage about four boiler makers earlier. By the time I got him, he was weepy and rubber-legged.

'I arrested Cody for first degree murder,' Jace said. 'I enjoyed telling him he was going to be charged with a Class A felony with special circumstances. He's looking at either the death penalty or LWOP, and since the new county pros-ecutor ran on a platform to protect the Forest's seniors, he wants to give Cody the needle.

'When I told Cody that he'd committed first-degree murder because he was trying to get "something of monetary value" from the victim – that's how the law reads – the creep started whining that it wasn't fair: he never got his TV back.

'At the jail, I passed the word that he'd killed an old woman dying of cancer. The other jailbirds are going to make his life very unhappy.'

'Did Cody confess?' I asked.

'Didn't have to,' Jace said. 'We got enough for an arrest. The Dollar General store had him on tape, buying that saw blade. We found sawdust in his shirt pocket. He's toast. We'll soon have the DNA to back it up. Cody's not getting out of this one. He's not cutting any deals, either.'

We all drank our coffee in the long silence. Finally, I spoke. 'Mrs Rawlins didn't have any living relatives. Did anyone claim her body?'

'Cynthia Lockridge,' Katie said. 'Mrs Rawlins went to the Forest Methodist Church, so her funeral will be there and Cynthia will make sure that Shirley is buried in the churchyard next to her husband.'

'That's very nice,' I said.

'You don't have to stare at me, Angela,' Jace said. 'I still think Cynthia Lockridge conspired to kill her husband.'

I chalked his angry tone up to exhaustion, and said, 'That's not why I was staring. I thought you needed a shave.'

'I do,' he said. 'I've been working this case non-stop.'

I changed the subject. 'Have you been able to dive into Cynthia's records?'

'A little bit,' he said. 'So far, the Christmas ball has taken in one-point-eight million dollars.'

Katie whistled. 'That much for a Christmas dance?'

'It's a big deal charity,' I said. 'I'm surprised they haven't roped in Monty as a sponsor.'

'If I'm lucky, his name will stay off the guest list,' Katie said.

'A sponsorship is ten thousand dollars. The money adds up quickly when all the fat cats are trying to outdo one another,' Jace said. 'If Cynthia is careful with the expenses, she could easily reach or surpass that one-point-four-million-dollar goal for this year. But, man, those records are tricky. There are almost two hundred vendors, from florists to the valet parking service to bartenders and more.'

'What can I do to help?' I asked. 'I'm still on call today.'

'It's not a good idea to have your fingerprints on this investigation,' he said.

'I realize that.'

'Why don't you two split the vendors list?' Katie said. 'Send half to me, and I'll forward it to Angela. That way you won't leave an electronic trail to her.'

'I can do that now.' Jace took out his cell phone and texted something. When there was an audible *ding!* from Katie's phone he said, 'You've got it. I'm bushed. Goodbye all.'

Jace left, dragging a heavy load of discouragement behind him. Katie texted the vendors list to me.

I sipped my coffee and Katie said, 'So you didn't spend last night with Chris?'

'What? How did you know?'

Katie grinned. 'This is the Forest, Angela. We all live in each other's pockets. I heard your honey sent you off to Mrs Rawlins's investigation in the wee hours with a warm cinnamon roll and hot coffee.'

'So what!' I sounded snappish, but I didn't care. 'I'm really not in the mood for this.'

'Chris is a good man,' Katie said. 'Don't let him get away.'

'You make me sound like some man-chasing old maid.'

'I know you're annoyed with me, Angela, but there's not much comfort in a dead man's arms.'

'I'm getting plenty of comfort,' I said. 'Take care of your own love life.'

'Has Chris said the L-word yet?' Katie asked.

'Which one: Lumberjack? Lemming? Lobotomy?'

'You're avoiding the subject, Angela. He's falling in love with you, and it looks like you're serious about him. Soon he's going to want you to start leaving your things at his place.'

'Leave, that's another L-word,' I said. 'I'm out of here.' I stood up and grabbed my purse.

Katie followed me to her door. 'What if Chris says he loves you, Angela? What are you going to do then?'

I reached for my favorite movie cliché. 'If I told you, I'd have to kill you, and right now, that idea sounds way too inviting.'

TWENTY-THREE

Back home after the meeting in Katie's office, I worked on the vendors list she'd texted me, mainlining coffee to keep me going. My half of Jace's list of party vendors had eighty-nine names. First, I set out to eliminate the fifty business names I knew, including the Forest Bakery, Chouteau Party Planners, and Dubois Valet Service. I confirmed the addresses and contact names, and checked the amounts billed. If the billing amount seemed reasonable, I crossed off the name. It was tedious work, but I was making progress when my work cell phone rang.

I looked at the display.

Damn. It was Ray Greiman. My heart sank at the prospect of working with him again.

'Who died and where?' I asked.

'Some housewife OD'ed.' I heard the contempt in Greiman's voice. 'She's in a McMansion in Chouteau Executive Estates.' He gave me the address.

'Any children?' I asked.

'One little girl. Neighbor saw the packages piling up on the front porch, went over to check, heard the kid crying and found the mother dead inside. She's keeping the kid for now. Husband works in St. Louis. He's at some big deal conference, and they're tracking him down. Well, it's been fun gossiping with you, sweetheart, but it's time for you to get your ass over here.'

He hung up after his usual rude farewell. I wanted to throw my phone against the wall, but I took a deep breath and told myself to keep it together. Greiman liked to set me off, and I wouldn't give him the satisfaction.

There was no point complaining to Chief Buttkiss. He and Greiman were buddies. He told the chief that I was 'over-sensitive and had a stick up my ass' – Greiman's words. The chief, a well-connected good old boy, dismissed my complaint about Greiman as 'a personality conflict.' If I wanted to make trouble, I could have called Monty Bryant, and the lawyer would charge in and defend me. But I liked my job here, and a lawsuit would end it, so I put up with the jerk.

One thing I did know: I'd work even harder to help Jace solve Tom Lockridge's murder. The prospect of even more work with Ray Greiman was intolerable.

It was a short drive to the Chouteau Executive Estates, a new subdivision for the Forest's up-and-comers. They didn't want their parents' and grandparents' grandiose nineteenth-century mansions. These new homes were lighter, brighter and more energy-efficient, but they were still the exclusive preserve of the one-percent. The mansions had new kitchens with islands, more bathrooms, and attached garages for four or five cars. The starting price was four million dollars, and amenities like wine cellars, infinity pools, waterfalls, hot tubs and saunas quickly added another two or three million. The lots were huge.

Allen and Barbara Blanchette lived in a brand-new redbrick mansion bristling with balconies and dormers at the end of a cul-de-sac. The house was so new, the shrubbery still had the landscaper's orange tags on it. The home on the east side was a wood-and-concrete skeleton, and the lot's denuded soil was washing into the street. The house on the west side was similar to the Blanchette mansion. After the spindly trees and shrubbery grew out, the street would be lush and tree-shaded. Right now the cul-de-sac looked like an awkward teenager who might be a real knockout in a few years.

The Blanchette driveway was packed with official vehicles, so I parked on the street and rolled my DI case up the gray pavers to the door. I was met at the entrance by Paul Burke, a new uniform. He about twenty-five, with pale skin, cornflower blue eyes and broad shoulders.

'Hi, Paul, how are you?' I asked.

Paul looked like a grateful puppy. I never used his hated nickname, 'Butt Face.' Greiman tagged him with that name because he said Paul's face was smooth as a baby's bottom. Naturally, the name stuck.

Paul signed me in on the scene log, and gave me booties

and the case number. The young cop was chatty, and I liked that. It meant I'd have to talk less to Greiman.

'The dead woman is in the upstairs master bedroom,' he said. 'The husband is at some conference in Clayton' – a city that bordered St. Louis – 'and they've finally located him. He's a big deal at Danvers and Dall, the marketing company. He should be here shortly.'

'What about the little girl?' I asked.

'Her name is Olive,' Paul said. 'Cute little thing, about three. She's with the neighbor lady, Lisa Kling.' Paul pointed to the house next door. 'Mrs Kling has a little girl about the same age. She's watching Olive until her father can take her. Mrs Kling found the body.'

That meant I'd have to talk to Lisa for my investigation.

'This neighborhood is plagued with porch pirates,' Paul said – the nickname for thieves who swiped Amazon deliveries. 'The neighbor lady saw a bunch of packages on the doorstep and thought she'd better take them in. Then she heard Olive crying. Mrs Kling had a key to the Blanchette house. She went inside, saw Mrs Blanchette was dead, and called nine-one-one. The paramedics said the vic couldn't be revived. They didn't even try. They pronounced her dead' – he checked the log – 'at 12:26. She was in full rigor. They think the mother had been dead at least twenty-four hours.'

I tried to keep the horror out of my voice as I asked the next question: 'And the little girl was alone with her dead mother the whole time?'

'Yes, Olive was hungry and tried to fix herself some food. Made a real mess in the kitchen.'

'Oh, man.'

'Just breaks your heart,' Paul said. 'I've got nieces her age.' He looked adorably sad.

'Who's doing the forensics?'

'Nitpicker,' he said.

'My favorite tech,' I said. At least there was something good about this assignment.

'Oh, one warning,' Paul said. 'The DEA is on the way.'

Interesting. The DEA was the Drug Enforcement Administration. 'Why are the feds being called in for an OD?'

'Because there may be fentanyl in here and they want to trace where the substance is coming from.'

'Not good,' I said. Fentanyl was a synthetic opioid painkiller, sometimes known on the street as 'drop dead' – and rightly so. It was related to heroin but far deadlier.

'Good luck.' Paul opened the front door, and I walked into a two-story marble foyer with a sweeping staircase leading to the second floor. Downstairs, through a series of arches, I glimpsed a living room, a gigantic open kitchen, and a study lined with books. The living room was crowded with furniture, upholstered in a soft gold color and covered with tassels and fringe.

I started hauling my suitcase upstairs. Greiman was at the top, dressed in his favorite camera-ready outfit: a Hugo Boss charcoal suit, light blue shirt and power tie. He was scowling and his arms were crossed. I'd be damned if I'd let him see me struggle. I faked carrying the heavy suitcase as if it were light as a purse. When I made it to the top, I was pleased I wasn't out of breath.

'Finally,' he said, as if he'd been waiting for hours. 'The stiff is in the master bedroom on the left.'

I entered the room and blinked. The bedroom was the size of a school auditorium and the walls were covered with yellow-and-black baroque wallpaper. The bed was white leather, and designed like a sled. The dead woman on the bed was almost lost in the white-and-yellow Medusa head emblem on the rumpled spread.

'Versace,' said a voice behind me, and there was Nitpicker. The tech's lime green hair was a welcome sight.

'The deceased definitely loved Versace,' she said.

'Right.' I was still slightly dazed by the screaming colors of the wallpaper and the bedspread. The room felt feverish and unsettled, like a drug dream. The trademark Versace Medusa, with her hollow eyes, would give me nightmares.

'This stuff is outrageously expensive,' Nitpicker said. 'That spread alone is twenty-two hundred dollars. When it's clashing all together like this, it's ugly as homemade sin.'

'Did Barbara Blanchette OD?' I asked.

'That's what it looks like. She was definitely an addict, and had the habits. I'm finding pills everywhere.'

'Mostly white ten milligrams?' I knew different dosages of OxyContin came in different colors.

'I've found the whole rainbow,' she said. 'White, gray, brown, pink, yellow, red and green.'

'Impressive,' I said. 'All the way up to eighty milligrams.'

'Her tolerance must have really increased. I found one 160 milligram pill. But when I found these, Greiman threw a hissy fit.' She showed me a bag with four pretty pale blue pills. On one side was a '30' and on the other an 'M.'

I grinned. 'Do tell. More oxycodone?'

'Worse,' she said. 'Mexican oxy – way deadlier. This stuff is fentanyl disguised to look like oxy. I did a quick field test and found out what it was. Fentanyl is about fifty times stronger than heroin. The ME will have to confirm it, but I bet this is what killed Mrs Blanchette, and there was no way for her to tell it wasn't real oxy.

'We'd been warned to be on the lookout for Mexican oxy. It's killed four people in this area – a high school basketball star in Ladue, two teenagers in Clayton and a twenty-six-year-old woman in Town and Country.'

'All the richer burbs,' I said.

'Right. Anyway, I did the test and it was positive. I told Greiman – in front of witnesses, so he wouldn't "forget"' – she made air-quotes with her fingers – 'and now the DEA is on its way. Greiman is so mad he can't see straight.'

'Dumb question, but is Mexican oxy made in Mexico?'

'Sort of,' she said. 'It's made by the Mexican cartels, but the fentanyl usually comes from China. Those pills are not only dangerous, they're way cheaper than oxy.'

The bedroom door slammed open, and Greiman was glowering at both of us. 'Sorry to interrupt the hen party, ladies,' he said. My fingers twitched and I imagined strangling him with his power tie.

'There's been a change of plans. The DEA is here and they have a search warrant for this place. They want to track down where the stiff bought the fentanyl. Meanwhile, they want you to find all the drugs in the house, bag them and tag them. Have fun, ladies.'

I rolled my DI case toward the vast yellow-and-white bed, and opened the DI Form on my iPad: Death Due to Ingestion of Alcohol and/or Medications.

Next, I checked the ambient temperature with my thermometer: sixty-eight degrees. I photographed the thermostat with my point-and-shoot camera. It read seventy degrees.

I gloved up and turned my attention to the small, thin body of Barbara Blanchette. She was in a king-size bed adjacent to the west wall. Her body was lying face-up on the right side of that fabulous Versace spread.

Barbara did not die peacefully. The rumpled spread showed she'd thrashed around on the bed, fighting death. She'd vomited three times. I measured the patches and took samples. I could see bits of blue pills in the vomit. I also found two small smears of diarrhea on the spread. My guess was Barbara hadn't eaten much in her last days.

On the pillow next to her body was an open book, 'The Adventures of Alice in Wonderland.' The paper pages were hollowed out.

'Hey, Nitpicker,' I said. 'Did you see this?'

The tech came over, holding a striped Kate Spade make-up bag in her gloved hands.

'Let me guess,' I said. 'You found more pills in the make-up bag?'

'Thirty even,' Nitpicker said.

'Take a look at this book,' I said. 'Under the circumstances, the title is almost a joke.'

Nitpicker examined the hollowed-out steel center of the book. 'A book safe. With real paper pages. The choice of discerning druggies.'

'Another ten pills in the book safe,' I said. 'Where would she get something like that?'

'Walmart. The internet. Twenty bucks. Some prefer Jane Austen or the dictionary.'

I bagged the book safe and went back to Barbara. The dead woman's mouth and brown eyes were open. Her sunken eyes had yellow whites, and nested in bunches of wrinkles.

Barbara's driver's license said she was thirty. I'd have to verify that. People often lied on their driver's license. She looked at least ten years older, but that may have been the drugs. Her height was five feet. I estimated her weight at seventy-five to eighty pounds. She was way too thin, even for a small-boned woman. Her feet were bare and bruised. I checked for needle marks between the toes or on her arms. Nothing. Barbara was a pill taker.

The rigor mortis was advanced: her entire body was stiff and unmovable. I agreed with the estimate that she'd probably been dead at least twenty-four hours, but the ME would have to confirm that.

I spread out a cheap, white sterilized sheet on the vast bed, and Nitpicker helped me turn the decedent. As we struggled with the stiff body, I noticed patches of purple on the victim's back and skinny buttocks – livor mortis, the pooling of blood in the body after her heart stopped pumping. She also had dark purple patches on the backs of her arms and legs.

But here's what bothered me the most about Barbara: she was unkempt, especially as the wife of a Forest executive. Her brown hair needed a wash. It looked like it had been cut with nail scissors and – most shameful of all – there were strands of gray in her brown hair. Forest women did not go gray naturally. Not in their early thirties.

Barbara's nails were chewed and her eyebrows needed to be plucked. She wore dirty gray sweatpants and a stretched-out pink sweatshirt, both two sizes too big for her. I checked the labels. Definitely not designer wear.

Barbara had died on a twenty-two hundred dollar Versace bedspread, but she looked like she'd been sleeping under a bridge.

What was going on here?

TWENTY-FOUR

'This pill search is turning into a real Easter egg hunt,' Nitpicker said. 'Check these out.'

She showed me a cardboard evidence box holding odd items in sealed plastic bags. She held up one evidence bag containing an open blue box of tampons. About half remained. 'Barbara hid pink and green pills in a sandwich baggie under her tampons.'

'I doubt anyone would go rooting around in a tampon box,' I said. 'Especially her husband.'

'That was the idea,' Nitpicker said. 'She was hiding even more in her dressing room.' She picked up another bag. 'This Versace candy dish was supposedly filled with coffee-flavor hard candy. Each candy wrapper really holds two to three oxy pills.'

'There must be thirty "candies" in there,' I said.

'Thirty-two,' Nitpicker said. 'For a total of sixty-seven pills. I photographed and documented each one. I'll help you with the count.'

'Thanks,' I said. This was a huge favor.

'Barbara had a three-year-old but still had time to fill all those candy wrappers with pills?' I asked.

'Never underestimate the dedication of an addict.' Nitpicker put the candy dish back in the box with a clank. 'Oops,' she said. 'That dish is four hundred bucks. I saw it on sale online. And those Versace throw pillows are four hundred each – and hid another thirty pills.'

Nitpicker held up three more evidence bags from the box. 'Barbara used some traditional hiding spots for suburban homemakers. I found fifteen pills in this purple sock, and twelve in her cute little red satin evening bag. She had another stash of thirty-one in the toes of these black winter boots.

'We're going to be here all day going through this house,' Nitpicker said. 'It has seven bedrooms and nine bathrooms, plus the living room, den, library and kitchen. I'll have to check the toilet tanks, the vents and cold air return ducts. With eight thousand square feet, this house has too many hiding places.'

'Don't forget the yard,' I said.

'And the three cars,' Nitpicker said. 'Oh, well, today's over-time may pay off my Visa bill.'

'Do you think Barbara's husband knew his wife was an addict?' I asked.

'He had to,' Nitpicker said. 'But he didn't want to know.'

'Are all the pills OxyContin?' I asked.

'Nope, she had quite a collection of opioids, including Demerol, Percocet, Roxicodone, and Vicodin. All meant to be short-term painkillers. My guess is this poor woman had some serious pain and got hooked quickly.'

'Where was she getting these pills?'

'So far, I've found prescriptions from seven different doctors,' Nitpicker said. 'Some of them are fifty or sixty miles away. She was shopping around and using false IDs. I found three driver's licenses, as well as her real one.'

'A sad story, and way too common,' I said.

'It's what helps keep us in business,' Nitpicker said.

I left Nitpicker rooting out more pills in the decedent's bedroom. I thought I'd looked everywhere, but she found three more oxys stashed in the battery compartment of the clicker on the nightstand. Nitpicker was suspicious about that clicker – there was no TV in the room.

I escaped the glaring yellow bedroom for the master bath-room. The Versace obsession stopped here. This room was fit for a Roman emperor. It must have had a thousand feet of marble tile. Three marble steps led up to the marble sunken tub, surrounded by palm trees. I stared at the luxurious room like a hick at a county fair. I saw two heated towel racks, four sinks, a glass-enclosed steam shower, and a stone sink to heat face and shaving cream. Framed mirrors and dark wood cabinetry covered a full wall.

Weirdly, in the midst of this magnificence, a plain old Coke can sat on the edge of the sunken tub. I carefully picked it up. The weight felt odd. Sure enough, it wasn't a soda can. It was a stash safe. I photographed it, then opened it, counted twenty-one oxy pills and bagged it.

The bathroom turned into a surreal treasure hunt. In another cabinet, I found ten oxy pills in an Aqua Net hairspray can, and twelve in a hairbrush. The weight of the round-headed brush felt off and when I held it up to the light, I saw the top of the round brush unscrewed. Also, there wasn't a single hair in the brush. Barbara liked hiding her stashes.

'Nitpicker,' I called out, 'Barbara uses stash safes. I've found three so far in the bathroom.'

'Check the wall outlets,' she said. 'I'll bet you'll find at least one is a fake.'

Nitpicker knew her business. I checked six outlets, before one outlet pulled out of the wall to reveal another oxy stash. Six pills this time.

Nitpicker joined me in the outrageous bathroom. 'Is there a clock in this room?' she asked.

'Nope.'

'I do a lot of drug cases. I'll bet she'll have a stash safe in a clock somewhere. This means we're really going to have to search the kitchen. She's going to have more soda can safes, as well as vegetable cans and cleaning products. Back to work.'

The bathroom also had a real medicine cabinet. Inside it, I found twenty-four white OxyContin tablets in an aspirin bottle, along with a bottle of Tylenol that actually contained Tylenol. Other shelves held Milk of Magnesia, Band-Aids, three kinds of mouthwash and more harmless nostrums. At least, I thought they were harmless. I bagged them all.

I searched the lavish bathroom for over an hour, checking the cabinets, the wall outlets, and the toilet, but I didn't find more oxy. Nitpicker said she'd go over the room after me.

'Do you want to check the little girl's bedroom?' she asked.

'You don't think Barbara would keep drugs in her daughter's room, do you?'

'She's an addict.' I heard Nitpicker's disgust. 'She has stashes everywhere.'

Olive's room was a little girl's dream – at least for little girls who liked princesses. The walls were bonbon pink, and framed posters of Disney princesses decorated the walls. Frilly pink curtains covered the windows. The small single bed had a sheer pink canopy held up by a gold crown. In an alcove was a pink adult-sized couch, along with a child's rocking chair and a forty-two-inch TV. Lined up on a shelf were dozens of Disney movies. I opened all the cases, but inside were nothing but DVDs.

In one corner was a white child-size crib, filled with stuffed animals and a baby doll carefully arranged under a pink coverlet. Over the crib was a pink battery-operated clock, well out of a child's reach. I took it off the wall. The clock worked, but there was another stash safe inside it. Barbara was keeping drugs in her daughter's room. The woman definitely needed help.

'You were right,' I called out to Nitpicker. 'There were drugs in the clock.'

'Check the stuffed animals, pillows and upholstery,' she said. 'This doper was far gone.'

I went back to work. In the crib, the ten stuffed animals, ranging from bunny rabbits to baby elephants, were drug free. So were the pillows and couch cushions.

When I checked in with Nitpicker again, she was going through the dresser drawers in the bedroom. She found a stash of oxy in a black lace bra cup.

'Should I start the kitchen without you?' I asked. Nitpicker doesn't give me orders, but on long difficult jobs like this one, we worked in sync.

'We should do that together,' she said. 'It's going to be a lot of work. What time is it?'

'According to the stash clock, it's a little after four,' I said.

'Where's Barbara's husband?' Nitpicker asked. 'If he really was at a conference in Clayton, he should have been home two hours ago.'

'Beats me.' I shrugged.

'You may want to talk to the next-door neighbor before the husband shows up. You might learn more when he isn't around.'

'Good idea.'

I rolled my suitcase next door to Lisa Kling's mansion. The front door had a silk flower wreath, the suburban salute to spring. Lisa answered the door herself. She looked tiny and delicate in her black jeans and pink cotton shirt. Like her dead friend, she was barely five feet tall. Lisa's long blonde hair was fashionably styled, her face was make-up free, and her blue eyes were red from crying.

She invited me into her sparkling kitchen, a room bigger than the first floor of my home. It was obviously her favorite place, and smelled of cinnamon. She treated me like a welcome neighbor.

'I've just made cranberry-oatmeal cookies for the girls,' she said. 'Would you like some? I have coffee, too.'

I sat at a round wooden table by a window overlooking the backyard, where I admired the avian action at her bird feeder. 'What's the cute little guy with the yellow breast?' I asked.

She glanced out the window. 'That's a pine warbler. A pair of cardinals hang out there. And a noisy blue jay. I love watching my birds. I'm still trying to figure out how to keep the squirrels out of the bird seed.'

After Lisa brought over a plate piled with freshly baked cookies and poured two mugs of coffee, she sat down across from me. The cookies were still warm.

'What can I do to help?' She added two spoons of sugar to her coffee. 'Barb was a dear friend. I tried to help her. I did.' She started crying. I brought over the box of tissues from the kitchen island. She thanked me and said, 'I'm sorry. I can't stop crying.'

'No reason to apologize. Barbara Blanchette was your friend.' I was grateful for the coffee. It was hot and freshly brewed. I opened my iPad to ask the required questions for my death investigation: 'When was the last time you talked to Barbara?'

'Two days ago,' she said. 'About three in the afternoon. We met in the driveway when we went out to get the mail. Her husband Allen was going to be at the Missouri Marketing Executives Conference for four days. She was looking forward to spending time with Olive. And, truth to tell, she was relieved her husband would be gone for a while.'

'How would you describe their marriage?'

Lisa stopped, and carefully chose her words. 'I'd say it was difficult. Barbara was proud of Allen's success, but they'd both changed so much since their marriage eight years ago.'

'How so?'

'Allen was obsessed with his career. He's a rising star. Allen felt Barb's role in their marriage was to help advance his career, and lately she wasn't doing it. Certainly, not this last year.'

'What was Barbara's mood like when you last saw her?' I helped myself to a second cookie.

'Happy. Upbeat. She told me she was going to make Olive's favorite lunch – toasted cheese and tomato soup. They planned to watch *Frozen* for the ninety-ninth time in Olive's princess bedroom. Have you seen that room?'

'Yes,' I said. 'It's really cute.'

'Olive had just made the transition from her crib to a "big-girl bed" and thanks to Barb's efforts, the move went well. Barb let Olive use her old crib for her dolls and stuffed animals. Olive loved that room. When I saw Barb that last time, she was with Olive. The little girl was tugging on her mother's hand. She wanted to go inside. Barb picked her up and kissed her.'

'She was such a good mother.' Lisa started sniffling, but fought back the tears.

'Did Barbara complain about any illness when you last saw her?'

'She said she felt like she had the flu. She said that a lot.' Another sign of opioid addiction.

'Do you remember what Barbara was wearing?'

'What she always wore: ratty sweatpants and a shirt I wouldn't use for a cleaning rag. I think the top was pink. It was definitely dirty. I believe the sweatpants might have been gray.'

Addicts often lost interest in their hygiene, I thought. Barbara fit the pattern. 'Shoes?' I asked.

'No shoes. It was a warm day and Barb was barefoot.'

'Did Barbara appear to be under the influence of alcohol or drugs?'

'Yes. Drugs. Oxy, I think. She was wearing sunglasses, but

not because it was sunny. She didn't want me to see her eyes.
She and Olive went inside and shut the door. That's the last
time I saw Barb alive.'

Now Lisa did cry – great, gulping sobs. I got her a glass
of water. She drank it down, and once again, apologized for
crying.

'This next question is going to be hard for you, Lisa, but I
have to ask it. How did you find Barbara's body?'

Lisa wiped her eyes, then steeled herself to talk.

'I saw a pile of packages on Barb's front porch. They'd
been there at least a day. Packages had been stolen off the
porches in this area and I thought I'd better take them
inside. I figured Barb might have gone on another short
trip somewhere while Allen was away. Lately, she's been so
secretive.

'I have a key to her house, and I went over about eleven
thirty this morning.'

She stopped and looked at me. 'Was it really this morning?
It seems like years ago.' Lisa took a long sip of her coffee,
and then spoke: 'Anyway, I opened the front door to put the
packages on the table in the foyer, and heard Olive crying.
Bawling her head off. I ran upstairs.

'That's where . . .' Lisa stopped, then started again after a
deep breath. 'That's where I found Barb, all stiff and cold.
Olive was on the bed next to her, crying, "Wake up, Mommy.
Wake up."

'I called nine-one-one. The paramedics and the police
came, and pronounced' – Lisa stopped and gulped, then said
– 'pronounced my friend dead. Olive was clinging to me
and crying. The police said I could take her home until they
found her father. Olive was hungry. Have you been in Barb's
kitchen?'

'Not yet.'

'Olive had tried to fix herself something to eat. She must
have climbed up on the sink to get the cereal, and managed
to pour it in a bowl, but she spilled the heavy gallon jug of
milk. I tried to wipe up the milk, but the police wouldn't
let me.'

'You can't. It's part of the scene,' I said.

'Olive wasn't afraid to come here to my house. She plays with Bella, my daughter, all the time. I fed her and Bella lunch and they're both upstairs napping.

'Once the girls were asleep, I called Allen's office. His secretary said he was at some important conference and the police had already called him. Allen was giving the keynote this afternoon at two o'clock. I hate to say it, but I think he's not coming home until after he gives that speech.'

'You're joking.' I was shocked. Nobody – *nobody* – ever refused to run home after they found out their spouse was dead. Certainly not because they're giving a stupid speech.

Lisa leaned in like a breathless woman at a kaffeeklatsch. 'That's Allen. He doesn't give a damn about anyone but himself and his blessed career. Not even his little girl. Most daddies adore their daughters. Allen basically ignores Olive because he wanted a son. I hope for that little girl's sake, she gets to live with Barbara's parents. They love her. I called them in Tampa and gave them the news. They're flying back here and will be in St. Louis about seven tonight.'

'Did Allen know his wife had a drug problem?'

'Of course he did. But he didn't want to know. She was dying, and he didn't care. He wanted a Stepford wife – in his eyes, Barb was defective.

'Once she died, he could get a newer, better model.'

TWENTY-FIVE

E ven in Lisa's warm, homey kitchen, I was chilled listening to her description of Barbara Blanchette's husband. How could any man neglect his wife like that? I wrapped my hands around my coffee mug to warm them.

'You knew about Barbara's drug problem?' I asked Lisa.

'Yes, of course. We all did. All her friends, I mean. Allen pretended nothing was wrong. Like I said, that man has an iceberg for a heart. More coffee?'

'Please.' Lisa brought over an insulated pot, poured us both coffee and set the pot on the table.

'When did Barbara's addiction start?' I reached for another cookie.

'About six months after Olive was born.' Lisa lowered her voice to confide the information. My interview was turning into a girl-talk session, but that was fine with me. It was a comfortable way to deliver difficult information.

'Barb and I were more than neighbors – we were good friends. Barb really wanted that baby, and she had a difficult pregnancy. She had to stay in bed for the last month. Doctor's orders. I'd go over to talk to her and bring her meals. I'd just had my little girl, Isabella. Our girls are only three months apart.

'In that last month of her pregnancy, Barb was big as a house. I mean, she waddled. She couldn't wait to give birth.'

'Did Allen help when she was confined to bed?'

'Help!' Lisa gave a small snort, like a miniature pony. 'He wasn't even in town. He was away on another so-called important trip, leaving his wife alone and frightened. Barb's parents had retired to Florida, and her mother, Cathy, flew in from Tampa to help.

'Barb called Allen when her water broke, and he told her to take an Uber to the hospital. Cathy and I went with her. Allen didn't show up until the baby was a day old. He'd wanted a boy, and he made it clear he was disappointed. He didn't like holding Olive and got angry when she cried. I don't think he ever changed her diaper.

'For Barbara, it was love at first sight. Olive was healthy, beautiful and smart, and they had so much fun.'

Lisa lowered her voice again to confide more troubling information. 'Allen wanted sex when Barb was one day out of the hospital, still hurting after Olive's birth. During her recovery, he complained about her looks. Said she wasn't losing her baby-weight fast enough. He called her a tub. Said she was fat.'

Fat. The ultimate Forest insult. Executive wives were required to be slim and pretty, even after they'd just had a child.

'That must have hurt Barb,' I said.

'It did. She only weighed a hundred and thirty pounds. Barb wasn't fat by any means, but she was having a hard time going back to her pre-baby weight of a hundred pounds. It didn't help that Allen kept nagging her. Barb was alone a lot and she was very close to Olive. They played games and . . . and . . .'

Lisa started crying again. 'I just realized how much Olive is going to miss her mama.' She wiped her eyes and blew her nose with a tiny honk, and then started talking.

'About six months after Olive was born, Barb had a pinched nerve in her back. The pain was excruciating. She couldn't drive or even walk up the stairs. She slept on the living room couch. A nanny helped care for Olive during that time. I took Barb to several doctors, and none could help with the pain. Finally, she heard about a doctor way up north in St. Peters.'

That's a suburb about forty-five minutes north of the Forest, and another world.

'Dr Lindell Delbert.' Lisa pronounced every syllable carefully. 'I hope he fries in hell. I drove her to his office. Delbert's the one who gave my friend OxyContin. He said he'd only prescribe it "until her back healed."'

'Barb got better almost immediately. With these new pills, Barb was almost her old self. We went shopping together and

had lunch. We joked that we were sisters separated at birth.
Barb had always been a worrywart, but now she was relaxed
and happy – and pain-free.

'And I was too dumb to know that her addiction had started.'
Lisa's face crumpled, and I was afraid she'd start crying again.
Instead, she pulled herself together and continued.

'After two months, Dr Delbert said he couldn't keep
prescribing oxy for Barb. She was furious. Then she was
frantic. When she ran out of her medicine she was sick and
sweating. She told me she had the flu.'

Lisa looked at me seriously. 'That's another sign of addiction,
you know.'

'Yes, I do.'

'Well, I didn't,' Lisa said. 'I thought addiction didn't happen
to people like us.'

I couldn't say anything. Nothing polite, anyway. The
Forest's one-percent believed they were exempt from the
problems that haunted ordinary people, including addiction,
suicide and crime.

Lisa continued. 'Now I see that Barb must have been
secretly looking for another doctor who would prescribe
more pills. I did know that Dr Bartlett here in the Forest
refused to give her more pills and warned her that oxy was
dangerous. Barb was so mad she quit going to her.

'Barb found another doctor in a dodgy neighborhood in St.
Louis. He prescribed the pills she needed. And she was fine
again.

'But as the months went on, I noticed more problems. Yes,
Barb lost the baby weight, but she kept on losing, until
she was too thin. She hardly ate. She didn't go to the gym or
have her hair done at Killer Cuts, and Barb was starting to
go gray.'

Lisa confided this last information in hushed tones, as if
refusing to cover gray hair was as bad as using oxy. This
time, I had to say something, or I might snap at this sheltered,
well-meaning woman.

'Did you notice any other changes, possibly in her
behavior?' I asked.

'Yes. Lots. We have a group of girls in the Forest – four of us, all about the same age – and we go to lunches, dinners, and our clubs. Barb quit going out with our group and dropped out of the clubs. She'd skip the meetings at the last minute, saying she didn't feel well. Also, Barb used to chair the neighborhood holiday party. She had the best ideas! She quit that, too. We miss her. I miss her.'

Lisa's voice was soft and sad. I realized she'd been mourning the loss of her friend for a long time.

'Did Barb like living in this neighborhood?' I asked.

'She learned to like it. She didn't really want a house this big. She would have been happy with a much smaller home.'

'Did Barbara do her own decorating?'

'Oh, yes.' Lisa eyes sparkled. 'She loved doing Olive's room.'

'The master bedroom was, uh . . .' I searched for the right word. 'Unusual.'

'No, it was horrible.' Lisa didn't mince words. 'I told her, "Barb, I don't know how you can sleep in that room – it's so loud." Barb laughed and said to me, "I know. I just turn the lights out when I want to sleep."' A ghost of a smile crossed Lisa's face as she remembered her friend.

'Why did Barb spend all that money to make an ugly room?' There didn't seem to be any connection between the loving mother who created the princess bedroom and that hideous master bedroom.

Lisa smiled, and almost looked like a young girl. 'Barb told me she did it on purpose, to keep Allen away. She said, "He won't come near me in that room." Allen hated the new master bedroom and slept in a guest room. That was fine with Barb.'

'Why?'

'This is really personal.' Lisa looked serious. 'I told you he wanted sex the day after Barb came home from the hospital. The day after! He said he'd gone without sex for months and it was her "duty." Like we were living in the 1800s. She refused, so he raped her. That's the only way to describe what he did. He raped Barb. She was still bleeding the next morning, and I had to take her to the ob-gyn.

'I told my husband – Dave's a lawyer, one of the good

ones.' She smiled at the mention of her husband's name. 'Dave wanted to help Barb file charges against Allen. He said she and Olive could live with us. Barb refused. Instead, she spent a fortune making that room ugly. She said Allen was very particular about sex. He only wanted it at night, right before bedtime. She made sure she was zonked at bedtime. I thought she was using sleeping pills to avoid him, but now I think she was drugging herself with oxy.'

'Was Allen always so bad?'

Lisa looked thoughtful, then poured me more coffee. There was only half a cup left. 'Oops. I better make us more.' She bustled around in the kitchen, preparing the coffee, then sat down.

'I suppose they were happy in the beginning. I mean, no one willingly marries a rapist. But then Allen's career took off like a rocket, and suddenly that was all he cared about. He went into work early and came home late. They had no social life unless it helped his job.

'Allen insisted on buying that huge house because it's next to the new Du Pres home.'

'Victoria Du Pres?' I said.

'Do you know her?'

'I've met Victoria.' I kept my answer noncommittal. I didn't want to discuss Tom Lockridge's death investigation. 'I heard she and her husband were building a new house, but I didn't realize it was here in the estates. When will Victoria's house be finished?'

'I don't know,' Lisa said. 'The contractor told me Victoria and her husband ran out of money.'

'A Du Pres ran out of money?' I couldn't keep the disbelief out of my voice.

'I know.' Lisa's eyes were wide with excitement. She loved imparting this juicy gossip. 'But the work on the house has definitely stopped. For at least two months.'

'Did Barbara know Victoria?'

'No,' Lisa said, 'and neither did Allen. But he was impressed by the Du Pres name.

'Allen wanted to have a big party to welcome the Du Pres to the neighborhood. Naturally, he expected Barb to do the cooking. She was a first-rate cook. Barb took lots of classes, and could make anything from Northern Italian to Thai. She would cook dinners for ten, twelve or twenty people from Allen's office. Her crown roast was famous.

'After Barb hurt her back, Allen started complaining she didn't want to host more dinners. He insisted on inviting the new CEO over for dinner, even though Barb said she was too sick to cook. So she served hamburgers – from McDonald's! Allen was livid, and this time I didn't blame him.'

'Really?' I raised an eyebrow.

Lisa gave me a small smile. 'OK, I sort of did. But he should have listened.

'Allen said the least Barb could do was go to the company events – the endless cocktail parties. She went to the last company event back in December. She pulled herself together to get ready and looked nice. Really nice. The party was at the Ritz in St. Louis. Barb passed out on a sofa in the lobby. Allen had trouble reviving her. He took her home and told everyone she was sick. His colleagues believe Barb has some kind of mysterious wasting disease.'

Sadly, that was true. But Barb's disease might have been cured if her husband had put her in rehab.

'Allen gets a lot of sympathy at work for having an invalid wife,' Lisa said.

'After the December party, Barb became more secretive. She would disappear for an afternoon, or sometimes over-night. She'd usually leave Olive with me. No matter how bad things got, Barb was a good mother.

'I figured out that Barb was going to more doctors to buy her pills. I'd check the odometer on her car. Sometimes she'd go as far as two-hundred-fifty miles.

'By this time, I realized that Barb didn't have the flu. She was using drugs.'

'How did you find out?' I asked.

'One day, I was at her house and she had to take Olive upstairs for a nap. Barb said, "Lisa, if you want another Coke, get a can out of the fridge." I did, but the top came off – the whole top. Inside were a bunch of gold pills. They had "40" on one side and "OC" on the other. I photographed the pills with my phone and looked them up online. Those were forty-milligram OxyContin pills. Barb was hiding them in a stash safe. I put everything back and found a real can of Coke.

'Now I was worried. Every time I went to Barb's house, I'd check another place. The aspirin bottle in the downstairs powder room had no aspirin, just white OxyContin pills. What if someone took those by mistake? The last straw was when I saw a cut-glass candy dish with different colored pills – yellow, green, pink, red – all different strengths of oxy, on a shelf in the den. Olive couldn't reach that high. Not yet. But what if she climbed up and got those pills? They looked like candy.

'Barb had a serious habit. I tried to talk to her about it, but she laughed it off. I wasn't laughing. Not any more. My once-pretty friend was wearing rags and she badly needed a bath. She looked like a homeless woman.

'I talked to my husband about the problem. Dave said Barb needed professional help and we should try an intervention. He knew the names of some good rehab clinics. We decided to wait until Allen came home from work for our intervention. It was nearly eight o'clock when he arrived.

'I said to Dave, "I might lose my friend if this doesn't work." Dave told me, "Barb is so bad, Lisa, you're going to lose her anyway. If she doesn't lay off the oxy, she's going to OD."

'Dave and I went over to Barb and Allen's home for the intervention. It went even worse than I feared. Far worse. Barb cried and denied she used oxy. Allen began shouting, "No wife of mine would abuse drugs!" He said I was crazy and should butt out of his life. Then he threw Dave and me out of their house and screamed that he'd sue us for slander.

'I went home and cried. Barb wouldn't talk to me for a week. If she saw me when she came outside, she ignored me.

'A week later, she came over here with Olive. I could tell Barb was on drugs. She was happy – too happy. More like euphoric. Her pupils were pinpoints. She acted like nothing was wrong. I didn't want to start a fight in front of Olive, and she must have known that. Barb was over here several more times, and she always brought Olive with her. I didn't know what to do.'

Lisa was crying again. She made no effort to stop the tears. I let her cry, and then said, 'Why do you think Allen wouldn't face his wife's illness?'

Lisa's face was a kaleidoscope of emotions: first anger, then pain, then sorrow. 'Personally, I think Allen wanted Barb to die, so he could have a more suitable wife. He—'

With that, the front door burst open, and a furious man stormed into the kitchen. He was almost as tall as me, and he wore a well-cut dark business suit. His blond hair was short, and he moved like a bully.

He was shaking with fury. 'Lisa, you interfering bitch!' he shouted. 'Where's my daughter?'

Lisa rose from her chair and fought to keep her voice level. 'Allen, you know perfectly well where Olive is. The police told you she's staying here with me.'

'You had no business taking my daughter! I told you to stay away from my family.'

'I found Barb's body.' Now Lisa's voice sounded small and fearful.

Allen made a grab for Lisa's shoulder, but I rose and stepped between them. 'Mr Blanchette, I realize you must be upset, but you need to calm down.'

'Who the hell are you?'

'I'm Angela Richman, the death investigator for your wife's case.'

'Why are you listening to this woman's lies?'

'She's a witness. She found your wife.'

'Why didn't you talk to me?' He was screaming again.

'You were called at twelve thirty today. Why didn't you come home as soon as you were informed about Mrs Blanchette's death?'

'I don't have to answer to you, but I had to give an important speech.'

'More important than the death of your wife?' I said. 'It's almost five o'clock.'

'Like I said, that's none of your business. But one o'clock

or five o'clock, she's still dead. Nothing's going to change that. Now, Lisa, give me my daughter!'

I didn't think Allen Blanchette should be anywhere near his little girl – not in this mood. But I couldn't call Greiman for help. He knew Allen was important in the Forest. The detective would do whatever this bully wanted.

'Why don't you let Olive sleep, Allen?' Lisa's voice was thin and quavery. 'Her grandparents are arriving tonight and they'll take her back to Florida.'

'Why should I leave my child here?' He was shouting louder. He loomed over Lisa.

I said, 'Because I'll make sure your employer knows you didn't go home for more than four hours after you were notified that your wife was dead. What will that do to your career?'

Allen stomped out of Lisa's house, slamming the front door so hard the glass rattled.

TWENTY-SIX

I watched Allen Blanchette stalk across Lisa's lawn to his own home and go inside. Lisa was still trembling from the bully's verbal assault after he'd invaded her kitchen.

'Are you OK?' I poured Lisa more coffee.

She nodded and tried to hold back her tears, but couldn't. 'You see what he's like. And Barb wouldn't leave him.' She took a long drink of coffee, but she was still shivering in the warm kitchen. I found a sweater on a hook by the door and gave it to her.

'Thank you.' She slipped into the sweater. 'I shouldn't get so upset.'

'Of course, you should. That man is frightening. Did Allen Blanchette physically abuse his wife?'

Lisa looked at me, her face streaked with tears. 'Isn't rape and intimidation abuse?'

Now it was my turn to apologize. 'Sorry. Dumb question.'

I checked my iPad. Lisa had answered all the questions on the form. I had to return to the scene. 'You've had some terrible shocks today, Lisa. You found your friend's body, and Allen Blanchette threatened you. Is there someone you can call to stay with you?'

'I just called my husband, and Dave's coming home. He'll be here any minute. Do you have to go back to that house now that Blanchette is there?'

'Yes. I have to interview him.'

'Don't be alone with Allen Blanchette.' She looked worried.

'I won't. There will be plenty of techs and cops around.' I gave Lisa my business card. 'If there's a problem, call my cell phone. If Blanchette comes back, call nine-one-one.'

She pasted on a brave smile and said, 'I'll be OK. Thank you.'

As I rolled my DI case back over to the Blanchette mansion, I saw a black SUV roaring down the street, way over the speed limit on the quiet cul-de-sac. Lisa rushed outside, waving her arms. As the vehicle pulled into the driveway, I heard Lisa calling, 'Dave! Dave! You're home.' Even this far away, I could hear the relief and joy in her voice.

At the Blanchette home, I stopped to chat with Paul, the uniform in charge of the crime scene log. He looked bored sitting on the porch, and he was chatty as ever. 'The husband just came back home,' he said. 'Greiman called him about twelve thirty and Mr Blanchette finally showed up around five. What a sorry excuse for a husband. I can't imagine why he was so late.'

I knew why, but I wanted more information. 'Couldn't the police find him?'

'Oh, yeah. They tracked him down at some conference in Clayton. He said he had an important speech to make. Can you imagine? What's more important than your wife?'

'What did Greiman say about Mr Blanchette's excuse?'

'Oh, he was real polite, like always.'

If you're important, I thought. I'm glad I didn't say it. I studied Paul's bright blue eyes and boyish face, but there was no sign of snark.

Paul had more news. 'When Mr Blanchette got home, he didn't seem shocked or surprised by his wife being dead. He just kinda shrugged. Then Greiman said their little girl, Olive, was staying with the neighbor lady next door and Mr Blanchette stormed out of the house.'

'I know,' I said. 'I was next door with Lisa. He yelled at her.'

'Why would he do that?'

I told Paul a condensed version and he said, 'I don't know, Angela. I heard that poor Mrs Blanchette overdosed, but it sounds to me like her husband is partly responsible. He should have at least tried to get her into rehab.'

'I agree. But he's done nothing illegal.'

'Maybe not. He won't get away with it,' Paul said. 'Your sins have a way of catching up to you.' He gave me a Sunday-school smile.

I wondered how long Paul would have that attitude now that he wore a uniform. I'd seen too many guilty people go unpunished and the innocent suffer. But I didn't want to turn bright, blue-eyed Paul into a cynic.

'Greiman let Mr Blanchette go in the middle of the interview?' I asked.

'Yeah. He just came back. The detective is talking to him in the living room.'

'Where's Nitpicker?'

'She's working in the kitchen. She's found a humongous number of pills so far, and she's still finding more.'

I put on a clean pair of booties and gloved up again, then headed for the kitchen. It smelled slightly of sour milk.

Nitpicker was emptying the kitchen cabinet to the left of the sink. On the kitchen island, which was bigger than a life raft, were ranks of items in evidence bags: canned goods, Clorox bleach, and a loaf of bread. The tech's lime green hair was drooping a bit this late in the day, and she looked weary.

I filled her in on Lisa's interview, as well as Allen Blanchette's threatening visit. I also told her the rationale behind the glaring Versace bedroom.

Nitpicker kept her voice low. 'That man talking to Greiman in the living room raped his wife?'

I nodded. 'According to Lisa.'

'He's the scum of the earth. But that explains why I found no men's belongings in the master bedroom.'

'Lisa says he's been sleeping in a guest room.'

'Yep. The one at the end of the upstairs hall. And he's not sleeping alone. I found a different kind of stash there. A secret compartment that contained condoms. I think he's got something on the side.'

'That doesn't surprise me. By the way, how come the DEA isn't using drug dogs?'

Nitpicker put down a real can of green beans, and laughed. 'Because there's fentanyl here. It's highly poisonous to dogs. A couple of sniffer dogs got sick searching for fentanyl during a bust in Florida – they accidently snorted small amounts and nearly OD'ed, so sniffer dogs aren't used in fentanyl searches. It's too dangerous.'

'But humans are OK?'

'There are more of us and we're cheaper.' Nitpicker laughed and ran her fingers through her green hair. Now it looked like an uncut lawn.

'This search is endless,' Nitpicker said. 'I checked the Roman bathroom and found two more drug stashes. Six pills in a tube of ChapStick and four in a Secret deodorant stick.'

'Love the name on that last one,' I said.

'I've hit the mother lode in the kitchen. Everything bagged on that island is a stash safe. It's all been photographed, videoed, bagged and tagged. So far, the pill count is two hundred and sixty-eight.'

I checked out the evidence bags on the granite-topped island. A round loaf of bread caught my eye. 'Is that bread real?'

'No, but it sure looks like it. The stash safe is in the bottom. Ten pills.'

'Those canned goods have authentic-looking labels.' I pointed to the bagged fruit cocktail, whole kernel corn, and green beans – all Del Monte brand.

'Those are real cans,' she said. 'But they have safes in their false bottoms.'

'It takes a truly twisted person to turn comfort food like Campbell's chicken noodle soup into a stash safe,' I said. 'Is nothing sacred?'

'Nope.' Nitpicker was enjoying this. 'Look at this Heinz baked beans safe. Potheads get a giggle out of that "baked." The Morton Salt and the jar of gourmet seasoning had more pills.'

Now Nitpicker was back pulling items out of the kitchen cabinet. 'Hey, Angela, here's an oldie but goodie. A Pringles potato chip safe.' She photographed the tube of chips, then pulled off the round plastic lid. 'See, real chips on the top, but if you unscrew the bottom . . .' Another rainbow of pills poured into her hands.

'I can't believe there are so many kinds of safes,' I said.

Nitpicker gave me a mischievous wink. 'Didn't you use one when you were in high school? To hide your weed?'

'No, I didn't smoke. I was too boring.' I felt slightly ashamed that I was such a goody-two-shoes.

'I had one,' she said. 'A Coke can. But I made my own safe and kept it in my room. These safes are parents' nightmares. Teens use them to hide their stash. Their older brothers and sisters take them to their college dorms.'

Nitpicker continued her tutorial. 'Most of the safes here in this kitchen are used by your garden variety suburban stoner.'

'Do they work?' I asked. 'You know what to look for, but what about other people?'

'Think about it, Angela. Have you ever said, "I'm dying for a can of fruit cocktail"?'

'Nope,' I said. 'Not ever.'

'Right,' she said. 'So it's unlikely anyone would stumble on your stash hidden in that fruit cocktail can. I've never seen a chocolate candy box stash safe.'

I checked the kitchen clock. It was almost six p.m. 'What can I do to help?'

I didn't like Nitpicker's grin. 'You get the fridge. If you want. It's loaded with canned drinks and every single one is suspect. Have fun.'

On the counter next to the fridge, an overturned gallon of milk had splattered and dripped on to the floor, next to a flipped over yellow box of Kix cereal, proclaiming the corn puffs were 'Kid tested, parent approved.' The cereal box was nearly empty. It looked like Olive had eaten some food while her mother lay dead upstairs.

I photographed the spilled milk and cereal, and took samples of both.

The silver refrigerator was a monster, probably twenty-eight cubic feet, with a narrow freezer on the left. On the right side, three shelves were crammed with canned beer, soda, water, and energy drinks.

I photographed the inside of the fridge. My fingers were numb with cold by the time I went through the drinks, but I found five safes: Dr Pepper, Bud Light, Red Bull, A&W root beer and Mountain Dew cans. Plus two more Coke can safes. In the side shelves, I found a Kraft Mayo safe. I counted the pills and bagged them all. There were about three cases of real drinks.

The rest of the fridge contained surprisingly little food – a dozen eggs, a loaf of wheat bread, butter, deli ham, American cheese slices, a plastic container of leftover pasta in red sauce, another container of apple sauce, and a full, unopened gallon of milk. Apples and oranges filled one produce bin.

I opened the other bin and saw a bag of green onions past their prime, a shriveled green pepper, and a head of iceberg lettuce.

'Ah, hah!' I said. 'Iceberg lettuce. I know that's a safe.'

Nope. It was real lettuce, and slightly slimy at that.

When I finished the fridge, it was going on seven o'clock. Nitpicker had found and bagged three more safes: a green can of Comet cleanser, a metal water bottle designed to hold water plus pills in a secret compartment, and a black Sharpie that really wrote, but had room for three pills.

'I've finished the fridge,' I said. 'Anything else?'

'I think we've almost finished with this kitchen,' she said. 'And I turn into a pumpkin – an unpaid pumpkin – at eight o'clock. I'll have to come back tomorrow. I still didn't get all the rooms.'

'That means a uniform is going to have to camp out here overnight,' I said. Chain of custody required that someone stay on the premises to keep the warrant legal.

'Are you coming back tomorrow, Angela?'

'Nope, I have the day off,' I said. 'And Evarts won't give me overtime for this project. I still have to talk to the new widower tonight.'

'He's a piece of work,' Nitpicker said. 'Do you want me in the room?'

'Yes, please. I don't want to be alone with him.'

Allen Blanchette was in the living room, sitting in one of the pale gold damask chairs, texting. Nitpicker was examining the volumes in a bookcase, searching for more book safes. I stood in front of him, and said, 'Hello, Mr Blanchette. I'm sorry for your loss.'

He ignored me and kept texting. He didn't seem upset or lost in grief.

'I have a few questions for my death investigation report,' I said.

He continued ignoring me.

'You can answer my questions now, Mr Blanchette. Or I can call your office and ask for their help. I'll also ask if they can help explain that four-hour gap between the time you were notified and when you arrived home.'

A long sigh. Then Blanchette began whining like a spoiled child. 'You don't understand. I'm the victim here. Barbara and I had an agreement: She would stay home and keep house and help my career, and I would let her have a child.'

Let her have a child, I thought. Like letting her have a puppy.

'The sooner you answer my questions, the sooner this will be over.'

'Go ahead.' He sighed dramatically again. His tone was martyred.

'What is Mrs Blanchette's age?'

'Thirty.'

'Her date of birth?'

'I don't have that information. You can call my assistant, Tracy.'

'You don't know your wife's birthday?'

'No. Tracy keeps track of that and buys Barbara a nice present. Same with our anniversary.'

'Do you know your wife's Social Security number?'

'Of course not. Tracy has that.' Allen gave me Tracy's phone number. I nodded my thanks so I wouldn't snap at the entitled jerk.

'When was the last time you saw your wife, Mr Blanchette?'

'Thursday morning, about seven o'clock. She was in the kitchen feeding Olive. I told her I'd be back Sunday night. As it is, I had to leave my conference early.' Resentment flared in his small, brown eyes.

'Did you know that your wife was addicted to OxyContin?'

Now he sat up, his face red with rage. 'My wife was not an addict. Say that again, and I'll sue you six ways from Sunday.' I could see Nitpicker hovering protectively nearby.

He jabbed a meaty finger in my face and said, 'I would never marry an addict. Never! So quit saying it.'

'I'm sure Barbara wasn't an addict when you married her,' I said. 'But she became one.' I tried to keep the fear out of my voice.

'No she didn't. She took OxyContin because she had a pinched nerve in her back.'

'That's how it started, Mr Blanchette. But your wife became addicted. She was sick. Addiction is an illness.'

He was seething with anger. 'No, it's not. Addiction is a weakness. We are people of good character and we live next door to the Du Pres. We do not have addicts in this neighborhood.'

He was screaming now – spitting, he was so mad. That's when Nitpicker brought over a Bible. Inside was a safe with a stash of pink OxyContin.

'Is that so, Mr Blanchette?' she said. 'Look at the Good Book. The truth is in the Bible.'

TWENTY-SEVEN

The next morning, I went back to working with my half of Jace's list of the Christmas ball vendors. I'd slogged through the rest of the fifty business names that I recognized by nine o'clock. My eyes were aching from studying the numbers, but I kept pushing. Working with Ray Greiman yesterday gave me an added incentive. Jace had to crack this case.

So far, all the vendors that Cynthia had hired for the Christmas ball were legit. All the checks were signed by her lawyer, Wesley Desloge, who had financial power of attorney for Cynthia. Nothing suspicious so far.

Now I started on the twenty-eight unknown vendors. The first two were fine. Then I got to the third: Brantham Consulting, Inc., which was paid a whopping 27,930 dollars.

Brantham Consulting? Never heard of it. I started a feverish search, and couldn't find a mention of the company anywhere. Brantham didn't seem to exist on the internet. Not even a website. Weird. What kind of consultancy didn't have a website?

Odder still, the company didn't exist on any social media, including Facebook, Twitter, Instagram, LinkedIn, and TikTok.

That 'Inc.' in the name was supposed to mean the company was incorporated, but there were no official documents filed with the Missouri Secretary of State about the status – or lack thereof – of Brantham Consulting, Inc. I checked Delaware, another popular state to incorporate, then Nevada and Wyoming. Nothing. Too bad the US didn't have a national registry of incorporated companies. As a last resort, I searched Google for anything related to this name: an article, a blog, a press release, even a hashtag on some site. Nothing.

Brantham was smelling fishier by the moment. Why was this anonymous company charging 27,930 dollars for consulting? What kind of consulting?

The file from Jace contained a scanned invoice that answered that last question. The invoice said, 'Brantham Consulting: Select Financial Services.'

It said Brantham billed the charity for:

42 hours of financial services re: Xmas Ball @ $700 per hour.

Minus 5% discount for charity = $27,930.

Those were select financial services indeed. Seven hundred dollars an hour? Definitely not minimum wage work.

The company had no address, just a post office box and a phone number.

I called the number and got a recording. A man's voice said, 'You have reached the offices of Brantham Consulting. Please leave a message.'

I hung up. I knew that voice. Wesley Desloge. He was the lawyer hired by Tom Lockridge to help his wife, Cynthia, with the Christmas ball's finances. The same lawyer who also helped himself to his patron's wife. Was this snake skimming money from a nonprofit? And generously giving them a five percent 'charity' discount?

I found the cancelled check in the file. Sure enough, it was signed by good old Wesley Desloge. He was paying himself.

I called Jace, nearly breathless with excitement. 'Jace! I think I've found something. On my list. Number sixty-two, Brantham Consulting. No listing, and no footprint on the internet.'

Jace cut in. 'Whoa, Angela, slow down. You're talking so fast I can't understand you. Can you take it from the top again?'

So I did. This time, I spoke slowly and told my story in detail: I believed that Wesley Desloge was skimming money from the charity ball using a fake consulting company. He was already being paid by Tom Lockridge, but now he was also paying himself. And quite handsomely, at the charity's expense.

'Terrific, Angela,' Jace said. 'We may get that scumbag yet. What was that amount again?'

'The bill says it's 27,930 dollars. And the check has been cashed.'

'Perfect!' Jace said. 'According to Missouri law, if anyone

steals more than twenty-five thousand dollars, it's a Class B felony. Wesley is looking at up to fifteen years in jail, and a twenty-thousand-dollar fine. This guy is an idiot. If he'd kept his bill under twenty-five thousand dollars, it would have only been a year in jail and a thousand-dollar fine.'

The discouragement had vanished from Jace's voice. Now he was energized. 'I want to talk to Cynthia, and then see Wes. Are you working today, Angela?'

'No, I have today off. I'm devoting it to helping you.'

'Then will you come with me? At least to see Cynthia? She may say more if you're there.'

'Of course, if she'll talk without her lawyer present.'

'She will.' I caught the determination in Jace's voice. 'I'll meet you at her place in twenty.'

I threw on my black DI suit and was out the door. As I drove to Cynthia's marble pile, I thought it was good to hear Jace sounding so confident.

The house had an oddly abandoned look today. Jace was already there, waiting in his unmarked car. We knocked on the massive front door, and the housekeeper, Mrs Timmons, answered. She was wearing her white uniform and looked strong and healthy. She smiled when she saw us.

'Mrs Timmons, you look so much better than the last time I saw you,' I told her.

'I wanted to thank you for your help,' she said. 'That asthma attack was scary, but I wasn't sick. Not really. It was the shock of poor Mr Tom's murder, God rest his soul.'

'Are you OK working here with Mrs Lockridge?' I asked.

'I need the money.' Her blunt words chopped off any further questions. 'I'll get Mrs Lockridge for you. Would you like to wait in the living room?'

We followed Mrs Timmons, our footsteps echoing in the vast marble hall, to the living room, ablaze with gold. Jace and I sat on cloud-soft damask chairs and watched the painted cupids frolicking overhead.

The detective was impressed by the overwrought magnificence. 'This is sort of a preview of heaven,' he said.

'Marie Antoinette's heaven,' I said, and Jace laughed. The spell was broken. Now he was the shrewd detective I knew.

Cynthia entered the room in full widow regalia. She wore a severe high-collared, long-sleeve black dress, no jewelry, and her dark hair was pulled into a tight bun. Her face and hair were covered by a shoulder-length black veil, suitable for a state funeral. The somber covering made her face more difficult to read.

She sat in the chair opposite us and spoke so slowly, I wondered if she was on tranquilizers. 'My attorney, Wesley Desloge, says I shouldn't talk to you unless he's present.'

'You can call him now,' Jace said. 'But I don't want you to talk. Just listen for a moment. Can you do that?'

Cynthia nodded.

'Did your husband pay Wesley Desloge to oversee the financial transactions for the Christmas ball?'

Cynthia nodded again.

'Did Wesley Desloge ask you to sign a financial power of attorney, so he could sign all the checks that pay the bills for the charity?'

She nodded a third time.

'Have you ever heard of a company called Brantham Consulting Inc.?'

Cynthia shook her head no. I couldn't get a read on her face, but the soft silk folds of her veil whispered sadness.

Jace kept his voice soft as he delivered the killer question. She had to lean forward to hear him. 'Did you know that the 27,930 dollars billed to Brantham Consulting actually went to a ghost company set up by Wesley Desloge? Do you know he's skimmed nearly thirty thousand dollars from your charity ball?'

Cynthia was silent. One beat. Two. Then she burst out, 'No! He wouldn't do that!'

'Oh, but he did, Mrs Lockridge,' Jace said. 'And word's going to get out to all your fancy Forest friends unless you cooperate.'

I waited for Cynthia to say the magic words, 'I want a lawyer.' Instead, she started talking.

'Wes knew how important this Christmas ball was for me,' she said. 'Tom wanted me to be a success in Forest society, and I've worked too hard to get to be the co-chair. I was surprised how complicated the job was. The Christmas ball has so much money and there were so many details – the decorations, the food, the music, the servers, the corporate sponsors. The list went on and on.'

The barrier of the veil seemed to make Cynthia feel safe. She kept talking and Jace and I didn't interrupt.

'Wes knew I was overwhelmed,' she said, 'and he said he'd try to make my life easier. He'd handle the financial part. If I gave him power of attorney, he'd sign the checks. I thanked him. I was so busy planning, that handling the finances was a big help. Besides, he gave me the list of companies to review before he signed the checks, so I knew what was being sent out.'

Except Cynthia didn't check that list too carefully, and Wes helped himself to nearly thirty thousand dollars.

'I can't believe Wes did that to me.' Cynthia was weeping now. She brought out a black lace handkerchief and lifted the veil to dab her eyes. I caught a glimpse of her pale face. I was pretty sure she wasn't crying for her murdered husband.

When the veil was safely back down, Jace asked another question. This one was bolder. 'You said you were overwhelmed running this charity ball. But you used to be the office manager of Mr Lockridge's construction company. You were paid to handle lots of details, including the financial ones. Didn't you work on the books at your job?'

'I was supposed to work on the books,' Cynthia said. 'That was part of my job description. But I didn't. Not really. Tom couldn't afford an accountant, but he was good with numbers. So we would stay late and work on the books together. That's when I started bringing him meals, and we became, well, close. My lack of math skills brought me my husband.'

I wasn't buying Cynthia's 'I'm a complete ditz' act. She struck me as a calculating little number. I took a chance and asked an awkward question. 'Cynthia, did you have an affair with Wesley?'

Jace's eyes bulged. Cynthia stayed stone silent.

I started talking again. 'I'm a widow myself. I understand how lonely life can get. And Wes is an attractive man. I'm not judging.'

More silence. Now I was afraid Cynthia would ask for a lawyer. Jace and I both held our breath.

Finally, Cynthia broke the silence. 'Yes. I did. I fell for his slick ways. I was stupid.' She sounded ashamed. 'My husband, Tom, was a good man, but he was so much older than me. Thirty-four years. At first, life was perfect. Tom treated me like a princess. Then, well, as he got older and heavier, he changed. He liked to wake up early and go to bed early. And there wasn't much going on in the bedroom. I'm still a young woman, and I wanted love, and Wes . . . well, I'm ashamed to say that I said yes to him. We had an affair, but then Wes got serious. He wanted to marry me, and I said no. I realized that I still loved my husband.'

And his money and your new social position, I thought. But this time I kept silent.

'So I ended the affair, about a month before Tom died,' Cynthia said. 'Wes was very angry. He kept trying to get me to change my mind, but I wouldn't. He threatened to tell the other members of the committee that we'd . . . we'd been more than friends. I said I didn't care. Our romance was over. Through.'

'Then why did you call Wesley Desloge when you found your husband dead, Mrs Lockridge?' Jace said.

'I panicked,' she said. 'I didn't know any lawyers except Wes. I was frightened. Wes came right over and took charge, and I needed that. I wanted it. But I don't want Wes, not any more.'

'Do you think Wes killed your husband, Mrs Lockridge?' Jace asked.

Another silence. Then she lifted her veil and showed her tear-streaked face.

'Yes,' she said.

'I *know* he did.' She emphasized that word 'know.'

'Wes paid those burglars – that horrible Spider-Man – to come here and kill poor Tom. Wes knew how to get inside this house and where I would be that night.

'Wesley Desloge killed my husband.'

TWENTY-EIGHT

Jace and I escaped the Widow Lockridge, wrapped in her woeful black. I was glad to leave the bizarrely overdecorated room with its ceiling of cavorting cupids. Once outside the opulent marble mansion, the morning seemed brighter and the genuine gold of the sun looked good. Jace looked surprisingly cheerful after being so dejected these last few days, and I felt encouraged by what we'd learned.

Standing by our cars in the driveway, I said, 'Well, that was useful, wasn't it? Cynthia Lockridge says Wes killed her husband.'

'Says. And she didn't give us a shred of proof,' Jace said. 'We can't arrest him on her word.'

Now my enthusiasm started melting away. 'Especially since Wes is her ex-lover,' I said.

'We can't even prove he's really her ex,' Jace said. 'Cynthia went running to Wes as soon as her husband was murdered. If their affair was over, why would she run to her husband's killer?'

'Her body language confirmed what she told us, Jace. Cynthia didn't like Wes, not any more. Remember when we interviewed her the morning Tom Lockridge was murdered? She was sitting as far away from Wes as she could, practically perching on the sofa arm.'

'In Wes's house,' Jace said. 'Where she spent the night. Would you spend the night with your husband's killer? She must have other friends. One of those society ladies would have taken her in. Or she could have stayed at the Forest Inn.'

'It was late,' I said. 'She wasn't thinking clearly.' And why was I making excuses for this woman's stupid decisions? 'But I could tell she didn't want him touching her when she sat next to him on that couch in his living room.'

'Too bad body language isn't admissible in court,' Jace said.

'Anyway, thanks to you, I now have some leverage when I talk to Wes. I can ask about the 28,000 dollar payment to that phony consulting company.'

'At least I've done something to help the investigation,' I said.

'You've done a lot. Far more than the new death investigator would do. Have you met her? Natalie Upton?'

'No, Jace. I rarely go into the office. Unlike most death investigators, I've lost my desk to my boss's Swedish shower.'

'Oh, yeah.' He laughed. 'I remember that story. Well, you will meet Natalie. She's very professional. And God help her, working in the Forest.'

'Why?' I'd been behind in my gossip. I'd have to check in with Katie. Anything to avoid the office.

'That's all I'm going to say. I'm heading to Wes Desloge's office next, Angela, but it's too dangerous for you to go with me.'

He was right. 'Normally, Jace, the phrase "it's too dangerous for you" would be fighting words, but this time I agree. If Wes complains to Chief Butkus that I was with you at that interview, we could both lose our jobs. Besides, you may not want me there when you "persuade" Wes to talk.'

Jace grinned. He had the old fire back now that he had a lead. 'Me? I'd never do anything illegal.'

'Right.' Actually, I wasn't sure. 'I have plans of my own. I'm supposed to meet Debbie Carlone, the office manager of the Chouteau Forest Construction Company, for lunch today.'

'Lunch,' he said, sounding wistful. 'I won't see lunch for at least another three hours. Where are you going?'

'I'm meeting Debbie at Luigi's, that little Italian place near her office. I'll see if I can find out anything useful for us.'

'Lucky you,' Jace said. 'I'd much rather be eating lunch at Luigi's than trying to shake something out of a slimy lawyer.'

'I'll eat some pasta for you.' I got into my car, waved goodbye and drove off.

I made it to Luigi's long before Debbie. I was nearly half an hour early. A dark-haired woman in her forties greeted me at the door. 'Welcome to Luigi's. I'm Anna. My husband and I own this restaurant.' Anna showed me to a corner table, with a view of the asphalt parking lot. I didn't care where Anna seated me, as long as I could inhale the glorious aroma of Luigi's homemade garlic tomato sauce. She delivered a basket of warm bread and a dish of garlicky olive oil. 'The bread is right out of the oven,' she said.

While I waited for Debbie, I dipped the crusty bread into the oil and thought about the office manager. Would Debbie kill her boss, Tom Lockridge?

I didn't think so, but she did shoot her stepfather. For good reason. At least, that's how I understood the story. Word was he'd been abusing Debbie for years, and one day she'd finally had enough and put three shots in his head with a .22, while he was sleeping. The police didn't charge her.

But did Debbie suddenly snap and shoot Tom, her boss? Why? She was grateful he'd hired her away from a low-paid job at a convenience store. She told me she'd have a hard time getting a job that paid as well as this one. No, Debbie wouldn't hurt Tom. Unless he was a hound who harassed her. And I'd never heard a whisper that questioned Tom Lockridge's fidelity. Cynthia, yes. But not Tom. And in a small town like the Chouteau Forest, word would get around.

By the time Anna showed Debbie to the table, I'd not only mentally cleared her of murder, I'd eaten the whole loaf of bread. Debbie ordered the homemade bow-tie pasta with red sauce. I went for the caprese salad with fresh basil. We both ordered a glass of the house red. I sheepishly asked for more bread. Anna graciously did not mention that I'd eaten the whole loaf.

Debbie wore a pink pantsuit that flattered her creamy skin, and oddly enough, looked good with her orangish hair. Today, she seemed subdued and sad.

'I like that color on you, Debbie. But you look kind of down.'

'I am,' she said. 'I'm waiting for word from Mrs Lockridge and Victoria about what's going to become of me. Right now, they've asked me to run the office. They still don't know if the company is going to be sold or if it will fold.'

'You said Mrs Lockridge and Victoria. Are they making this decision jointly?'

Debbie looked surprised. 'Oh, yes. Mrs Lockridge under-
stands that Victoria feels very sentimental about her father's
business. She also knows that Victoria is good with money.
So they're working together.'

'It must be hard to plan anything when you're in limbo,' I
said. Anna brought our wine glasses, and Debbie took a good
stiff drink before she answered.

'Tell me about it. I don't know whether to look for another
job or try to hang on to this one and hope they'll find a good
buyer. My prospects aren't good for another job. I'm forty-one
and don't have a college education.'

'But you have experience,' I said. 'How long have you run
the construction company office?'

'About seven years.' She started to say something else, when
Anna arrived with our food. She grated Parmesan cheese over
Debbie's steaming plate of pasta, brought more bread, and
then left.

We ate our food in respectful silence for a few minutes.
Finally, I said, 'You were going to tell me something when
our food arrived.'

Debbie said, 'Can you keep this quiet?'

I had a mouthful of tomato and basil, so I nodded yes. I
didn't want to mention that I'd be telling Jace anything
important, and I didn't consider a nod a full lie. What if
Debbie didn't say anything useful?

I leaned in to listen. Debbie lowered her voice, even though
we were the only customers in the restaurant. 'As you've
probably guessed, our company isn't doing that well. We've
got the new CoffeeTime building and that's about it. Most of
our equipment is leased or rented. About all we have is the
goodwill and our name.'

'But it's a good name,' I said.

'Yes,' she said. 'Everyone loved Tom. But now that he's
gone, I'm not sure it's worth much. What I couldn't say when
you were at the office with that detective was that Tom has
been selling off our assets right and left to keep up with Mrs
Lockridge's demands for more money.'

'So the company's not worth as much as it was seven years
ago?' I took another forkful of tomato and mozzarella.

'Heck no,' Debbie said, dredging a piece of that new warm loaf through the olive oil. The bread looked tempting, but I'd already eaten an entire loaf. 'Not by a long shot. Most of his money was spent decorating that house. That's why he'd get so upset when Cynthia called and asked for more. He couldn't make her understand that he didn't have an endless supply of money.'

'Do you think Cynthia killed her husband for his money?' I was still eying that fresh, crusty bread.

'Oh, no,' Debbie said. 'Cynthia was greedy, but in her way, she loved her husband. She just loved money more.'

'And what about his daughter, Victoria?' I reached for the bread. Heck, life was short. No one knew that better than me.

'You do know that Victoria is my friend.' Suddenly Debbie's eyes looked hard. 'I would never say anything to hurt her.'

'Of course.' I backtracked quickly while I dredged my bread through the olive oil. 'I'd heard that Victoria didn't inherit anything from her father. Everything went to Tom's wife, Cynthia.'

Debbie smiled. 'That's right. Victoria wasn't greedy like Cynthia. She has her faults, but she cared about her father. She tried so hard to get him to eat healthy, but that was a lost cause. Tom enjoyed food – his kind of food. Her efforts to save him were all for nothing.'

'Right.' I could be dead tomorrow, I thought, as I helped myself to more bread.

'In a way, Tom's death turned out to be a blessing for Victoria.'

'A blessing?'

Debbie looked confused, and tried to erase her words with her hand. 'No, I didn't mean that. Victoria was heartbroken when Tom died, but his death did work out for her.'

'What do you mean?' Should I take that last piece of bread? I eyed the warm crusty treat, but Debbie got it first.

As she soaked her bread in olive oil, Debbie said. 'Tom had a two-million-dollar life insurance policy, and it's all going to Victoria. She's the beneficiary. He never changed that after he married Cynthia. Tom was about to cash in that policy to keep the business going.'

'So now the two million dollars goes to Victoria?' I finished up the last bite of my caprese salad. Debbie was also looking at an empty plate.

Anna appeared and said, 'Could I get you ladies any dessert?'

'Lunch is on me,' I said to Debbie. 'How about some tiramisu and coffee?'

I saw the first smile on her face that afternoon. I wondered if she'd been worried how she would pay for this lunch.

'Yes,' she said. 'Dessert sounds perfect.'

We played catch-up while we waited for our desserts – I told Debbie which of our classmates were married, divorced, or had babies on the way, and who was working and where.

When our desserts arrived, I asked Debbie, 'Did Victoria know that she was still the beneficiary of her father's life insurance?'

'Oh, yes. She was smart enough to keep quiet about it. Victoria knew if she ever mentioned the life insurance to Cynthia, she'd want that, too.'

'And Victoria knew her father was going to cash in the life insurance?'

'Yes.' Debbie took the last bite of her tiramisu, and I waited impatiently for her to finish it.

'Victoria and her father often talked about his business when they had their breakfasts. She tried to warn him he was spending too much on the house, but Tom was desperate to please his wife.' She looked and me and smiled. 'I think it's because as he got old, he couldn't please her in other ways, if you know what I mean.'

I nearly choked on my coffee. 'You knew he had problems in the bedroom?'

'Victoria told me. Tom was taking double amounts of Viagra. She was afraid her father would have a heart attack. And then he did have one, and he quit using the Viagra.'

Good lord. The Forest really was a fish bowl. Everyone did know everything about their neighbor. I took a long sip of coffee to recover from my shock that Debbie had such intimate knowledge of her employer.

'Do you know the name of Mr Lockridge's life insurance company?' I asked.

'Hm, not sure. Pacific Life. Prudential. Is it important?'

'It could be.' I shrugged. 'If it's not too much trouble, the name would be helpful.'

'I'll get it for you,' Debbie said. 'I'll check the files and text you the name later today.'

I asked for the check and paid it. We both agreed it was good to see each other and made a date for another lunch.

On the way out, I bought two loaves of that crusty bread. I had a date with Chris tonight. He was fixing dinner, but we could enjoy that bread together.

He didn't mind crumbs in bed.

TWENTY-NINE

I stopped by Supreme Bean and picked up two large black coffees – one for me and one for Katie. I could always bribe my friend with good coffee – she only drank the witch's brew at the ME's office out of desperation. It was only three o'clock. I had time for a quick gossip visit.

Katie was at her desk, working her way through a pile of paperwork. She smiled when she saw me – or maybe it was the coffee.

'What brings you here?' Katie grabbed for the coffee as if it would keep her from slipping off the edge of the world. She took a sip. 'You saved my life. I was seriously short of caffeine. But you're not the coffee fairy, Angela. Why are you here?'

Katie knew me too well. 'I have a gossip emergency. I need information.'

Katie savored her second sip of coffee. 'Anything. Within reason, of course.'

'I hear we have a new death investigator.'

Katie gave me her trouble-making smile. 'Yes, the Forest has hired Natalie Upton.'

'Upton, Upton,' I said. 'Who's she related to?' To get a job in the Forest, you usually had to know someone.

'Harrison Upton, president of Upton Industries.'

I raised an eyebrow at that news. 'Why would the daughter of a widget-making bigwig want to be a DI? Why isn't she at an Ivy League school?'

'Don't you start with the racist comments,' Katie said. 'Not all Asians go to college.'

'Natalie Upton is Asian?'

'Half Asian. Harrison married a California woman who was third-generation Chinese.'

'OK.' I stretched out my word. 'So what's the problem?'

'It's not a problem. Well, it is, but you know what I mean.

Natalie is beautiful. Movie star beautiful. She has her mother's Asian features.'

A light was dawning in my dim brain. 'And she's hearing every possible racist insult.'

'You guessed it. The half-wits she's encountered have asked her: why aren't you a doctor? What kind of Asian are you? Oh, and Trudi, the department secretary, thought she was complimenting Natalie when she said, "You speak English really good."'

'Oh, jeez. They're hitting all the racial stereotypes.'

'And Natalie's hitting back,' Katie said. 'She's definitely busting the quiet Asian stereotype. She told Trudi, "Thank you. I do speak English well." She hit that "well" hard. "Your English, however, sucks out loud. Did you go to school in the US?"'

'Ouch. Has it come to blows?'

'Not yet, but we're expecting her to punch someone any day now.'

I was still puzzled by this information. 'If Natalie is from a Forest family, shouldn't she be used to these remarks? I don't mean she has to put up with them, but the Forest should be past making those stupid comments if she's lived here a while.'

'She hasn't.' Katie paused for another long drink. I waited for the rest of the sentence. 'Natalie's parents separated when she was twelve, and she went with her mother to live in San Francisco.'

'Which is more enlightened than the Forest. Got it. Why did Natalie come back here?'

'First, she's a damned good death investigator, Angela. Takes amazingly detailed notes. Very thorough and accurate. We had an opening and we hired her – and she could have been hired even if her father wasn't important. She's that good.'

I felt a slight twinge of jealousy, and tried to ignore it. The ME had two other death investigators, and one was Detective Greiman's sister, who reported everything to her brother.

'Second, Natalie has this dingbat notion that people in the "heartland" – that's what she calls the Midwest – are sensible, down-to-earth types.'

'Some of us are, but Natalie should know about stereotypes.'

'You'd think so, but she said she was tired of "the California granola eaters."'

Hm. Another stereotype. 'Natalie may be lonesome for them after she spends more time here in the Forest.'

Katie stopped to savor her coffee, then said, 'I hope not. She's almost as good as you.'

That 'almost' soothed the sting of jealousy. 'So can I meet my new colleague today?'

'Nope,' Katie said. 'She's out on a case. Traffic fatality. You can introduce yourself later.'

Katie and I sipped our coffee in companionable silence, until I asked about her golden retriever, Cutter. At six months, the energetic forty-pound pup was too big for Katie to bring to her office, which wasn't much bigger than the average dog run. My question produced a flood of cute puppy photos, and I enjoyed admiring them on her phone. It was funny to see my hyper-rational friend gaga over a puppy, but I'd never mention that.

Too bad the puppy photos ran out and Katie started questioning me. 'How's Chris?'

'Wonderful.' I was on high alert now. Katie was about to grill me about my love life. 'We're having dinner tonight. He's making spaghetti carbonara for dinner. That's really hard to make. It's difficult to get the egg yolks right.'

Katie snorted. 'As if you would know anything about pasta except how to eat it. What's your contribution to this dinner?'

'I'm bringing the bread. Real Italian bread from Luigi's. I had lunch today with Debbie Carlone, the late Tom Lockridge's office manager. Debbie and I went to school together.'

I thought Katie might take the bait and ask about Debbie, but no luck. She was focused on Chris and me.

'Has Chris said the L-word yet? Or made room for you in his closet?' Katie pinned me with a laser gaze.

'Uh, not yet.' I shifted uneasily and wondered if I should run for the door.

'He will, and soon,' she said. 'Just be prepared. It's about time—'

My phone rang. Saved by the bell. I checked the number. It was Debbie Carlone.

'Excuse me, Katie. I have to take this.' I would have taken the call if it was a telemarketer, but now I had a good excuse to avoid the subject I didn't want to think about. I asked Debbie to hold on a minute, grabbed my purse and waved goodbye to Katie. 'Sorry, Katie, this is going to take a while.'

And I was out the door, sprinting for the parking lot. Once I was in my car, I settled in to talk with Debbie.

'Angela!' She sounded upbeat and excited. 'I have the name of that life insurance company. The one that Tom Lockridge has the policy with.'

'Oh, good. I'm glad you found it.'

'Well, I didn't exactly find it. I couldn't locate it in my files. I had to call Victoria, but she knew the name right away.'

'I'm standing by,' I said.

'The information comes with strings, but good strings. Delicious strings, even.'

'Now I have to know.'

'Victoria stopped by the office with a basket of her home-made brownies. She made me promise not to tell you the name until after we each ate at least one. Come on over.'

'Sorry. I can't, Debbie. I have a date tonight.'

'Trust me, you won't need a date. Victoria's homemade brownies are better than sex.' She giggled like a teenager.

I wondered about people who said that. Were they having really bad sex, or hadn't they had sex in a while? No brownie was a match for a night with Chris. Then I remembered that Debbie had been abused by her stepfather. Maybe for her, brownies were better than sex.

'I really can't, Debbie. He's making dinner for me.'

'Oh.' That single syllable held so much loneliness.

'How about this? I'll take you to lunch tomorrow, Debbie. Any restaurant you want.' I upped the bribe. 'How about Solange?' That was the best restaurant in the Forest.

'Seriously? You would? You'd take me to Solange?'

'I'll love to. I'll make the reservation as soon as we hang up. You're close by. How about if I pick you up at noon?'

'Perfect,' she said. 'I can't promise I won't eat some brownies now.'

'Well, they are calling your name,' I said. 'I won't tell if you give me the name of the life insurance company now.'

'Really, you won't tell Victoria?' I heard the hope in her voice.

'My lips are sealed. You can break into the brownies if you give me the name.'

'Hawbley American Life Insurance. Hey, Angela, the coffee is done. I'm going to have coffee and brownies now. You don't know what you're missing, Angela. You've never sampled Victoria's cooking like I have. I've gotta go.' She sounded in a hurry. Those brownies must really be good.

'Then I'll see you at noon tomorrow,' I said. 'Enjoy!'

After I hung up, I called Solange and made an appointment for twelve thirty, asking for a corner booth.

Then I went home to get ready for my date with Chris. I spent extra time with my hair and make-up. Before I left, I stuffed a fresh change of clothes and a toothbrush in my oversized purse. The Forest busybodies would check to see if I did the Walk of Shame when I came home tomorrow morning. They kept track of the clothes I wore, and loved to cackle if I wore the same clothes the next day. Some people seriously needed a life.

While I was getting dressed, Victoria Du Pres's name was buzzing around in my mind. I wasn't quite sure why. Jace was convinced that either Cynthia or her maybe-ex lover Wesley Desloge had killed Tom Lockridge. Still, Victoria's name kept coming up too often in conversations. Plus, I wanted to know why a Du Pres would be too broke to finish construction on a new house. That family was supposed to be endlessly rich.

One person could answer that question: Clare Rappaport, an eighty-something who belonged to the cream of Forest society. Clare knew my mother. Mom had worked for her before she became Reggie Du Pres's housekeeper, and they became friends, in the way rich older women were friendly with former staff. Clare must have had some genuine affection for my mother, because she stayed in touch with me after Mom died, and stopped by from time to time for coffee and a chat. I'd managed to save her life with the timely use of an epi pen when she'd accidentally eaten peanuts, and Clare felt she was in my debt.

I called Clare and she sounded happy to hear from me. 'I'd love to catch up with you, dear.' Her voice was soft but she sounded strong. 'Would you be able to stop by for coffee tomorrow morning, say about ten o'clock?'

That would give me time to have breakfast with Chris and still pick up Debbie at noon. 'I'd be delighted, Clare,' I told her. 'I'm looking forward to seeing you.'

I was, too.

Finally, it was time to see Chris. He greeted me at his door with a kiss. A kiss so ardent and insistent we went straight upstairs to his bedroom. An hour later, I was sitting on one of the black leather chairs at his kitchen island, wrapped in one of his robes, watching him make spaghetti carbonara. Chris was letting his hair grow out a little, and it was adorably tousled.

There was something sexy about a man cooking for a woman, I thought dreamily. Donegan, my first husband, wasn't—

Suddenly, I snapped awake. Did I just call Donegan 'my first husband'? He was my only husband! What was I thinking? I felt the blood drain from my face and grabbed the counter to keep from falling.

Chris looked up from dicing the pancetta. 'Angela, what's wrong? You look a little pale.'

'Nothing. I'm fine.'

'You're not fine,' he said. 'When's the last time you've eaten?'

I thought for a moment. Did I have lunch? All I had for breakfast was coffee.

'You can't remember, can you?' Chris said.

I shook my head no. 'Wait, yes. I did. I had lunch at Luigi's.' I wasn't that hungry after all the food I'd eaten with Debbie, but I couldn't let Chris know the real reason why I was dizzy.

'Well, you need something to eat now.'

He opened the fridge, brought out a wedge of Vermont Cheddar, put it on a plate, then added wheat crackers and green grapes.

'Here. Eat this while I finish our dinner. I shouldn't have

let you go this long without food.' Then he poured me a glass
of water and filled a wineglass with red wine.

I cut a slice of Cheddar, and put it on a cracker. After another
cheese slice and some grapes, I was fully recovered. I
convinced myself I'd simply been hungry when I'd had those
traitorous thoughts about Donegan.

I watched Chris silently, sipping the glass of water. He
worked with quick, precise moves. Now he was beating the
eggs in a bowl, then grating Parmesan cheese into the eggs.
When they were mixed, he added the pasta to the pan. Next,
he tossed in the pancetta, and poured in the Parmesan eggs.

His hands were a blur of motion as he kept the mixture
moving, adding splashes of the pasta cooking water.

'That looks difficult,' I said.

'Not really. The trick, Angela, is to make sure the pan isn't
too hot. If that happens, we'd have scrambled eggs. That's
what carbonara is, you know, fancy scrambled eggs.'

He divided the carbonara into two huge portions in blue
bowls. We took our bowls back upstairs, along with the bread,
wine and garlicky olive oil. And yes, we got crumbs everywhere. Oil, too.

The next morning, after breakfast in bed, Chris asked me to
leave my things at his place.

It was just a toothbrush, I told myself. It doesn't mean
anything.

But I knew I was lying.

THIRTY

'You're positively glowing, my dear,' Clare said. 'You must tell me your beauty secret.'

Lots of exercise, I thought. In bed.

I quickly turned the conversation back to her. 'Thanks, Clare. You're looking especially well.' And she was. Clare's elegant white hair was in its usual French twist. She looked regal in a powder blue St. John knit pantsuit.

This morning, Clare presided over a pretty table in her breakfast room that was gleaming with crystal and silver. She poured me another cup of strong coffee from a Limoges pot.

'You need to have more of these lemon bars, Angela. Cook made them this morning.'

I did need them. For my health. I didn't want to feel faint like I did last night. I helped myself to one more. 'These are an amazing blend of sweet and sour, Clare.'

'Cook is a marvel,' Clare said, and I agreed.

We'd already discussed Clare's children and grandchildren, as well as her health. Having made the rounds of all the customary polite topics, I finally asked my question.

'Clare, I've heard an interesting rumor about one of the Du Pres.'

'Really.' The patrician woman leaned forward, eager for me to spill the details.

'I had a death investigation at the home of Barbara Blanchette.'

'Oh, yes, I heard about her death.' Clare looked sad. 'The poor woman was addicted to opioids. I was surprised that she lived in the Forest Executive Estates. That's too upscale for drug use.'

'You'd be surprised, Clare.'

'I suppose I would.' She sighed. 'Sometimes I feel so old-fashioned, Angela. I don't understand how things work any more. In my day, well-bred women did not get addicted to drugs.'

This wasn't the time to remind Clare about the society women who made it through their days swigging 'cough medicine' with an opium content that could fell a horse.

I reached for another lemon bar. After all, they were healthy. 'Next door to the Blanchette house is a new, unfinished home. A neighbor told me it belongs to Victoria and Ashton Du Pres.'

'Yes, I remember their wedding.' Clare smiled. 'Such a lovely bride. She wore her grandmother's lace veil. Victoria and Ashton make a handsome couple.'

'I've met her,' I said. 'Victoria is definitely a beauty. But the neighbor says work has stopped on their new house. Completely. She says Victoria and Ashton Du Pres ran out of money and can't finish their home. A Du Pres who's broke? Is that even possible?'

'Let me think.' Clare used her silver fork to break off a few crumbs of her lemon bar. It wasn't enough to feed a mouse. Then she took a dainty sip of her coffee. I felt like I was at a doll tea party. After Clare patted her mouth with her linen napkin, she said slowly, 'Ashton is the son of Wade Du Pres, a first cousin of old Reggie.'

I could almost see Clare constructing the Du Pres family tree in her mind. 'Old Reggie likes to be in charge,' she said.

No kidding, I thought. He runs Chouteau Forest.

'Wade is quieter, but just as rich. He stays out of the spotlight, and gives a lot of money to charity. He's had three wives and each one gave him a son. Ashton is the youngest.

'Wade's sons all work in some branch of finance. Wade told me he got tired of the boys waiting for him to die. "They're sitting around my table at the holidays like a flock of vultures," he said.'

I must have raised an eyebrow, or twitched, or something. I don't have a poker face.

Clare said, 'Don't look so shocked, Angela dear. Great wealth is a burden as well as a privilege. And if you're young and due to inherit a princely sum, like Wade's boys, you can't escape those thoughts, no matter how much you love your father.'

I nodded, mostly to keep Clare talking. Her faded blue eyes sparkled as she told her story.

'So Wade had what he called "the Great Divide." He gave each of his sons five million dollars, outright.'

'Five million? He could spare fifteen million dollars?'

'Pocket change.' Clare sounded proud.

'There were no strings on that money, either. Wade told them to use it any way they wanted – enjoy it while he was still alive.

'I heard Wade Junior very sensibly put his money in gold and cannabis – he's doing well. Milton bought Tesla and Apple stock, and well, we all know how that's doing. He's making money hand over fist.

'As for young Ashton, I heard he didn't do quite as well. He put his money into real estate, which is generally a good idea, but the young man chose to invest in shopping malls. Since the rise of Amazon, the malls are becoming dinosaurs. I don't know what he was thinking. Our mall off the interstate is practically a ghost town.'

Clare was old, but shrewd. She managed her own financial affairs and knew her way around a bank statement.

'So, yes, Angela, it's possible a Du Pres – at least that one – may need money. Ashton will inherit more money when Wade dies, of course, all the sons will. But for now, he might be a bit short.'

I had the information I needed. I lingered a bit longer with Clare, and she told me a story about my mother – a story I hadn't heard before. 'When you were a little girl, your mother found a baby bunny on the path to my home. The mother rabbit was nowhere around. Your mother couldn't bear to see it die, so she kept it in a shoe box and fed it with an eye dropper. Finally, the little rabbit recovered and she set it loose in a field. She was the kindest person I've ever known.'

Stories about my mother always made me feel good. I left Clare's home with a smile, and set out to pick up Debbie Carlone for our lunch at Solange. Before I left Clare's driveway, I texted her, *On my way for lunch. Be there in fifteen. Hope you left me some brownies.*

No answer. I figured she was on the phone. I was looking forward to lunch with Debbie. When I arrived at her office, I parked next to her car and texted again, *I'm here. Come on out.*

The sunny morning was not kind to the Chouteau Forest Construction Company building. The low-maintenance yellow brick was dingy and needed cleaning. I could see the gutters were clogged with leaves and the glass door needed to be cleaned. The sun revealed enough fingerprints for an FBI lab on that door. And the blacktop parking lot had some serious potholes.

I checked my phone. I'd been waiting more than five minutes. We were going to be late for our reservation at Solange if Debbie didn't leave soon. I'd better go in and get her.

I tried the door handle, and the office wasn't locked. Odd. On our last visit, Debbie kept the door locked. I walked inside and the office was strangely quiet – no ringing phones, no fax machine whirring, no computer hum. And no Debbie.

'Debbie?' I called. 'It's after twelve. Are you ready?'

No answer.

I saw the light on in the bathroom and the door partly open. Maybe she was combing her hair.

'Debbie?' I knocked on the door and it swung open. The bathroom was empty, but there was the stench of vomit. Someone had vomited on the floor. Something dark had made them sick.

The bottom dropped out of my stomach. Something was seriously wrong.

Was that blood in the vomit? I couldn't tell, but I saw a dark handprint on the floor.

Where was Debbie?

I ran through the long office. The seating area was empty, the couch pillows and coffee table magazines undisturbed.

'Debbie?'

Still no answer.

Her desk was still precisely arranged: papers neatly stacked in IN and OUT boxes, framed photos of her calico cat on the right. Only the vase of fresh flowers was missing.

Wait! Her chair was overturned. Next to the chair was her favorite coffee cup, the one that said, 'Bloom where you're planted.' Coffee was spilled on the carpet.

Where was Debbie?

I was moving faster now, but I couldn't seem to gain any traction. I seemed to be running in slow motion, though my heart was pounding in my chest. I ran past Debbie's silent desk, the coffee maker with a tarry substance in the bottom of the pot, and the row of file cabinets. I kept calling her name, hoping for an answer, a sound, even a muffled groan. It felt like I'd been running for hours, but I knew I hadn't.

At last, I was in Tom's section of the office, with the Cardinals' baseball memorabilia. The top drawer in the file cabinet closest to Tom's desk was open.

And underneath it was—

No! I stood frozen to the spot. My eyes didn't want to believe what I was seeing.

Debbie was on the floor, stiff and cold, her flaming hair in a pool of blood and black vomit.

I heard someone screaming, and realized it was me.

THIRTY-ONE

I called 911 with shaking fingers. The paramedics arrived first, though I knew their visit was a lost cause. Next I called Jace, and the detective said he was on the way. He'd caught the case. I felt a little better: Debbie's investigation would be in good hands.

Two fridge-sized paramedics rushed through the door, and I led them to the back of the office, where Debbie was lying dead on the floor, in a pool of blood and vomit. They made no attempt to revive her. Debbie was pronounced dead at 12:37. She'd been dead at least twelve hours, the paramedics estimated, and was in full rigor. Rick, one of the newer uniforms, arrived next. I gave him a quick explanation – I was supposed to meet Debbie for lunch, and I found her dead. Rick immediately treated the area like a crime scene, and started stringing yellow tape.

I couldn't stop shaking. It was a warm day, but I felt cold. And the room seemed to spin. I grabbed the edge of the desk. One of the paramedics, Farrell, a strapping young man in his twenties, wrapped me in a blanket and hustled me outside to a gurney near the ambulance. He made me lie down with my feet elevated and gave me oxygen.

He sounded apologetic for rushing me outside. 'I had to get you away from the crime scene. You left fingerprints on the desk. I didn't want you destroying evidence.'

'Thanks,' I said. 'I wish I could make my teeth stop chattering.'

'You're in shock,' he said. 'You have all the symptoms – cold, clammy skin, dizziness, and your fingernails are blue.'

I checked my fingers. The nails did have a bluish tinge.

'Now breathe deep. That oxygen is good for you.'

The oxygen did help, but I hated its snakelike hiss. 'I don't understand why I'm reacting like this, Farrell. I'm a death investigator. I see dead bodies all the time.'

'But you didn't see a dead body,' Farrell said. 'You saw your friend, Debbie. Someone you were planning to have lunch with. Now she's dead, and you didn't expect that. That would shake up anyone.'

'It did. It does. That's why my teeth are chattering and I'm shivering like its ten degrees outside.'

I saw Jace's unmarked car pull in next to mine. As the detective got out, I pulled the oxygen prongs out of my nose and tried to stand up. The parking lot spun around me, and I quickly sat down on the gurney.

'Whoa, Angela,' Farrell said. 'Take it easy. Lie back down.'

'OK, but I don't need the oxygen.'

Jace charged over, his face a mask of worry, his brown striped tie flapping against his beige wash-and-wear shirt. 'Angela, what's wrong? Are you hurt?'

'No, no, nothing like that.' Suddenly the day's events rushed in on me and I could barely hold back the tears. 'It's Debbie. We were going to lunch at Solange. I stopped by to pick her up and she didn't come outside. I went inside to get her, so we wouldn't be late for our reservation, and I found her . . .' I stopped and gulped for air. I wasn't going to cry, dammit. 'I found her dead. She was murdered, Jace.'

'Whoa, whoa, whoa,' the detective said. 'Where are you getting this murder business? I was told it was an unexplained death. Was Debbie shot? Stabbed?'

'Poisoned.' I looked him in the eye. 'She was poisoned, Jace. And I know who did it. Victoria Du Pres. Victoria gave my friend poisoned brownies. She wanted me to eat them, too, but I didn't. Victoria tried to kill us both.'

I could see that Jace didn't believe me. Heck, he looked ready to get out a jacket with wraparound sleeves and haul me off to a rubber room.

'Victoria Du Pres wanted to murder both of you? You'd better explain yourself, Angela.'

I sat up – Farrell helpfully adjusted the back of the stretcher – and started my story. 'Debbie called me last night about five o'clock. She said Victoria Du Pres brought over a basket of brownies and they were incredibly delicious.'

I left out the 'better than sex' part. I didn't want Debbie to
seem silly. Death was enough of an indignity.

'OK,' Jace said. 'That sounds harmless.'

'But it wasn't. At lunch yesterday, Debbie told me that
Tom Lockridge, Victoria's father, was about to cash in a two-
million-dollar life insurance policy right before he died, and
Victoria was the beneficiary. If Tom had cashed in that policy,
Victoria was out two million dollars.'

'Wait a minute,' Jace said. 'I thought Tom Lockridge left
everything to his wife, Cynthia.'

'He did. The life insurance policy was an exception. Debbie
knew about the policy, because she handled some of Tom's
financial affairs. Debbie told me that Tom was nearly broke
and needed the policy money to keep going. I wanted the
name of the insurance company, and Debbie said she'd look
it up.'

I stopped. I had trouble telling this part of the tale.

Jace nodded, waiting for me to go on. 'Debbie couldn't find
the company's name in the office records, so she called
Victoria,' I said. 'Debbie said Victoria was her friend, and
often stopped by this office. Victoria was helping her stepmother sell the company. Sometimes Debbie and Victoria had
lunch together. Other times, Victoria brought Debbie treats.
She's a world-class cook.'

I must have stopped again, because Jace prompted me. 'So
Victoria brought over a basket of brownies yesterday, about
five o'clock.' It sounded strange when he said it, like something
from a fairy tale.

'Right. And Debbie called me. She said Victoria gave her
the name of the insurance company, but the information
came with strings – I had to eat the brownies, too. I told
Debbie I couldn't come over last night because I had a date.
Debbie said the brownies were so good, she couldn't wait
until today to eat them. I told her to go ahead and break out
the brownies. I swore I'd never tell Victoria. I also invited
Debbie to lunch today. She gave me the name of the insurance
company, and then she ate the brownies . . .'

I stopped. My request had signed Debbie's death warrant.

She was too trusting. So was I. But Debbie had paid the price for my clumsy amateur investigation.

'And?' Jace said.

'And now she's dead. And I escaped.' I knew my tale sounded absolutely crazy. Jace was treating me like someone who'd flipped out.

'How do you know the brownies were poisoned?'

'Because I saw Debbie's body. She'd vomited and had bloody diarrhea.'

'Angela, that doesn't mean Debbie was murdered. Those symptoms could also mean she died of natural causes.'

'She didn't,' I said. 'She was poisoned by Victoria Du Pres.'

'Really,' Jace said. 'Did you see Debbie actually receive these poisoned brownies from Victoria?'

'No.'

'Did Debbie send you a photograph of this basket of goodies?'

'No.'

'When you entered the office this afternoon and found Debbie's body, did you see the basket of brownies?'

'No.'

'Was Debbie clutching a half-eaten brownie in her cold, dead hand?'

I winced when he said that. Debbie's death wasn't a joke. 'No.'

'Then where is this fatal food?'

'Victoria must have sneaked back in and taken it away,' I said. 'Both the leftover brownies and the basket. Yes, that's what she did. You can check the CCTV footage.'

I realized I sounded like one of those loonies who believes the Moon landing was staged, but my story was true. I had to find some way to persuade Jace.

'Angela, help me out here. Why would Victoria want Debbie dead?'

'Because Debbie was talking about Tom Lockridge's two-million-dollar life insurance policy. Victoria and her husband are building a mansion in the Chouteau Executive Estates – I saw it, next door to the Blanchette house – and the Du Pres's have run out of money. They can't continue construction without that two million.

'You have to believe me, Jace.' I sounded desperate, and I knew it. Worse, I was clutching the sleeve of his light brown jacket.

He carefully removed my fingers, and spoke softly but distinctly. 'I have to go inside, Angela. You just rest up here for a while.'

I hated being patronized. I tried to get off the gurney. 'I'll do the death investigation.'

'You can't, Angela. You're a witness. I've called for another DI. Natalie Upton is on her way. I'll take your statement later. Don't leave.'

He patted my hand. I was completely humiliated.

Less than two minutes later, a shiny black Beemer pulled up and parked beside Jace's car. The woman who got out was tall and slender, with delicate Asian features. Her straight black hair was pulled into a low, tight knot. She opened her trunk and brought out a new black leather suitcase, which I guessed was her DI case.

Natalie Upton, the Forest's newest death investigator.

I thought she might come over and I could introduce myself, but Natalie went straight to the door. Rick the uniform was now in charge of the crime scene log. Natalie signed it. The young cop attempted a bit of flirtation, but Natalie breezed past him. She was all business.

I waited outside more than an hour. After half an hour, Farrell decided I was OK, and the paramedics left. I bought coffee for myself and Rick from a little shop nearby, and sat in my car.

Jace came out and found me in my car, with the window rolled down, drowsy with sleep on the summery May afternoon.

'Are you feeling better, Angela?'

'I'm fine.' I sounded snippy, which wasn't what I intended. I got out of my car and leaned against the front bumper, waiting for Jace to speak first.

'Natalie found what might – accent on "might" – be a bit of brownie or some kind of chocolate cake in the vomit. But that's all. There's not a crumb of brownies anywhere in the room.

'However, based on your statement, I'm investigating this as a possible homicide. Katie will be doing the autopsy and she can give us the cause of death.'

'Anything on the security cameras?'

'The cameras in the office appear to have malfunctioned yesterday afternoon.'

'How convenient,' I said.

'We're checking the neighboring cameras,' he said. 'The ones that cover the parking lot. If Victoria's comings and goings are at times that are inconsistent with her regular trips, well, that will raise suspicion. And if the security cameras show her carrying anything about the time Debbie says the brownies were delivered, we'll have something.

'Also, if Katie finds any food in the victim's stomach we can see if the digestion time coincides with the daughter's visit on the security cam.'

'Can you get a search warrant for Victoria's house?' I asked.

'Probably not with the information we have now, but I could subpoena her credit card records for her store purchases and look for say, brownie mix or poison.

'I could certainly tip off the insurance company and ask them to slow any payout on that policy. They'll be more than happy to do that – maybe even get their own PI on the case.'

'That could stop her from spending the policy money,' I said. 'Anything else we can do now?'

'We could also grab her trash once it is out at the street for pickup.'

I liked that 'we.'

'I can do that tomorrow,' I said. 'It's trash pick-up day in some parts of the Forest. If Victoria has any trash out, I'll toss the bags in my car. I'm feeling better.'

I was, too. Jace was taking me seriously. In fact, he was getting downright enthusiastic. 'I can also subpoena her internet records for searches relating to death by poison,' he said. 'If we find any video of Victoria delivering anything to this building, or if Katie finds poisoned brownies during the autopsy and there are no other signs of trauma, we might actually have enough for a search warrant. Especially if we find stuff in the trash, and with the credit card searches.

'Meanwhile, I need you to write and sign a statement for me. Natalie will want to know if you have any demographic information on the victim.'

'I can do both,' I said. 'How did your interview with Wesley Desloge go? Did he implicate Cynthia in the murder of her husband?'

Jace sort of shuffled his feet, and I guessed he didn't want to answer. 'Not yet,' he said, 'though Wes did admit to skimming "a little money."'

'A little money? Twenty-eight thousand dollars?'

'There may be more,' Jace said. 'That's all we can find so far. I want to bring in a forensic accountant. At least now I can arrest him for felony embezzling.'

Next, I asked the important question, the key to ending this investigation. 'Any way to tie Wes and Cynthia to Spider-Man?'

'Not yet.' Jace still sounded hopeful. 'And if we're going to get Victoria for this murder, we have to find a way to tie her to Spider-Man. I doubt that a Du Pres would have him over for tea.'

'I'll find a way,' I said. Now this was personal. My friend was dead and I was determined to nail her killer.

THIRTY-TWO

The next morning, Jace and I met at Katie's office for the news about Debbie Carlone's autopsy. The meeting was short and businesslike. Jace looked worn and tired, and I assumed I didn't look much better. I'd had a restless night, my sleep disrupted by flashes of poor Debbie's body, and the realization of my own guilt. I'd played amateur detective and now my friend was dead.

Only Katie, the assistant ME, looked alert and ready for work.

We each had our own coffee. Jace and I perched on the edge of Katie's desk, and the assistant ME started right in.

'Angela, I'm sorry about the loss of your friend,' she said. 'The information I'm going to deliver is short and brutal. I heard you had a hard time after you found her body yesterday. Are you sure you want to stay for this?'

'Yes.' I was determined to find Debbie's killer. It was time to woman up and face the facts.

Katie's face changed suddenly. Her eyes were hard and her voice was quick. She was angry. 'Debbie Carlone ingested a massive – and fatal – amount of antifreeze. The poison was in the brownies that she ate. And she ate quite a few of them.'

I looked at Jace and felt vindicated. He kept studying his cooling coffee.

'This was an ugly way to die. The victim would have had blinding headaches, fatigue, lack of coordination, grogginess, nausea and vomiting. And that's just for starters. After that, she'd have massive organ failure and convulsions. Somewhere along the line, she lost consciousness and fell into a coma. She had a number of chronic health problems due to her weight, and that hastened her death. I'd say she died between midnight and three a.m.'

'If the victim ate that much antifreeze wouldn't she taste it?' Jace asked.

'The natural taste of ethylene glycol, the major ingredient in this brand of antifreeze, is supposed to be sweet,' Katie said, 'and these brownies were loaded with sugar, chocolate chips and thick fudge icing. Also, they had lots of walnuts, which have a slightly bitter taste. That combination could have accounted for any tastes that were "off." She must have liked the brownies because I'm guessing she ate a dozen.

'That's about all I can tell you. Except that judging by the stomach contents, I'd estimate that she ingested the poisoned food between five and six o'clock. And the killer is an evil SOB. That woman suffered.'

Poor Debbie. I felt angry about her cruel murder and her final agony.

Jace and I thanked Katie and left her cramped office for a conference in the parking lot. The morning sun glared down at us. It was going to be another hot day, but for now, the sun felt good.

'I'll work on obtaining the CCTV videos for the parking lot,' Jace said. 'I'll check them and see if Victoria Du Pres delivered those brownies before the victim died.'

'Do you still think Cynthia conspired with Spider-Man to kill her husband?' I had to ask.

I saw the confusion on his face. 'I don't know any more. I need proof, Angela. I need connections. Right now, there's no connection between Cynthia and Spider-Man or Victoria and that same killer.'

'I'll help,' I said. 'I can go to two places. First, Fairdale Manor, where Spider-Man used to live. I'll talk to the longtime residents and see if I can find a connection between Spider-Man and Cynthia or that creep and Victoria.'

'I can do those interviews,' Jace said.

'You can, but I might get more information. And you have to check those CCTV videos.'

'You do have a way with people,' he said. 'So if you don't mind.'

'Not at all. After that, I'm going Dumpster diving at Victoria Du Pres's home. I want to get the evidence that that witch baked those killer brownies.'

'You don't have to go digging in the trash, Angela,' Jace said.

'Yes, I do. My friend Debbie is dead, and I want her killer caught.'

'Then be careful,' Jace said. 'Call me after you leave Fairdale, and also when you grab the Du Pres garbage. Promise me. These are dangerous people.'

I agreed, and meant it. I had no intention of being the idiot female who ran recklessly into danger.

Twenty minutes later, I was at Fairdale. Once again, I was struck by how pretty the mobile home park looked. I heard the distant sound of a lawn mower and saw a chunky man riding one, cutting the wide swath of grass past the shade trees.

The crime scene tape flapped sadly on the broken stairs to Mrs Rawlins's mobile home, but her flowers in their painted tire planters were blooming. In fact, Peggy Nolan, the woman who'd found Mrs Rawlins's body, was watering the flowers with a garden hose. She was dressed for yard work in a blue overall and a green T-shirt. She greeted me with a smile and a wave.

'I'm glad you're taking care of things,' I said.

'Bob and I have lived here for more than twenty years,' Peggy said. 'That's him over there, mowing the lawn. This is our home and we want it kept up. You have to do that to keep out the riffraff.'

'Do you know who inherits the mobile home park?'

'Shirley left it to Cynthia Lockridge, but we haven't heard from her yet. We're doing this on our own.' She turned off the faucet and coiled the hose in its holder on the side of Shirley's home.

Sweat was rolling off Peggy's forehead. She pulled out a pocket handkerchief and wiped her brow. 'This heat is getting to me. I need a break. Want to come in for some iced tea?'

The inside of Peggy's home was dim, cool, and comfortably neat. She collected salt and pepper shakers and they were displayed everywhere. I was admiring a set of china palm trees on her kitchen table. Peggy poured me a tall glass of iced tea, then gave me a paper napkin and a spoon. 'Sugar bowl's on the table,' she said, and handed me a plastic lemon. 'In case you'd like a squirt of lemon juice.'

After we fixed our tea and Peggy had cooled down, she said, 'I'm glad that Cody Ellis was caught. Killing poor Mrs Rawlins over a stupid TV! I hope he never sees daylight again.'

'Me, too.' I sipped my tea. 'I have a question about another crook who used to live here. Spider-Man.'

'Him.' Peggy gave a contemptuous snort. 'Gives himself a silly nickname and thinks he's big time.'

'Was he friends with Cynthia Lockridge when he lived here?'

'Cindy? Not when she was younger. She avoided that man like a dose of the clap.' Peggy stopped, then said, 'Pardon my manners, but I tell it like it is.'

'That's good.'

'Well, that boy was no good even then, and he tormented little Cindy – that's how I knew her, as Cindy. Wouldn't leave her alone. And Cindy's mother, well, I'm sure Shirley told you, she wasn't much use. Anyway, Shirley had a big heart, and she let Cindy move in with her. So no, that little girl wouldn't go near Spider-Man. Not then. She was afraid of him.'

'Has she changed her attitude?'

'Yes. I never said anything to Shirley, because she loved that girl like a daughter, but about eight to ten weeks ago, Cindy started seeing Spider-Man.'

I sat up, startled. That was before the death of Cindy's husband.

'I spotted him sneaking around here at night after Shirley was asleep,' Peggy said. 'At least twice. One night, I found a note sticking out from under Cindy's doormat. I photographed it. Let me show you. It's on my cell phone.'

Peggy got up and found her cell phone on her sink counter. She swiped through her pictures until she found one and handed it to me. 'Here's the photo of the note under the doormat on Cindy's porch,' Peggy said. She swiped to another photo. 'And this one, see, is the note itself. I made sure the doormat was still in the photo.'

I read:

Leave the last of the ten thousand in the flower pot under your porch.

What?

My heart was pounding. Didn't Spider-Man say Cynthia was going to pay him ten thousand dollars to kill her husband? I read the note several times, but the words didn't change. Was I holding the proof Cynthia had killed her husband?

'Well?' Peggy said. 'What do you think?'

What did I think? I couldn't. My brain was spinning. 'So you kept this photo?' I said.

'Yes, ma'am.' Peggy looked proud.

'But you didn't take the note itself?'

'I was too scared. Something wasn't right about that note.'

'Could you text me that photo?' I gave her my cell phone number.

'No problem.' My work cell dinged and I had it.

'Did Spider-Man ever come back for the money?'

'Not that I could tell,' Peggy said. 'Not before he was arrested for murder. But you can't go by me. My Bob was sick and I was taking care of him. All I can say is, I don't want to see hide nor hair of that Spider-Man ever again.'

'I don't blame you. I hope they lock him up and throw away the key. I have one more question. Do you know a Victoria Du Pres?'

Peggy sipped her tea and repeated the name. 'Victoria. Victoria. It sounds sort of familiar, but I don't think I know a Victoria Du Pres. Now wait a minute. I do know a Victoria Lockridge.'

'That's her!' I did everything but yell 'Bingo!' 'Victoria Lockridge married Ashton Du Pres. How did you know Victoria?'

'Oh, we all knew her. Everyone at Fairdale who had dealings with her back then knew Victoria. She was the insurance adjuster after the tornado hit this place some years ago. A good one, too. That's how we got this nice new home. Our single-wide didn't have that much damage, but Victoria totaled it so we could get this big double-wide.'

'Did Victoria know Spider-Man?'

'Of course she did. His home was crushed nearly flat. I

have no idea how he survived that hit, but he did. Maybe he was drunk. Anyway, he crawled out of the wreckage alive and Victoria got him a nice new double-wide.'

'Was she afraid of Spider-Man like Cindy was?'

'Oh, no. Victoria didn't have any reason to fear him. Spider-Man was busy sweet-talking her because he wanted that double-wide. He got it, too.'

'Did they stay in touch?'

'Who? Victoria and Spider-Man? Sure, why not? I know she liked to smoke a little weed and she'd call him from time to time. Victoria wasn't involved in the wild parties at Spider-Man's new home, but he was her dealer. But it was small-time. Just like Spider-Man.' Peggy frowned and said his name as if she'd bitten into a lemon.

I left there slightly dazed. I came hoping for a little information – and left with too much.

THIRTY-THREE

As soon as I left Fairdale Manor, I called Jace with my news. My call went straight to voice mail.

Rats.

Well, I'd call him when I got closer to Victoria Du Pres's house. It was past three o'clock, and I had to hurry. The Forest trash haulers followed the same route – the trucks started on the working side of town and finished up in the fancier neighborhoods. The rich folks complained about the trash sitting out in front of their homes all day, and wanted the trash haulers to come around the back of their mansions to pick it up, but the haulers refused. I suspected the homeowners were too cheap to offer them an incentive.

I'd stopped by the side of the road to make the call to Jace, and while I was parked there I prepared for my search of Victoria's trash. I took a sheet from my DI case and spread it over the bottom of my trunk, in case Victoria's trash was drippy. I hauled out my point-and-shoot camera and put it on the passenger seat. I was ready for my mission.

From Fairdale, I was fifteen minutes and light years from the Du Pres home. All the way there, I thought about what I'd learned. Peggy Nolan had implicated both Cynthia, the murdered man's wife, as well as his daughter, Victoria.

The issue came down to Cynthia's freedom and Victoria's greed. Yes, Victoria needed money to finish her mansion, but she was married to a Du Pres. Even if Ashton had squandered his five million, there would be more money in the couple's future. Maybe Wade would give them the rest of the money for the house as a present.

By all accounts, Victoria had been a model daughter. We knew Cynthia was a less than perfect wife. I didn't want the killer to be Cynthia, but I wasn't sure about Victoria, either.

The answer could be in Victoria's trash.

Victoria and Ashton Du Pres lived out in the countryside,

about five miles down the road from Wade Du Pres's estate. Their home was a charming white brick Cape Cod house with green shutters. I estimated the two-story house had four bedrooms.

All the home owners on Wilshire Road had wheeled their green plastic trash bins to the curb. As I drove by Victoria Du Pres's home, my work cell phone rang. I parked under a nearby stand of trees and checked the display: Jace.

'Angela!' There was a world of discouragement in that one word.

'What's wrong, Jace?'

'I've wasted too much time on these damn CCTV videos.' Hm. That mild cuss word told me Jace was nearing the end of his rope.

'The closest cameras were dummies, so there was no footage.'

That happened a lot. Business owners cut corners during a money crunch, and security was an easy cut to make. They were betting that if their building was bristling with cameras and fierce signs that would stop the crooks.

'There is a set of cameras on the other side,' Jace said, 'but the business was locked up and it took me all morning to track down the owner. He made me wait until his tech guy came in half an hour ago – claimed he didn't know how to operate the system. I've wasted the morning.'

'Not entirely. You have the footage,' I said. 'I have some information, but I'm afraid it will add to the confusion. I talked with Peggy Nolan, the woman who found Shirley's body. She said Spider-Man was sneaking around the place about eight to ten weeks before Tom Lockridge was murdered. He was leaving notes for Cynthia under the door mat of her mobile home. Peggy photographed one, and the note is very damning. It says something like "Leave the last of the ten thousand in the flower pot under your porch."'

Jace was suddenly on high alert. 'Does Mrs Nolan still have that photo?'

'Yes,' I said. 'And she texted it to me.'

'God bless her,' Jace said. 'Text it to me. I'll go talk to her. This is great news, Angela. I knew it was Cynthia. We've got her!'

Something stubborn stirred in me. I wanted to crush Jace's glee with my newfound facts.

'I'm not so sure, Jace. There's also a connection between Tom's daughter, Victoria, and the killer. Peggy says she was the insurance adjustor for the mobile home park, when it was hit by a tornado. Victoria negotiated new homes for a number of residents, including Spider-Man. He's also her weed dealer.'

A grinding roar and a prehistoric screech blocked Jace's answer. When the noise stopped, Jace said, 'Listen, Angela, where are you?'

'Half a block past Victoria's house. I'm going to get her trash.'

'No! Angela! That's too dangerous. I'm on my way. Go home.'

'You'll be too late, Jace. The trash truck is almost here. No one is around. I'll grab Victoria's trash before we lose it for good.'

'Angela, I'm on my way. And I'll have dispatch send the closest uniform. Be careful. This woman could be a cold-blooded killer.'

'So could Cynthia. I'll be fine, Jace.'

'Then leave your phone on. Please!'

Fair enough. I stuck the phone in my front jacket pocket so he could hear everything. Then I grabbed my camera off the seat and ran toward the Du Pres's trash bin. I photographed it – long shot, medium and close-up. The bin had the Du Pres's house number on it (3946) and I made sure their home was in the background of some shots. The trash truck roared again, grinding its way up the road toward me.

I checked that no one was around, and opened Victoria's bin. Inside were four black plastic trash bags. The one on top clanked and when I lifted the bag, it was heavy. I sprinted with it to my car and tossed it into the trunk. The second bag was lighter and crackled – boxes and paper, maybe. The third was also heavy and dripped a nasty brown substance. I hoped it was coffee grounds, but it seemed too greasy.

As I grabbed the fourth trash bag, the plastic tie came loose, and I saw some of the contents: an empty yellow bag of chocolate chips, a brown can of cocoa, and a red box of Aunt Dora's Secret Recipe Brownie Mix. 'Tastes just like homemade' proclaimed the box.

Was that Victoria's secret? She used a box mix? Didn't she bother to make her poisoned brownies from scratch? I searched the bag for an antifreeze jug. Nothing. What was going on?

The trash truck gave an earsplitting shriek. The lumbering beast was only one house away. Time for me to move. I heard a car coming down the road. Great. Just what I needed. I high-tailed it to my car and threw in the last two bags. One landed with a crunch, the other with a wet splish. Before I could close the trunk, a black Beemer pulled up behind my car.

The driver was Victoria Du Pres. I quickly slammed my trunk.

'Angela,' she said. 'Is that you? Are you having car trouble?'

'No, no.' I hoped my voice didn't shake. 'I'm fine. I heard a rattling noise in my trunk and wanted to check that nothing was wrong.'

Victoria had the face of a Christmas angel – long blonde hair, china white face and perfect features. Looking at her clear, untroubled eyes and kind smile, I couldn't believe she'd cooked up a mess of poisoned brownies and killed Debbie. But I knew she did. Just like I knew that except for Cain, most killers weren't marked by their crimes.

I edged toward the driver's side, slid inside, locked the door and started my car. Only then did I glance over. Victoria was standing next my car, pounding on my window. Her pretty face was transformed. Rage flickered in her eyes and she had a demon's smile. I didn't dare roll down the window.

'Liar!' she screamed. 'I saw what you were doing. You stole my trash.'

'I didn't steal it. If it's out on the road, anyone can take it.'

'Give it back.'

'No!'

She took off her high heel and pounded on my window. I roared off, leaving her in the dust.

In the rearview mirror, I saw her kick off her other heel, run for her car and start it up. I pressed down on the gas, and hoped my Charger could outrun her Beemer.

'Jace!' I shouted. 'Can you hear what's going on? Victoria is chasing me. I just left 3946 Wiltshire Road. I'm heading west toward the Wade Du Pres estate.'

'Copy that. I'm on my way. So is another unit.'

This section of road was twisty, and I was going a hundred miles an hour. At that speed, the car seemed to float over the road. I prayed there were no other cars on this road.

Victoria was coming up behind me. I saw the white wooden fencing of a farm just around the curve, and slowed down.

And there was Victoria, fury burning in her eyes, her Beemer next to my car. She hit the side of my car, scraping the back quarter-panel with a horrifying screech of metal. I managed to hang on to the wheel, and my Charger stayed on the road. She hit me again as I rounded the curve, and sent my car careening through the white fence.

That fence saved my life. The airbag exploded. I stood on the brakes and my car slowed, skidding wildly across the pasture until it plowed into a tree and died with a hiss. Dazed from the airbag, I crawled out of the car and saw Victoria's Beemer coming straight at me, bumping across the grassy field.

'Jace! I'm in a pasture. I've crashed! Help!'

I heard something that sounded like 'on my way,' but I didn't stop. I had to keep running.

Victoria's Beemer had been damaged. She couldn't drive it quite as fast. It rattled and coughed, but it still moved faster than I could run. I quickly scanned the field. No place to hide.

Rattle. Cough. Roar. Victoria was coming after me.

Then I saw it – salvation! A tree stump about three feet high, hidden by a clump of tall weeds. I ran toward it, and Victoria pushed her car to its top speed, which wasn't much. Soon I was standing directly behind the stump and Victoria was aiming straight for me. And the hidden tree stump.

She revved up the crippled car, engine rattling, gears grinding, and pushed her car to the limit. I ducked and ran so the car didn't flip on top of me. The Beemer hit the tree stump, and debris flew everywhere. I was hit with a piece of something and blacked out. Just before I heard the blessed scream of sirens.

I awoke in the arms of Officer Chris Ferretti. He was kissing me and saying, 'Angela, talk to me. Please, Angela! I love you. Let me know you're OK. Say something.'

'The trash is safe,' I said, and my world went black again.

THIRTY-FOUR

I awoke to a bright light. Where was I? Was I dead and entering the tunnel of light to the Great Beyond?

Then I heard Katie's enraged voice, so I assumed I didn't die and go to heaven.

I was in the hospital, with Katie pacing back and forth and yelling, 'What the hell were you thinking, Angela Richman! Risking your life for garbage! A bag of garbage!'

I winced. Her words rang unpleasantly in my head and her face was blurry, but I could see she was mad.

I felt the sandpaper bed sheet beneath me. Yep, I was in a hospital bed.

'We needed that trash for the case.' Was that mouselike squeak really me?

'There were other ways to nail Victoria Du Pres's ass.' Katie's voice was still furious.

'What's wrong with me?' I tried to sit up, but the room swirled around like a carnival ride.

Katie finally quit pacing and sat in the chair next to my bed. Her voice was softer now. 'You needed your head examined for starters, Angela. The CT scan showed you have a slight concussion. You're damned lucky. You barely survived six strokes and brain surgery two years ago and now you're in a fatal car chase.'

I tried to figure out what else was damaged. I wiggled my toes. They seemed OK. My midsection felt like I'd been punched in the gut. Was that from the airbag? My right arm had an IV line sticking out of it. And I couldn't move my left arm.

'What's wrong with my arm?'

'Your left shoulder was hit by a chunk of BMW bumper. Your shoulder was dislocated, but the docs fixed that when you were out cold.'

Good. The way to fix that dislocation was to pull hard on

my arm, and that would hurt like hell. In fact, my shoulder was hurting now. A whole lot. And my left arm was in a sling. The kind that was strapped around my body to immobilize the arm.

'You also needed twenty-three stitches.' That made sense. I tried to move that arm and pain shot straight up to my neck.

'You have assorted other bumps and bruises, but nothing else is broken. Like I said, you're damn lucky.'

'How long have I been out?'

'About four hours.'

'I remember Chris found me. Did that really happen?'

I also remembered he tried to kiss me back to life and he said he loved me, but I wasn't about to tell Katie.

'Yes. He was the first uniform on the scene. He pulled you away from the wreckage, and called an ambulance. By that time, Jace was on the scene and he let Chris ride with you to the ER. Chris stayed here about four hours, but then he had to go back to work. Chris called me and I promised to stay with you.'

My head was clearing by the minute.

'Did they get Victoria Du Pres?'

'She died at the scene,' Katie said. 'Her car hit that tree stump head-on and flipped.'

'I didn't mean to kill her.' I started crying.

'Angela, you're not making a whole lot of sense. She was chasing you, going more than a hundred miles an hour on a country road. Then she drove after you through a pasture and tried to run you down.'

'Yes. But I got behind that hidden tree trunk on purpose. I knew she'd go for it. She hit it and died. It's all my fault.'

Katie sounded angry and impatient. 'Spare me the drama queen nonsense, Angela. Victoria killed herself. Her death was quick. If you want to cry for someone, cry for your friend Debbie. She had the terrible death. I'll read you her autopsy report if you want inspiration.'

'OK.' Katie was saying something else, but I drifted off.

Later, I heard voices. Someone was calling for Dr Lovett to call extension 630. My room was dark, except for the light over my bed. And Jace was there, sitting in the same chair by the bed. Jace looked so tired *he* should have been in a hospital bed.

'Angela, you're awake. I've been so worried. Katie told me you were OK. Well, except for your shoulder. You were lucky.'

I hurt too much to debate my luck. I sat up, and this time, the room didn't turn into a Tilt-A-Whirl. 'What happened? I missed a lot, Jace.'

'Victoria turned out to be the killer. She killed her father because he was cashing in that two-million-dollar life insurance policy. I found her in the car wreckage, right before she died. "He promised it to me," she said. "He promised. And then he was going to give it to that bitch for that trashy house. I had to stop him."'

'Those were her last words?'

'Yes,' Jace said.

'What a hate-filled way to go,' I said.

'As far as I'm concerned, it's a confession. I don't think the Du Pres family will accept it, but I found more than enough evidence to back up her words. You got the garbage with the brownie ingredients. That was enough for me to get a search warrant for Victoria's house. I found antifreeze in the kitchen pantry.'

'That's an odd place to keep it.'

'Especially when we found two jugs of special BMW Coolant Antifreeze in the garage.

'Oh, and Victoria's credit card receipts showed she bought the brownie ingredients and the antifreeze the day she delivered the poisoned treats to Debbie.'

'Sure looks like she was guilty,' I said.

'Oh, she was. We can see that. The video showed Victoria driving into the parking lot of the Chouteau Forest Construction Company at 4:35 p.m., carrying a basket into the office, bold as can be. She came out of the office at 4:57 and drove off.'

'That settles it, then.'

'No, there's more,' Jace said. 'Victoria came back the next morning at 9:12 in jeans, a T-shirt, and sneakers.'

'Not her usual high fashion and high heels,' I said.

'Not at all. She didn't leave until 10:17 that morning.'

'So she cleaned up the poisoned brownies,' I said.

'Yes, she did, and she left carrying another trash bag. She took that one home, and dumped a lot of greasy leftovers in the same bag.'

'So that was the squishy trash bag I threw in my car.'

Jace smiled. 'It was indeed. We found the remains of the poisoned brownies and the gift basket in it.'

'Victoria cleaned up the office with poor Debbie lying right there dead on the floor.'

'Victoria was cold,' Jace said. 'And I'm hoping she's somewhere hot now, and I don't mean Miami.'

'I agree,' I said. At least I think I said that. All I know is I felt much better about Victoria's death.

When I woke up again, the sun was shining, and every part of me hurt, even my fingers. And there was Chris, behind an enormous bouquet of spring flowers.

'Chris, I'm so glad to see you.'

He set the vase of fragrant flowers on the nightstand next to my bed, and took me in to his arms.

'Ouch.'

He quickly backed away.

'No, come here,' I said. 'Let's find a way to do this where you don't grab my left shoulder.'

So we did. Soon we fit together nicely, despite the sling. Chris began kissing my forehead. 'Angela, I was so afraid you were dead when I found you.'

'I'm pretty hard to kill.'

Chris looked serious. 'Don't joke about that, Angela. When I thought you might be dead, the bottom dropped out of my world.' He kissed me again.

I was touched. 'You really feel that way, Chris?'

'I love you, Angela. I mean it.' He looked so handsome and so earnest. I liked his strong arms. I liked the crinkles around his eyes. I could hear his heart beating in his chest. 'Say you love me.'

'Chris, I . . .' I stopped, confused. I didn't know how I felt.

Did I love this man? I'd loved another man. Donegan. No, I loved him still. But Donegan was dead, and all I had were memories of his love. Memories that grew more perfect with each passing year.

And Chris was here. I felt like my future hung in the balance. Was I going to live with the shadows of my lost love, or embrace the future?

I reached for Chris with my good arm.

'Yes. I love you.' I was crying now, but these tears felt good.

EPILOGUE

As Jace and I expected, the Du Pres family refused to believe that their sweet Victoria murdered Thomas Lockridge and Debbie Carlone. But the rest of the Forest did. The evidence of Victoria's guilt was overwhelming. The case was closed and Detective Jace Budewitz's job was safe. For now.

But the fallout continued. Consider Roland 'Rolly' Roget III, the drunken nitwit who killed Danny Morton, while that young man was walking a dog. Rolly's lawyer thought the law-abiding citizens of Chouteau Forest would buy the argument that Danny's death was 'collateral damage in the war on crime.'

To Rolly's surprise, he was convicted of second-degree involuntary manslaughter. He was sentenced to four years in the state pen. Susannah Morton, Danny's mother, filed a wrongful death suit and was awarded a million dollars. The money was used to fund a scholarship in Danny's name.

Cordelia Du Pres Wellington, the drunken socialite who ran down bank teller Rose McClaren, had her driver's license revoked for a year. During that time, Cordelia enjoyed being chauffeured. She discovered she could drink while she was being driven. She never sat behind the wheel of a car again. Cordelia was convicted of a felony for driving while intoxicated and causing the death of Mrs McClaren. The judge said because of 'the defendant's extreme age' she would serve only a year's probation. To Cordelia's horror, her actual age, along with that phrase, was published in the Forest and the St. Louis newspapers.

Rose's husband, William McClaren, hired Montgomery Bryant to sue Cordelia for the wrongful death of his wife. Katie was right when she said the photos of Rose McClaren's semi-nude body would have a big impact on the jury.

William McClaren was awarded two million dollars.
The money was placed in trust for their grandchildren's
education.

When the dust settled, I had coffee again with Clare Rappaport,
and told her more about Barbara Blanchette, the woman
who'd overdosed. I may have mentioned that her ambitious
husband Allen didn't come home for more than four hours
after he learned his wife was dead, because he wanted to give
a keynote speech. It turned out Clare went to school with
William Danvers, the CEO of Danvers and Dall, the marketing
company where Allen Blanchette was a rising star. Clare may
have mentioned something to her old friend.

Anyway, Allen Blanchette's career stalled. His superiors
said he needed to improve his 'work-life balance.' His daughter
Olive went to live with her grandparents in Tampa, Florida.
She misses her mommy, but she's growing up in a loving
family.

Forensic accountants found out that Wesley Desloge, the sleazy
lawyer, embezzled more than fifty thousand dollars from the
accounts of the Chouteau Forest Christmas Ball. Wesley
received the maximum sentence – fifteen years in the state
pen and a twenty-thousand-dollar fine. Wes was also ordered
to make restitution. He filed for bankruptcy.

And what about that note Peggy Nolan found under the front
doormat of Cynthia Lockridge's mobile home? The one
where Spider-Man demanded the rest of the ten thousand
dollars? Turns out he was running a con. Spider-Man knew
that Cynthia wanted to know the name of her father.
Spider-Man confessed to Jace that he told Cynthia he'd
found her father, and he'd give her the name for ten thousand
dollars.

'I didn't mean any harm by it,' he said. 'I was going to pick
out some nice old dude at the VFW Hall. He could be her
daddy and they'd both be happy.'

Apparently, Spider-Man never considered that DNA might
ruin his scheme.

But he'd lied when he'd blamed Cynthia for plotting the murder of her husband.

Jace had an illegal recording of Spider-Man's confession. He swore me to secrecy and played it for me when I was in the hospital. The recording gave me the shivers.

Spider-Man's voice sounded sandpaper-rough, and scratchy. 'Victoria hired me to kill her old man,' he said. 'She swore she'd kill me if I mentioned her name if I got caught. I admit she's one scary chick, but I ain't afraid of her.

'When I got caught, I knew it was a chance to get even with that bitch Cindy. She was puttin' on airs, marrying a rich old guy and living in a mansion.

'I asked her out when she lived in the trailer park, but she ran to Shirley and Ron, the owners, saying she was afraid of me. She lied, and that made me angry. I never touched a hair on her head. I was gonna ask Cindy out on a real date, take her to a movie and fried chicken at the Dew Drop Inn. I even bought a new shirt. But she acted like she was better than me, and she wasn't.'

I could hear the venom dripping from his next words. 'Who did Cindy think she was to turn me down? Her momma was nothing but a common hooker. Everybody used her like a toilet. Even me. And Cindy didn't have no daddy. Not that anybody could name. My momma was a respectable church lady, and she was married to my daddy. So that made me better than Cindy. But she thought she was so high and mighty. A big-time society lady. So when I got caught, I thought, "This is how I'll bring her down. If I'm going to prison, so is she. It's payback time for hurting my feelings."'

Jace reminded him, 'You know when you lied in your first confession, you violated the agreement with the county prosecutor. You're facing the needle.'

'I don't care,' Spider-Man said. 'I took her down with me. She's ruined, too. No fancy friends any more. She's broker than shit.'

His laugh sounded like the devil dragging a soul off to hell. I know that seems melodramatic, but it's the only way I can describe it.

*   *   *

But Spider-Man was right about one thing: Cindy's old life was over. Why didn't Cynthia mention that she'd paid Spider-Man ten thousand dollars to find her father?

More bad advice from her lawyer, Wes. He told her to keep her mouth shut because the payment 'would make her look guilty.' Cynthia was not guilty of Thomas's murder – only of panicking when she found his body. She joined Narcotics Anonymous to quit her coke habit.

After Thomas's death, Cynthia was quietly dropped from the important committees, including the Christmas ball. She did inherit Thomas's estate, including the two-million-dollar life insurance policy.

Except there wasn't any estate. Thomas had barely been keeping his company going, as Debbie told me. He'd been spending way more than he earned on Cindy and her wild ways. All the houses and the boat were sold for debts. The jet and the flashy red Jaguar were leased by the corporation, so Cindy didn't have those, either. The Forest was stunned that the Lockridges were so overextended.

By the time the estate was settled, the lawyers got most of it. Cynthia wound up with about a hundred thousand dollars.

Cynthia was tired of being a society woman. 'I don't have any real friends here,' she told Jace. She took the money and bought a luxury double-wide in an attractive mobile home park in Festus.

She gained about twenty pounds and started calling herself Cindy again. Cindy married a mechanic named Jake. She and Jake manage the Fairdale Manor Mobile Home Park and live happily together.

My shoulder recovered, but it took longer than I wanted, and I had physical therapy besides. I had to wear that hellish sling for four weeks. I took sick leave while I wore it, and during that time I saw a lot of Chris Ferretti. When the sling finally came off, we celebrated with a picnic in the park. It was a perfect June day, and the air smelled of honeysuckle.

Chris made an exquisite meal: a cheese board with olives and nuts, caprese pasta salad, cherry tomato and ricotta tarts, and a chocolate-pomegranate cake, along with iced mango-peach sangria.

Afterward, we went for a walk. Chris kissed me, and said, 'I love you, Angela.'

'And I love you,' I said.

Would our love grow into something permanent? I didn't know. But nothing was permanent. I knew that, and my job confirmed it daily. I did know that I was happy. And that was enough.

THE INSIDER'S GUIDE TO CHOUTEAU COUNTY PRONUNCIATION

Missourians have their own way of pronouncing words and names. We're called the Show Me State, and you don't tell us how to say something. The French were among the first settlers, but we resist Frenchifying words.

Chouteau is *SHOW-toe.*

Du Pres is *Duh-PRAY.*

Gravois is *GRAH-voy.*

Detective Ray Greiman is *GRI-mun.* His name is mispronounced German.

So is my name. It's pronounced VEETS, and rhymes with *Beets.*

Missouri can't even decide how to pronounce its own name. The eastern part, which includes St. Louis, calls itself Missour-ee. That's how Angela pronounces the state's name. In the west, which has Kansas City, it's called Missour-uh. Politicians have mastered the fine art of adjusting their pronunciation to please whichever part of the state they're in.

Elaine Viets